STRAIGHT UP

STRAIGHT UP

A DAN STAGG MYSTERY

BY JAMES LEAR

CLEiS
PRESS

Published in the United States by Cleis Press,
an imprint of Start Midnight, LLC,
101 Hudson Street, Thirty-Seventh Floor, Suite 3705, Jersey City, New Jersey 07302.

Cover design: Scott Idleman/Blink
Cover photograph: iStockphoto
Text design: Frank Wiedemann

First Edition.
10 9 8 7 6 5 4 3 2 1

Trade paper ISBN: 978-1-62778-120-6
E-book ISBN: 978-1-62778-142-8

Library of Congress Cataloging-in-Publication Data is available on file

01

Have you ever fucked a married guy? If the answer's yes, then you know the score: he's all over you in emails and texts, you make a date to see him next time the wife's out of town, and then if you're lucky and he doesn't cancel, you get an hour of clumsy sex during which he probably won't kiss you or even look you in the eye. Afterward he talks about work, sports, the family, even the weather—anything but what just happened. Then you won't hear from him for months until that itch needs scratching again, and if you're fool enough you'll go back for more. Fun if you get off on dishonesty, bad news if you actually like the guy. I had enough of this bullshit in the military—and I was just as guilty as the next closet case of pretending it wasn't what I really wanted. I don't need it in civilian life. It happens, I admit. Sometimes I can't resist. But it's a waste of time.

And that's what I thought this was—at least, to start with.

I got an email from an old Marines comrade—he

found me through one of those forums that Jody encouraged me to join. "You can't just wipe the past out," Jody told me, which is pretty rich from someone who's already had about five identities by the age of twenty-five. "You've got to come to terms with it. Connect with people. It's part of your life." So, unwillingly and incompetently and with lots of help, I created a profile on a veterans' website and said something like "always happy to hear from old jarheads." I had a cursory glance at who else was on there, recognized a couple of assholes who would still be assholes out of uniform, and forgot all about it.

Then, one day: *You have a new message in your VetsWeb inbox. Click the link* (blah blah blah). I clicked, and there he was: Alan Benson. That was one name I was not likely to forget. We were in training together, just about: Al Benson was a couple of years ahead of me at Naval College, and already he was the star of the show. Six feet two, shoulders that could barely fit into a standard-issue uniform, the kind of looks you might find on a Midwestern farm boy, topped off with hair so red that he looked as if he was on fire. People called him Carrot Top, or Rusty Nuts, but only behind his back. To his face, if they didn't call him Sir, they called him Red. Red Benson. Football hero, athlete, natural leader, everyone's big brother. Of course I was crazy about him, and of course he barely knew I existed. The body, the looks, the hair, the milk-white skin covered in freckles, and on a couple of memorable occasions when we were in the shower block together, the bright-red bush and the long white cock with its branching blue vein... Yeah, I had it bad. Then he graduated, distinguished himself in combat zones around the world wherever the US Marine Corps was needed, we served together once or twice, and, in the way of these things, we lost touch. For all I knew he was dead.

Apparently not.

"Hey, Dan." Dan? He never called me Dan. "Lieutenant Stagg," yes, but "Dan," never. "How are you doing, buddy?" *Buddy?* He wants something, I thought, but it took me a long while to figure out what. "How's civilian life treating you? I'm coming to Boston on business next month and it would be great to catch up. Let me buy you dinner? Cheers, Al."

Okay: so he knew I lived near Boston, and he knew I'd left the Corps: that much was clear from my profile. He knew that I was short of cash, or he wouldn't have said that about buying me dinner. How did he know? Had he heard about the circumstances of my dismissal from the Marines—the honorable discharge, hushing up a scandal, a vicious last bite from the dying beast of Don't Ask, Don't Tell? Gossip spreads fast in military circles. Remember Dan Stagg? Quiet guy, dark hair, balding? That's him. Well, you'll never guess what happened. Got caught with his pants down—yeah, with a junior officer. A corporal. Sure, he told them everything. Kicked him out. It's a shame, really—he was a good marine. Made it all the way to Major. But you never can tell, can you? You never can tell.

That's part of the story—the part I don't care if people know. What the gossips of Pendleton and Lejeune don't know is that the corporal was killed by a sniper's bullet in Helmand, that Major Stagg fell to pieces from grief and guilt, and that he didn't give a shit what his senior officers thought, he just wanted it all to be over, to join Will in death. A spotless record down the toilet without a second thought.

I had a rough time: so did thousands of other veterans. PTSD, lost limbs, broken marriages. Adjusting to a world in which killing people isn't your everyday reality isn't easy. I sat around feeling sorry for myself, and then I kind of pulled through, thanks to a guy named Jody who had a suitcase full of problems even bigger than mine, and a set of circumstances crazier than anything I met in wartime. And now I have a relationship of sorts, and a future of sorts, and I try real hard not to over-think it.

How much did Al Benson know? I'm a suspicious bastard. I never take things at face value—that's Marine training for you—and I didn't believe for one moment that he just wanted to reminisce about the good ol' days. He wanted to gloat, or to preach, or possibly—yes, the suspicion flickered for a moment—to taste my cock. Experience has taught me that the most cast-iron straight man has secrets. Even Red Benson, the poster boy for the USMC. Unlikely, but possible. In my experience, if you've got a cock, anything's possible.

I wrote back in the same vein. "Hey, Al. Great to hear from you. Sure, I'm near enough Boston. Let me know your ETA and we'll hook up"—no, not hook up, that sounds too pushy—"we'll get together. Plenty of good chow in Beantown! Best, Dan Stagg." That'll do. Regular guy stuff, nothing faggy, no suggestion that we could go to the symphony or the ballet or the baths. Good chow, a few brews. Two veterans, old comrades, nothing more. Maybe he's a nice guy, heard I'd had some trouble, wants to lend a helping hand. That's what these networks are meant for. Informal support, taking care of each other. Well, I can always use a helping hand. Especially from Red Benson, with his hair and his smile and his freckles. SEND. Off it went. Dispatched and forgotten.

It's not like I didn't have other stuff to think about. Earning a living, for one thing. Building bridges with my family. Trying to sustain a long-distance relationship with a guy who's fifteen years younger than me, so cute that anyone with a pulse wants to fuck him, and not exactly famous for keeping it in his pants. Jody's gone back to school, doing the one thing he loves as much as sex: he's studying fashion at the Pratt Institute in Brooklyn, catching up on the years when he was making a living with his ass. He's smart, he's talented, and from what he tells me he's having a great time. He's grateful too: without the dirty money I made from a bunch of crooks who tried to frame me for murder, he wouldn't be able to afford Pratt's fancy fees. I don't mind. I'd never spend it on myself. Might as well buy Jody a future.

But it's not easy living apart. For one thing, I worry about him: when he was recovering from his brain hemorrhage, the doctors said he might experience some kind of epileptic seizures. If that happens, I want to be there to take care of him, but I'm not. Then there's the whole question of where we'd live. Jody loves the city: I'd be happy if I never set foot in the five boroughs again. He's got a room in one of the campus residence halls that he shares with another fashion student: two single beds, two desks, and a landslide of magazines and fabric and empty coffee cups. I visited him a couple of times when his roommate was out, and fucked him so hard his neighbors would have called the resident advisor if I hadn't put my hand over Jody's mouth.

He suggested once that we might get a place together, somewhere commutable, best of both worlds, but unless he sells his first collection to Saks Fifth Avenue or I win the Massachusetts State Lottery, there's not much chance of that happening. That kind of rent is way beyond my means. I'm living cheap in a house that belongs to my uncle in Lowell, Mass.—hasn't been fixed up since the seventies, no central heating, and the roof leaks so much he can't even rent it out as a meth lab. One step up from a barn: does just fine for the black sheep of the family. I pay him a hundred bucks a month, I keep his insurance premiums down and the junkies and squatters away. It's a one-sided deal, but I kid myself that it's better than a motel. At least it gives me the illusion of living with my family.

My parents are a few miles down the road in Groton, a nice little community where disgraced battle-scarred gay veterans don't quite fit in. I visit on weekends, or when Dad needs the roof fixed, or Mom wants a tree cut down in the yard. The neighbors probably think I'm the help. When they moved there a couple of years ago for a peaceful retirement growing squash and apples and tomatoes, I guess they didn't mention me much. I wasn't the hero anymore, the son they'd been so proud of they stuck pictures of me in the front window of the old family home. I came back different, and the pictures were put away—even the framed pictures that used to stand on the mantelpiece. My sister's there, with her kids. My brother, twice divorced, is there. But not me.

I'll give them time. I've got plenty of it. I'm not quite forty yet, they're only just in their seventies, and we could be looking at ten, even twenty years of avoiding the issue if I don't do something about it. So I'm here, living in a shithole, working in a rundown gym in Lowell that just about pays enough to cover the rent and put food on the table. God only knows what I'll do if I get sick or unemployed. Jody says he'll look after me, whisk me off to Paris and Milan when he's a famous designer. I'm not holding my breath. But one of these days I'm going to pluck up the courage to say, "Mom, Dad, sit down. There's something we need to discuss."

Somehow, that hasn't happened yet. I've stormed enemy positions with guns and grenades, I've killed more men than I can remember, but having an adult conversation with my parents scares me.

A week later: *you have a new message in your VetsWeb inbox*. It was early in the morning, five o'clock, my turn to open up the gym for the pre-work crowd. I usually shower and shave at work, since I prefer hot water and no bugs living behind the bathroom tiles. I was still in the sweatpants and T-shirt I sleep in, barefoot, puffy-eyed. Quick email check in case Jody sent me a nice message to start the day. Sometimes it's to arrange a Skype session. Sometimes it's a photograph. Like most people, I acquired IT skills in order to jerk off.

Not today. Too busy making pretty dresses.

But there was Al Benson again. *Arriving in Boston tomorrow (Thu) afternoon. Staying at the Marriott, Back Bay. Meet me there at 1800? Al.*

Almost sounded like a military briefing. No "buddy"

or "cheers." A time and a place, and if it wasn't for the question mark it would have been an order.

I didn't have to check my diary. I was on earlies, and if I'm not working, I'm free.

I wrote "sir, yes sir!" and hit send.

I just about had time to wonder what exactly Benson wanted—a buddy? A fuck? A gun for hire?—and then it was time to jump in the car. I keep a gym bag packed and ready, of course. Some things stay with you.

Now, those of you who know me well probably rolled your eyes when I said I worked in a gym. Oh, yes, Dan, a gym. A place where guys come and take their clothes off. How convenient. I might bust your chops for that, or I might say, You've got me all wrong, I'm in a relationship now and I don't fool around, and you'd pretend to believe me because you'd prefer to keep your limbs intact. But of course, you're absolutely right. My official job at the Strong Box—"Lowell's Premier Fitness and Martial Arts Facility" (i.e., the only gym in town)—is personal trainer, specializing in kickboxing and other legitimized forms of violence. In between clients, who are sparse, I sit at the front desk, answer the phone, pick up wet towels in the locker room, mop the floors, and generally clear up other people's shit. It's kind of like working for Uncle Sam, without the killing.

Of course there are opportunities, and yes, I've taken them. Not with the members: I can't afford to lose this job, and the boss made us sign a piece of paper agreeing that any fraternizing with the clients would lead to instant dismissal. I guess a few too many horny housewives got banged up by their personal trainers. They're safe from me, but their husbands might not be. Nobody needs to know that. I'm not what you'd call out at work.

I didn't sign anything about coworkers, though. People move around a lot in the fitness industry—there's a high staff turnover even in a little joint like the Strong Box: college grads trying to get a toehold in the business, former athletes whose competition days are over, even a few ex-military men like me. They're all physically fit, and at a rough guess I'd say about forty percent of the men could be persuaded. You get talking about your bodies, you hit the showers after locking up at night, you compare abs or delts or whatever fucking muscle you like, and that's all it takes. And just as I was putting the key in the ignition, I remembered I was sharing a shift with Lee, the young English guy who was doing a masters in sports science in a college over toward Boston. Like me, he was living in a cheap rented apartment in Lowell; like me, he was paying the rent by working at the gym; and in his first couple of weeks we'd enjoyed complaining about stuff. He was twenty-one, his first time abroad, his first time living away from home, and he was homesick. I guess I should also mention that he was tall and lean and had played rugby back at home, and hoped one day to play for his country. He had the English rose tattooed on his left pectoral muscle. "I want to wear that on my shirt one day," he said, the first time I saw him naked. If I had my way he'd never wear clothes again, but I just nodded and said something about sports.

He was already waiting when I pulled up to the curb, leaning against the wall, wearing jeans and a thick sweater and a beanie; it was September—the days were still warm but the mornings cold as ice, a promise of the winter to come. He'd found a patch of thin early sunshine and was basking in it like a lizard, soaking up the warmth. His face was striking rather than handsome, particularly with the strong shadows accentuating his high cheekbones and deep brow. His eyes were close-set, his mouth large; in repose, he could look quite stupid, a brainless meathead. I liked this. I spent my career giving orders to guys like Lee, and I always had a soft spot for the dumb ones. When he heard the car door slamming he opened his eyes and smiled.

"Dan!"

He stood up straight, pulled off his cap and ran a large hand over his head. The hair was cut in some crazy style, buzzed at the side but long at the top and back, a kind of modified Mohawk that would look fucking awful on anyone over twenty-two. When you're Lee's age you can get away with it—barely. His nails were bitten down to the quick, and he had a Band-Aid on his right middle finger.

I shook his hand, then inspected his fingers. "What's the matter, Lee? Can't you afford regular food? Been eating yourself?"

He pulled his hand away, stuffed it into his pocket, ashamed of the childish habit. "Yeah, right, I know." He had a habit of mumbling that, combined with a thick English accent and an unfamiliar vocabulary, which made communication interesting. "How are you, mate?"

"I'm good. You?"

"Yeah." He did a nervous little sidelong smile, hissed between his teeth. "All right. Cold, innit."

"Let's open up." I checked my watch. "Half an hour before we let 'em in."

"I need a shower." He sniffed his armpit and grimaced. "I fucking stink."

I scratched my twenty-four-hour stubble. "And I need a shave. Come on."

The Strong Box occupied the basement of two retail units, an outdoor clothing store and a bait and tackle shop, accessed by a metal staircase and a tiny front area into which garbage always blew. Our first job was to clear out the night's debris.

"I'll do this," I said, opening the door: as the senior employee, I was entrusted with the keys. "You go get the water running."

"Cheers, mate. I owe you."

Yeah, and I can think of a thousand ways to make you pay, I thought, watching his ass recede into the gloom of the interior. I kicked the trash into a little pile and dumped it in the wastebasket, hoping there were no sharps. Usual stuff: burger wrappings, cigarette butts, cans. I needed to wash my hands.

I could hear the shower as soon as I walked in; good boy, he'd done as he was told—first thing in the morning it could take five minutes for the water to get up to a bearable temperature. The boiler was always breaking down, which made for pissed-off members and smelly employees. The Strong Box was not exactly high-end.

"Lee?" I stowed my kit in a locker. "Where are you?"

"I'm having a shit." He left the tops and tails off words: *avin' a shi'.*

I peeled off my shirt. The cheap fabric crackled as it went over my head, making the hair on my chest and stomach (there's a lot) stand up with static.

"Fuckin' 'ell, it's Bigfoot."

I laughed and growled, showing my teeth. "Keeps me warm in winter."

"Not like me." He pulled up his sweater to reveal a perfectly smooth, perfectly flat stomach. "Like a baby's bottom, me."

"You're young. And I bet you do all that trimming shit that kids do these days."

He shrugged. "Yeah. A bit." He rubbed his head again. "Clippers. Can't afford them salons."

I dropped my pants. "Clippers don't really work on me." Lee took in my hairy legs, and his eyebrows shot up, furrowing his forehead—the expression that male models and pop singers try on in photo shoots.

"You look like our family dog."

"Woof," I said, wondering what he'd do when he saw my ass. It's starting to look as if I'm wearing hair underpants.

"I miss him," he said, with complete sincerity. "He's a nice old boy." I thought I detected a bit of moisture in his eyes, but then he pulled his shirt over his head. Lee's skin was the very pale, smooth type that always makes me think of marble statues, the kind that decorate hifa-lutin military establishments. Apart from the tattoo, the head of the rose as big as the palm of my hand, he was flawless. Big pink nipples, enough definition to make him look masculine, but not one of those skinny muscle freaks who end up looking like anatomical models. I licked my lips, and felt my dick stirring; it hadn't been completely limp ever since I got out of bed, even when I was picking up the trash. He unbuttoned his jeans and dropped them down his thighs; there was nothing underneath, just young flesh.

He sat down to remove his shoes and socks, looking up at me.

"What you do at the weekend then, Dan?"

"Saw my folks," I said. Sat in miserable silence around a dinner that nobody wanted to eat. Cleaned the gutters. Chopped wood for winter. Drank beer at home, alone. "How 'bout you?"

"Nothing." He looked down, struggling with a knot in his laces. "Can't afford to go out."

"Come on. Young guy like you should be having the time of his life."

"I don't know anyone."

"What about the other students?"

"They all run around in cars and shit. They never ask me out."

"Well, I tell you what, Lee," I said, pulling my underpants down and very conscious that my dick was well on the way to half hard. "Next weekend let your Uncle Dan take you out for a burger and a beer."

"Would you?"

"'Course. Now, come on. Let's get clean for the people." I couldn't stand there looking at him much longer, or he was going to get jabbed in the eye.

"Fucking things," he said, and kicked his shoes off, laces still knotted. He trotted after me into the showers, where steam was thickening the air.

The Strong Box, I'm happy to say, was one of the few remaining gyms to hold out against screened-in shower cubicles; it had a wall with five faucets and a drain down which soapy water ran. No sauna, no steam room, nothing but running water and some pegs on which to hang your towels. No obstacles to a clear and uninterrupted view of your fellow washers.

We stood, as is usually the case when two men share an open shower, with an empty space between us: close enough to be friendly, far enough to avoid intimacy. For a few moments we both faced the wall, getting our heads wet, rubbing our faces, but as we started to soap up we turned to face each other. I was definitely half hard now, my dick sticking out at about forty-five degrees from my body, water jetting off the end. I lathered up my armpits, my chest, my stomach. Lee's hair was plastered to his skull, his body covered in a film of white bubbles. There was a small thatch of hair above his cock, trimmed to almost nothing; apart from that, he was smooth. His cock, which I had never seen before, was long and uncut and, unless I was mistaken, starting to wake up.

"You lived around here a long time, Dan?" He wiped soap out of his eyes.

"On and off, all my life."

"Never wanted to travel?"

I laughed and washed my ass, making no effort to cover my dick. "Oh, I've been here and there." Afghanistan, Iraq, Bosnia. All the glamour spots.

"I always wanted to travel," he said. "See the world, right? Meet interesting people."

"Yeah, well, there's plenty of them."

"That's why I came to the States."

"Right." He was sneaking downward glances, which suited me fine. He wanted to see the world? I'd show him. "And does it live up to your expectations?"

He laughed. "Well, Lowell's not exactly Vegas." He ran his hands down his wet, slippery stomach. "But it's okay. I like it here."

"Me too." I rested my hands on the small of my back and pushed my hips forward a little. My dick swayed from side to side. He watched it like a mongoose watching a cobra. I guess he was missing his girlfriend back home as much as he was missing the family dog. "As long as you've got friends."

He looked up into my eyes. "This okay?"

"I've got the keys. And there's twenty minutes before we let anyone in."

"Twenty minutes."

"Yeah."

He stepped across the tiled floor, under the spray from my shower. "I'm not, you know. Gay."

"Right." I grabbed his dick. "Me neither." He gasped as I started to stroke him, and buckled at the knees. "I just like fucking guys." He was fully hard now; it took about twenty seconds. The joys of youth, right? "You like fucking guys, Lee?"

"I... I don't..."

"Or don't they do that back in the Old Country?"

He opened his eyes and frowned. "What?"

"Doesn't matter. Now, come here." His hands hung limp at his sides; I took one of them and placed it on my cock. "Time to learn."

He didn't look too happy about having a dick in his hands—in fact he was positively pouting. But then again, he didn't take his hand away. We stroked each other for a while, slicked up with soap, water coursing down our bodies. There wasn't time to fuck him—all that business with condoms means I allow at least half an hour even for a quickie—but I wanted to stake a claim on his ass for future reference. With Jody away, it made sense to have a regular buddy, especially one who wasn't going to fall in love with me, and wasn't going to be around for too long. I pulled him close so our cocks were touching, reached around and grabbed his right buttock. It felt like a basketball wrapped in a blanket. Lee was so intent on the feeling of two hard soapy dicks jousting around that he didn't complain about my invasion of what, I assumed, was virgin territory. Some guys yelp if you so much as look at their asses. Not this one. He grabbed both our cocks with one hand, squashed them together, rolled them around.

"Mine's bigger than yours," he said, and smiled.

"I guess it is."

"You want to suck it?"

"Sure." Let him think he's in charge. There's a lot he doesn't yet know—but he's going to find out. I dropped down to a squat, made a circle of thumb and forefinger around his balls, and started sucking his dick. He gently lathered my head, and once I'd got my lips as far down as they'd go he fucked my mouth. I could tell from the hardness in his shaft and the tightness in his balls that he wasn't going to take long; time to teach him lesson number one. My index finger found his asshole and pressed.

"Fuck."

There was enough soap around the place to make it easy. I slipped in to the first knuckle.

"Bloody hell."

I looked up, wondering if bloody hell was a good thing or a bad thing. His lips were parted, and a thick vein was bulging in the middle of his forehead. Good, I guess.

I pressed in further, still sucking, still squeezing, getting a kind of head massage from his big white hands. And bang, there it was, the prostate. I drew a circle on it with my fingertip, letting him know what I'd found, and then pressed.

"Jesus, Dan... Jesus..."

He was coming now, fucking my mouth hard, pressing me down on him. I pulled on his balls, making the sac tight, as semen pulsed into my throat.

When he'd finished, I slipped slowly out of his ass and let go of his dick. My thighs were cramping up little, and I stood. Lee looked stunned, and leaned against the shower wall.

"What the fuck was that?"

"Did you like it?"

"Yeah, but—"

"But nothing. Now, you just lie on the floor, pretty boy, and let me look at you."

He did as he was told, a quality I greatly value, and I planted a foot on either side of his hips. Water splashed down on his chest, in his face, but he wiped his eyes and watched.

I took my cock in my hand and started jerking myself off, taking in every contour of his beautiful wet body. The thick neck, the sculpted shoulders, the deep grooves from his hips to his groin, and that red rose blooming on his chest. He was playing with himself, gripping the base of his cock between two fingers, flapping it around from side to side; if we'd had more time, I could have made him come again. He crooked the other arm behind his head, lifting it off the floor, tensing his abs.

"I ain't never done this before," he said, "but it's all right."

That was all I needed to hear. My dick jumped in my hand and sprayed him with jizz from neck to navel, one big glob landing directly in the heart of the rose. It glistened for a moment before it was washed down the drain.

We dried and dressed quickly, quietly, pulling on our nylon Strong Box shirts and shorts, tidying the locker room, making sure the place looked respectable.

I checked my watch: six o'clock sharp.

"Time to let 'em in, Lee. You all set?"

He nodded, said nothing. Shit, I thought I was going to have a confused, sulky coworker all day. And then, as I was unlocking the front door, he came up behind me, pressing himself against me. "You really mean that about the weekend, Dan? I mean, you know, about going out and stuff?"

"Maybe."

He looked crestfallen. "Oh. Just maybe."

"If you kiss me."

He smiled. "Go on, then." He grabbed my neck, opened his mouth and kissed me, pushing me into the door, pumping his hips. He was hard again.

"Get behind the desk, Lee, and don't come out until that's gone down."

He vaulted over the reception counter and greeted the early birds with a particularly warm smile.

02

I've been in a few high-class hotels in my time: operational briefings and press calls in war zones often take place in surprisingly ritzy locations. I know how to behave. Admittedly these days I'm in civilian clothes, but I don't look like a bum. I don't get thrown out.

"Here to see Alan Benson."

"Yes, sir. Just a moment." The receptionist was a cute blonde girl, perfect scarlet nails, good skin. She tapped a screen. "Room 249. Who shall I say—"

"Dan!" A booming voice from across the lobby, a figure rising from the depths of a large, soft armchair. "That's okay, sweetheart. I'll take it from here."

Two strong arms were thrown around me, squeezing hard. I smelled soap and mouthwash, felt a smooth cheek against mine. I'd taken care too. Old soldiers never want to look as if they've fallen on hard times. It's a matter of pride.

"Let me look at you." Al stepped back, holding on to my shoulders. The smile was the same, dazzling and confident. He was wearing a well-cut tweed sports jacket, an open-necked shirt from which a few tufts of red hair sprouted, expensive-looking brogues. His blue eyes still twinkled despite the surrounding lines. "My god, Dan, you're wearing well. You don't look a day older."

I nodded. "Still bald."

"Still in shape." He slapped his own stomach, where a little roundness swelled like a pitcher's mound. "I got fat."

"Hardly."

"And look." He bent down, revealing a circular spot of skin around his crown where once had been thick copper hair. "Catching up with you."

"Time goes by, Al."

"Yup. How long's it been?" He looked up at the ceiling. "Fifteen—no, more than that. Seventeen years?"

I honestly didn't remember. We served together in some almighty fuckup, but I hadn't had time to recall which. "If you say so."

He looked into my eyes and frowned. "You forgot?"

"I guess."

"A lot of guys make themselves forget."

"Hey. I'm not one of the fuckups."

"'Course not." The smile was back, the teeth gleaming white, a hand on the back of my neck. "Let's get out of here. I booked a table for us. Hope you don't mind."

"Am I suitably dressed?" I was wearing the nearest thing I own to stylish clothes, a blazer and slacks.

"You look fine, Dan. Just fine."

He steered me firmly out of the lobby and into the street.

The restaurant was one of those places I'm never

going to be comfortable in, not if I live to be a hundred. Pastel walls, linen tablecloths, flowers in old-fashioned vases, waiters hovering like sandflies. Okay, I don't pick up my food in my hands and start gnawing the bones. I don't goose the staff. But I can do without the *jus de this* and the *crème de that*. I can do without the constant interrogation—is everything Okay for you gentlemen? Yes. Now, fuck off and let me eat.

But it was Benson's treat, and if he wanted to show me how prosperous he'd become, that was fine by me. For the first half hour he barely drew breath. "Leaving the Corps was the best thing I ever did. Jesus, Dan, imagine at our age having to take orders from the fucking Pentagon! I'd had enough. They get you when you're young and they brainwash you, right? But I always wanted more than that. I wanted all the things we were fighting for, and I reckon I did enough fighting to earn them. I know, I know, I was one of the lucky ones. I have a great wife and two fantastic kids." He opened his wallet and showed me the photos: Mr. and Mrs. Benson and two perfect American children, a boy and a girl, celebrating a perfect Thanksgiving, having a perfect skiing vacation. "Jesus, they grow up so fast. Al Junior is twelve now. Twelve! And Jeleen is ten. Look at her. She's going to be a beauty."

Yeah, I thought—once she gets rid of the braces and the glasses. Once she sheds about twenty pounds of puppy fat.

"I've got more on my phone." He reached into his jacket pocket and may have seen me wince. "But hey, I'll save those for later."

This was the point at which I expected him to say,

"And you, Dan? What have you done with your life?"
But no, he kept going, unable to stop the momentum.

"I've got to show you this." Another photo from the
wallet, this time of a house. A fucking house. "We just
moved into this amazing place in South Fayette, just
outside Pittsburgh. I took this the day we moved in. I
have to carry it around with me because I can't believe
we got it."

"Very nice."

"You should come out sometime. Loads of guest
accommodations. Hell, you could practically have your
own wing!"

"Great." I share my apartment with some bugs.
Plenty of room for them too.

"I figured if you're going to move, you might as well
buy the place you want to live in, right? This is a proper
family home. We can stay there forever. At least till I
retire—but that's a way off yet, right? Even if I am older
than you."

The waiter took our orders, which meant a further
fifteen minutes of intricate discussion: cuts of meat,
methods of cooking, appropriate wines. I was beginning to wonder if I could fake a duodenal ulcer in order
to cut and run.

"But hell," he continued, once the waiter finally left,
"I work hard for the money and I'm going to enjoy it.
People think that just because I work for a university
I get six months' vacation every year. Bullshit! I take
two weeks, that's all, and I spend every minute with my
kids. Every minute!"

He smacked the table, as if someone was contra-
dicting him.

"Who am I kidding? I love my job. I wouldn't do it if I didn't. Had enough of doing stuff I hate when I was in the Marines. I've got a lot to be thankful for, I got the software training on Uncle Sam's dollar and I took it all the way to the top. Here." He produced a business card. "Keep it. Maybe you'll need it."

Alan Benson
Head of Software Design
University of Pittsburgh Medical Center

"Great," I said, and put the card in my pocket.

"The money's good, I admit that, but by the time the school fees are paid, not to mention the fucking mortgage on the house, there's not much left for me. I mean, we were lucky. Brenda's father died a couple of years back, left her a little. Only child. That helped."

I bet it did, I thought, wishing I had a couple of wealthy relatives at death's door.

"No regrets, not me. Some of the guys, the top brass, told me I was crazy when I left. Could have climbed right up the promotion ladder, four stars on my shoulder, big player. But that's not what I wanted. They can't see outside their own little world. I left because I wanted a real life, okay? Not rank and promotion and all that crap. I've got a family! It was the best decision I ever made. Ten years ago, Dan! I just told them I was going to walk, and I walked."

This was getting tedious, so I said, "I was thrown out."

Clang! You could practically hear the echo of my words in the ensuing silence. Benson busied himself with his napkin, then continued.

"It takes a long time to adjust to civilian life. At first I was kind of confused—but my kids got me back on track. I hardly got to see Al Junior; I missed the baby years. I wasn't going to make the same mistake with Jeleen. Every night I was there to put her to bed. Every damn night."

And he was off again. I could feel that phantom ulcer starting to smart.

"I never had kids."

"Ah, man…" He rubbed his head, rearranging his hair. "You don't know what you're—" He stopped abruptly. His eyes darted around the restaurant looking for a safe topic of conversation. "Where's that damn waiter?"

"You know why I was thrown out, I guess?"

"I'm hungry."

"Al? *Buddy?*"

If he ignored me this time, I was going to walk.

"Yeah. I know."

"I fell in love."

Benson reached across the table, squeezed my arm. "Listen, Dan, that kind of stuff doesn't matter to me. You know? I don't judge." He wouldn't look me in the eye. "Ah! At last. Food."

The dinner looked good, so I ate it. I listened to Benson's monologue, and said "sure" and "right" when necessary. I would let him pay the bill, then make tracks.

Then, as we were looking at dessert menus, the conversation took an abrupt swerve.

"You heard about Dick Coburn?" He looked up at me, his eyes bluer than ever.

The name rang a faint bell. A marine, yes. But who and when I couldn't say. "What about him?"

"He's dead." He looked back down, pretending to scan the menu, but I could see that he was blushing, nervous.

"That's too bad."

"You don't remember him, do you? Just another of the things you've forgotten."

"Sorry, Al. My memory isn't as good as yours."

"Remember that special ops mission in Iraq? Ninety-eight?"

That was it, of course: the last time I'd seen Al Benson. He was a first lieutenant, I was a second lieutenant, we were sent ashore to take out an Iraqi surveillance station. A messy mission that involved a lot of shooting and dead bodies. We were under the command of a particularly nasty officer, a sadistic shit whose name was—

"Harry Armitage," said Benson. "That's who you're trying to remember."

"Armitage. Jesus. That's right."

"I've spent the last seventeen years trying to forget him. He was a bastard."

"He sure was."

"And look at him now." His mouth turned down in disgust, as if he wanted to spit. "A fucking general. That's why I had to get out: because shit like that floated to the top."

"It doesn't matter, Al. There were always psychos in the Corps. I was one of them."

"It does matter, though, because he's going to become a very powerful man."

"Is that so." There was a glint in Benson's beautiful eyes that I didn't much like: it said obsession.

"Tapped for a job in the West Wing."

"Really?"

"Don't you read the papers, Dan?"

"Not if I can help it." I had a sudden flash of Lee's wet, white body, the look of amazement on his face as I swallowed his load, the feeling of his young body pressing against mine as we unlocked the gym. "I have better things to do with my time."

"Well, good for you, because—" Benson took a deep breath and put his hands on the tabletop. "Okay, I'm sorry. My wife always says I take this stuff too seriously. You want dessert?"

"Just coffee."

"Me too." He beckoned the waiter over and ordered.

"So what happened to Dick Coburn, then? Was he still serving?"

He shook his head, looked at his fingernails, sighed. "Dick was the one who got away."

This sounded interesting. "What do you mean, Al?"

His eyes pleaded for understanding. He paused a while, then said, "You know what I mean. One of the guys that slips through the net."

"Which net is that?"

"Dick left the Marines a year before I did. He was having a few problems. Emotional problems."

I thought I detected a tear in Benson's eye, but he blinked it away. "Go on."

"He had a kind of breakdown. Went back home to Kentucky and stayed with his folks for a while, but that didn't work out. He never really got along with his folks."

This was starting to sound familiar. I wondered how

much Benson knew about my circumstances? How far did news like that spread?

"I lost track of him. His mother said he moved to Chicago, though fuck knows why he'd go there. He didn't know anyone in Chicago. He should have got in touch with me."

"Maybe he didn't want to."

"Of course he—" Benson was almost shouting. The coffee arrived and he calmed down. "He was a good buddy. He knew he could have come to me for help."

"We don't always like to. I don't."

"I know. But Dick was different. I mean, we were close."

"Right."

Benson fiddled around with his coffee spoon, weighing something in his mind. My heart was beating fast, waiting for the revelation. This was certainly more interesting than Al Junior and Jeleen and that adorable property in South Fayette.

"He was found dead in New York City."

"Oh."

"In a house fire."

"Shit."

"It was a derelict building in Queens. The kind of place that—" He had to swallow hard. "Where junkies hang out."

"I'm sorry, Al." His grief was genuine, whatever the motives. It was my turn to reach across the table and squeeze his arm. "I can see he meant a lot to you."

Benson hung his head; I could see that bald patch in its circle of red-gold hair. It made him look vulnerable. Is that what all the bluster and bravado had been about? A cover for his weakness?

He looked up. "I want you to find out what happened."

"What?"

"I'll pay you." He reached for his wallet.

Benson was certainly full of surprises. "Hey! Put that away. I don't need your money."

He looked me straight in the eye. "Yes, you do."

Part of me still responded to the senior officer, the Naval College hero. I wanted to obey. More than that, I wanted to help a brother in pain. But to be offered money like that, as if I was desperate—I mean, I was, kind of, but Benson didn't have to remind me. "How much do you know about me, Al?"

"I know why you left the Corps."

"You know about Will Laurence?"

"Yes. I'm sorry."

"And you know what I'm doing now?"

"Working in a gym."

"You did your homework."

"It's on your profile."

"And why would I suddenly give up a perfectly good job to become your private investigator?"

"You've done it before."

So he knew about that too: the dirty money I took from Julian Marshall and the chain of events that nearly ended up with Jody and me dead. "News travels."

"Like I said, Dan, I read the papers."

I'd done everything I could to keep my name out of the reports of Marshall's trial and the scandal surrounding the collapse of his property empire, but without much success. "Fame at last," I said.

"That's what got me thinking. Maybe you could use another commission."

I finished my coffee. "I see." I dabbed my mouth on the napkin, folded it, and dropped it on the tabletop. "So it wasn't just the pleasure of my company you were after." I stood up.

"Sit down, Dan, for Christ's sake. Stop being such a diva."

"What the fuck is that supposed to mean?"

"Look, I was as glad as anyone when DADT was thrown out. It was a fucking ridiculous ruling and it screwed up a lot of very fine men. Okay? I'm not one of the bad guys. I understand and I'm trying to help."

"You scratch my back, I scratch yours." I sat down. "So what's your offer?"

"Go to New York. Ask around. Talk to people who might have known Dick. I want to find out what happened to him and why. I can afford to be generous."

"Did you talk to the police?"

"Of course. They told me the official version. Dick was sleeping rough in the wrong place. House got burned down—probably an insurance job, maybe a turf war, but there's no proof. Nobody was charged."

"And what makes you doubt the police account?"

Benson shook his head. "I don't know what to think, Dan. I just want to know what happened. I want to know how Dick ended up in such a...bad..." His voice faltered, and he pinched the bridge of his nose.

"It's okay, Al. We all lost people."

"Thank god," he said, looking up at me as a single tear ran down his face. "I knew you'd understand. All right. That's enough of this." He blew his nose on an immaculate cotton handkerchief. "Now you show me your side of town. I need a proper drink."

* * *

We took a cab to the South End, and I took Benson to a sports bar that, to the casual observer, didn't seem particularly gay. Groups of men watching the game—nothing to frighten the upright family man. A few women even, in case he panicked. We found a table near the back, as far from the TV as possible, and ordered beers.

At first he jabbered on about nothing—sports, politics, work. While I waited, I took a good look at him. Large, ruddy hands coated with golden hair and a big gold band on the appropriate finger. Sturdy thighs that stretched his pants, and a package that did likewise. A face that was still handsome, if no longer the boyish beauty of 20 years back—strong jaw, cleft chin, big mouth. When he spoke, even when he was talking crap like this, it was hard not to hang on his words. He took care to look me in the eye as if my opinion of the rainfall or the Red Sox really mattered to him. He was a charmer. I'm sure his colleagues' wives competed to get him over for dinner. I wouldn't mind having him over myself. Over a chair. Over my knee. My dick started stirring, and I tuned out of his talk.

"Dan?"

He'd asked me a question, and I didn't even hear it. "Sorry. Miles away." Wondering if you have red hair on your ass, and what it would look like with my dick in the middle.

"I said, Is there anyone special in your life right now?" He'd taken his jacket off and rolled up his shirtsleeves; his forearms were thick and freckly and covered in golden fur.

I swallowed some beer. "Yes."

"Well?"

"His name's Jody."

He didn't miss a beat, just kept looking steadily at me. "And what does Jody do?"

"He's a student." I didn't want to say "fashion student." I'm not ashamed, but... Okay. I am a little ashamed. So sue me. "In New York."

"A student?" His eyebrows went up.

"He's twenty-five, to answer your question. Precisely fourteen years younger than me."

I thought he might look away and change the subject, but he smiled and said, "Wow. Lucky Dan. A piece of twenty-five-year-old ass. Very nice." And he actually licked his lips, ostensibly to wipe away the foam from his beer.

"How old is..." Shit: I couldn't remember his wife's name. He must have mentioned it a hundred times, but I wasn't really listening. "Mrs. Benson?"

"Brenda is seven years younger than me. She's thirty-five." He drank. "But she's a very beautiful woman."

"Yeah, I can see that."

"You ever...?"

"With a woman? No."

"Not even when we were posted abroad?"

I thought about Will Laurence, our nights in the desert and in cheap hotels in hot countries, and the countless other jarheads I'd fucked and forgotten all over the world. "Especially not when we were posted abroad. Guys get horny when they're far from home. They'll try stuff." Like Lee.

"Yeah." He rubbed his head, a gesture I'd already

learned meant that he was thinking hard about something. "So how often do you get to see Jody?"

"Not often enough. We're spending spring break together. He's coming out to Lowell, god help him."

"Must be frustrating."

"It is." I wasn't quite ready to tell him about Lee and my other occasional distractions. Gay men have a bad enough reputation without me adding fuel to the fire.

"I know that feeling." He laughed quietly and scanned the bar. "Lot of guys in here tonight."

"No shit. It's a gay bar."

"Thought it might be."

"You okay with that, Al?"

"Of course I am."

Now, if this wasn't the perfect opportunity for him to spill his guts then I don't know what is. He rubbed his head again, almost spoke, had some beer, fiddled with his beermat. Jesus, Benson, you weren't like this when we stormed that Iraqi surveillance station. As I recall, you shot first and thought later. So come on! Shoot!

"I can't help feeling," he said at last, "that I let Dick Coburn down."

Around and around in circles. "Okay. Why?"

"I should have been there for him."

"Come on, Al. We can't look after every single person we ever served with."

His blue eyes flashed anger. "Dick wasn't just anybody! Dick was..." He stopped, and looked down.

"He was your friend."

"Yeah."

"More than a friend?"

He drew wet circles on the tabletop, said nothing.

"Okay, Al. We can play hide and seek all evening. We can pretend that you just happened to get in touch with me to find out what happened to Dick because you know I need the money. We can pretend it's just a coincidence that I'm gay, and that we're sitting in a gay bar. You just feel bad about an old buddy. Fine. Make a donation to a homeless charity, if that helps. But leave me out of it."

"Jesus, Dan." He reined his temper in, and took a deep breath. "All right. You want the truth? I know all about you. I know why you left the Marines, and I know how they treated you. I thought it was shit, and I wanted to help you. That is true. But I also thought that you might understand what I went through. How difficult it is."

"I do." I put my hand over his. He sighed, a deep, grateful sigh of relief. "And I guess Dick Coburn did as well."

"Yes."

"Want to tell me more?"

"Shit." He drained his beer. "It's time somebody knew. Dick left the Corps because he couldn't stand it anymore. The secrecy and the lies, always watching your back."

"It sucked."

"And that wasn't all. He couldn't stand...me. What I was doing to him."

"And what was that?"

"We were lovers." That obviously took a lot of effort. "Any chance of getting another beer in this place?"

I caught the server's eye, signaled "two more."

"It went on for about two years, maybe a little

more. After Iraq. We were both posted home to do some training at Naval College. Back to school, can you believe it? But this time we were the teachers. We were living in the same house—you know those officers' quarters with four or five bedrooms? We became friends at first, talking about our experiences, going out for beers, bitching about the generals. Usual stuff. Then one night we... I don't know. Had a lot to drink. Got talking about deep stuff, parents, relationships, buddies we'd lost, the meaning of life. And suddenly, out of the blue—" He stopped as the beers were delivered.

"He told you he was gay."

"What? Christ, no." Benson laughed, took a big swig and smacked his lips. "Suddenly, I looked at this guy, this fellow marine, and I wanted him. Like nothing I've ever wanted before. No woman."

"Right." Benson was staring into space, as if reliving the memory in his mind's eye. I was starting to get very interested. "Go on."

"I felt sick with the intensity of it. So I told him I needed some fresh air, and we started walking back to the house, arms around each other's shoulders as if we were drunk, but we both knew what was going on. When we got to a dark spot up the street I kissed him."

"Wow."

"I mean, really kissed him." He scowled. "It felt weird: the stubble, the way his body was hard, all that. But you know, don't you?"

"Yup. I know."

"And after that we got back home as quickly as we could."

"And how was it?"

"It was..." Another tear formed in his eye, but this time he didn't bother to conceal it, and it spilled down his cheek. "Like nothing else I've experienced. Before or since."

"I see." My dick was hard now, partly because of the thought of Red Benson discovering what his dick was really for, partly because this handsome man, the Marine hero, was crying in front of me. I'm a sucker for vulnerability.

"For the first couple of weeks I didn't think about anything or anyone else. We were in love, simple as that. The rest of the world could go up in flames and I didn't give a fuck. Dick felt the same. It wasn't so new for him. He was always that way."

"Gay, Al. You're allowed to say it."

"Yeah. Sorry. Gay. But then after a while I got scared. I noticed people looking at us. I heard one or two remarks—you know the kind of shit. I got into a fight with one guy, nearly knocked his head off, because he said something about fags. And after that it changed."

"You started pulling away?"

"I wanted him as much as ever—more, probably, because now I felt we had to hide it. I moved into a different house, and we started sneaking around, trying to be discreet. Fuck, what a waste of time."

"I know. I did it too."

"Dick wanted us to leave the service, but I wouldn't hear of it. Throw away my career for something that I could never explain to my folks? No way. We'd keep carrying on in secret, and that was as good as it was going to get."

"What did Dick say?"

"He went along with it. What else could he do? Poor bastard was in love with me, and I knew it. After 9/11 we were in Pakistan together. Ever been?"

"Yes. No hurry to go back."

"Yeah. Can you imagine what it was like trying to have a secret relationship with another guy in Pakistan?"

"Yes."

"Of course you can. Sorry. Well, it was tough. But I made it tougher than it needed to be. I started finding reasons not to see him. I'd cancel arrangements at the last minute. Screwed up our leave a couple of times. At the time I told myself it was because I was trying to break off with him, but you know what? I enjoyed the power. God help me, I punished Dick Coburn for loving me, so I punished myself for loving him. I knew how much he suffered when I pushed him away, and it made me feel better. I just wanted to...to hurt somebody..." He put his hands over his face. "Oh, Christ, what did I do?"

I moved next to him and put my arm around his shoulders. "It's okay, buddy. It's okay." A preppy couple at the next table were looking kind of alarmed; I glared at them.

When Al spoke again, his voice was ragged. "And that's how it went on. Another posting, and another. And in the end, Dick couldn't stand it anymore. He resigned his commission, no explanations, nothing. They tried to talk him out of it but he wouldn't listen. Nothing I said... Well, why the fuck would he listen to me? I was the problem, not the solution. You know the truth? I was glad. I hardly even said goodbye to him. Acted like it was nothing—just some guy I'd been friendly with who was getting posted home. He tried to tell me how he felt, and I laughed at him. And that was the last…"

He couldn't speak anymore. I let him cry, rubbing his broad back, trying not to think how good it felt. How solid.

"Okay, that's enough." His eyes were bloodshot, and he blew his nose. "I'm done. A year after Dick left, I had to get out. I was going crazy. I think if I'd stayed any longer, I'd have had a nervous breakdown. I came home, and within a few months I was engaged to Brenda. She's a great woman, Dan, believe me. And the marriage is real. A partnership. A family."

"But it's not the same."

"I don't fucking know. Sometimes I think it is. We make love. I mean, we make love a lot, even after all these years, with two kids. Perhaps it was the secrecy and guilt that made it so intense with Dick. Perhaps I'm just one of those guys who want the best of both worlds. Bisexual." He laughed, and blew his nose again. "It's not a word I particularly like."

"Tough shit, soldier. It's what you are."

"Yeah. It's what I am." He sat up straight and squared his shoulders. "My name is Alan Benson, and I am a bisexual."

The preppies next door smiled and raised their glasses. Al and I saluted back in perfect unison, snap to the brim, snap down. Al threw back his head and laughed, his Adam's apple bobbing up and down in that great column of a neck. Suddenly, he was happy.

"So, what now, Dan? Disco dancin'?" He snapped his fingers. "Let's go where the boys are."

"Seriously?"

"No. But it's good to know that we could."

"Jesus, Al, I wish I'd known about you. I wish we'd all known about each other."

"There must have been thousands like us."

"Living in the shadows." I thought about Will, and the grave in Tennessee that I've never been able to visit. "Never speaking."

"It's over now, thank god," said Al. "Times have changed."

"Too late for us."

"Bullshit." He looked me straight in the eye, and the years suddenly dropped away. He was the first lieutenant, the football hero, and I was the starstruck junior officer who'd have done anything for a second of his attention. "Come here." He put a hand on the back of my neck and drew me in. We kissed for a long time, still for a few moments and then with passion, almost fury. When we finally came up for air, we both drained our beers and picked up our jackets.

Benson hailed a cab. "Marriott Hotel. And make it quick."

03

There was nothing fancy about room 249. It was right at the end of a corridor, which meant we only had one set of neighbors to annoy, and it had good views over the city, which I barely glanced at. It wasn't a suite: there was a bedroom and a bathroom, and that's it. However, I doubt if many guests have got as much value out of a hotel room as Benson and I did in the next eight hours.

There's an art to fucking straight men. It's a little like fly-fishing: you lay out your lures carefully, you play the line, you let them take charge for a while, and then, when they think they've got things their way, you land 'em gasping on their back. With a gay man you can say, "Okay, buster, get your legs in the air, I'm coming in." A straight man will run a mile first, even if that's what he really wants. You have to play to their expectations. Take control in a way that looks as if you're submitting. Too complicated? Then stick to your own kind.

I learned the art in Naval College, and in various theaters of war around the world, and I've reached the stage where I could run courses. My encounter with Al Benson was textbook stuff. Read and learn.

We kissed in the back of the car—nothing too heavy, because even though Boston cab drivers have seen it all I didn't particularly want to be thrown out on the street. Benson was breathless as we walked through the lobby, moving fast, head down, but once we were safely in the elevator he was all over me. Tongue in my mouth, hand on my crotch, pressing me against the wall with the result that my elbow jabbed several buttons, fortunately not the alarm. He practically ran down the second-floor corridor, fumbling with his wallet to find the keycard. I strolled behind him, enjoying his nerves. This was going to be fun.

"Fucking things," he said, trying to jam the wrong end of the card into the slot. "What's wrong with a key?"

"Here." I took the card, pushed it into place and opened the door. "After you."

Once inside, he got cold feet. There was no urgent kissing, no groping for my dick. He fussed around with his watch, taking it off, putting it down, putting it on again. He hung his jacket over a chair—I was gratified to see a patch of sweat on the back of his light blue shirt—and then thought better of it, and hung it in the closet. He emptied his pockets of change, and if I'd left him to his own devices I think he'd have deployed the ironing board and started pressing his trousers.

"Sit down," I said, pointing at the bed. "Let me take your shoes off."

He did as he was told, and looked up at me. "Thanks," he said, and had to clear his throat.

I looked down: god, he looked appealing with those big blue eyes, the bedroom light glinting off his bald spot. But it was too early to whip my cock out and slap him around the face with it. That would come later, when he was broken in.

I knelt at his feet and untied his shoelaces, noting with pleasure that the leather was polished to military standards. Just like mine. I cradled each foot in my hand, caressing the heel, and then peeled off his socks—conservative black wool socks, no patterns, no monograms. His feet were big and broad, red hair on top, thick veins under white skin. Toenails properly cut. A few callouses from walking and—what? Playing tennis at the country club? Jogging? Not from slogging around the desert in boots, that's for sure. Not for many years.

I ran fingers over the top of his feet and heard Benson sigh as he lay back on the bad. "You just relax, Al. Take it easy."

My hands worked up his legs, feeling the mass of muscle in his calves and thighs. Perhaps not as hard as mine—but then I work in a gym, and Benson pushes buttons in a software department. By the time I got to his belt he was starting to squirm a little. I undid the buckle, popped the button, and started on the zip. He lifted his hips. He was ready.

I grabbed the waistband and pulled his pants down past his knees, hobbling him at the ankle. There would be time for all that later. First I had to get a good look at his shorts—white cotton boxers, a million miles from the fashionable little briefs that Jody wears. These were high-waisted and full in the leg, and they looked brand new. The fly had a single button, but a good deal of stress was being placed on that fastening by pressure from within. One of the things I really like about white cotton is its tendency to become translucent when wet, and where Benson's cock tip touched the fabric there was a spot about the size of a nickel through which I could see his pisshole. I rubbed it with my thumb, and he moaned.

Time to get it out.

That little plastic button was starting to get on my nerves, so I grabbed either side of his fly and yanked hard. There was a tearing noise, and the button rolled onto the floor.

"Hey! My shorts!"

"Relax, soldier. You won't be needing them."

I drew his prick out of the fly; it was, I'd say, about sixty percent hard, in other words not standing straight up all by itself, but not lying down either. It flopped over to the right, a thick white shaft with a border of orange hair at the base, burning bright against the white cotton. I spat in my hand, slicked Benson's cock up with saliva, and gave it three firm tugs. We then both watched as it rose, pulsing, to full erection. It was impressive. Benson looked mighty pleased with himself. The unworthy thought crossed my mind that I could understand Dick Coburn committing a long, slow suicide when this piece of meat was withdrawn from his reach.

"Well, well," I said. "That's a big dick."

Benson, propping himself up on his elbows for a better view, nodded his head and smiled.

Okay, buster. You can have your moment. Just wait till you see what Dan's got for you...

I gripped the base—not too hard, just enough to

know that this was a man taking care of business—and licked him from base to tip.

"Oh…"

And when I got to the head I ran my tongue in circles before zeroing in on his pisshole, already wet from within. There was a clear drop of goo there, and I tasted it.

I'm not the world's greatest cocksucker. In my book, it's better to receive than to give. I prefer to leave it to the experts, like Jody. If sucking cock was an Olympic event, Jody would podium every time. But I know my way around, and I can do it without throwing up or inflicting injury with my teeth.

Benson was in no position to judge the finer points. When he felt my lips encircling his cock, sliding over the ridge and down the shaft, he said, "Aaaaaaaagh" and thumped his head back against the mattress. One hand caressed the back of my skull, applying gentle pressure. He hit the back of my throat, and was in no hurry to let me come up for air. Well, I can hold my breath for over a minute. Let him enjoy himself. He'll pay later.

I squeezed his tensed thighs and then, when I needed to breathe, moved slowly up, parking my lips just behind his glans. Down again, up again. I don't need to describe every single move: I'm sure you've given as many blowjobs as I have, and far better.

"Stand up."

He did as he was told; already the tables were turning. His dick stood straight out.

"Now drop your shorts."

He bent over, snapped the elastic waistband and touched his toes. Now he was really hobbled. I took one buttock in each hand, kneading his ass like warm, yeasty dough, and started sucking again. His dick was as hard as it was going to get, and I didn't want him coming yet—not for a long time. If they come too soon, they tend to bolt.

When I judged that we were entering the danger zone I pushed Benson backward; unable to move his feet, he toppled and fell onto the bed. I kicked off my shoes, pulled off my shirt, and started to unbutton my pants.

"Jesus, you're hairy," he said. "And in terrific shape."

Terrific, indeed. I slapped my stomach, which is hard and flat beneath the fur. Benson sat up.

"Can I?"

"Sure." My pants were half open now, enough for him to see my thick black bush. He ran the back of his knuckles down my torso from chest to groin, brushing the hair, feeling the definition. I put my fists on my hips and let him play. Things were going well. Any minute now he'd want to see more—but first, I wanted him naked.

"Get your shirt off."

He looked up with misgiving in his eyes. Surely he wasn't going to run away now? I've had runners before; in my service days, when I wasn't quite as nice as I am now, I used to lock the door if I thought they looked nervous. "I've kind of…let myself go."

Ah, that was it: intimidated by my rock-hard physique. I can't deny that it pleased me to be in better shape than the former football hero. A comfortable job and a happy home life are all well and good, but when your waist size starts catching up with your age you're in trouble. I'm still 34", just as I have been since the wiry teenager filled out in his twenties.

The shirt came off, and in truth he wasn't so bad. A little saggy—but a month in the gym and a sensible eating plan would fix that. His skin was still beautiful, pale and taut. And from his collar bones downward there was that glowing fuzz of hair, parting to reveal his rose-pink tits. My dick was as stiff as a pole, and my briefs did nothing to conceal it. I tugged at them to allow my cock to stand out straight, stretching the fabric to its limits.

And then I got it out.

Well, he didn't run. If he'd tried he'd have fallen flat on his face, since he was still hobbled by his pants. He just sat there staring, and licked his lips. Okay, I thought. Enough pussyfooting. Enough of the playing-the-fish-on-the-line bullshit, this one is hooked. Reel him in. I placed a knee on either side of his ribs, and pushed him backward. The fur on his torso tickled my balls, made my cock jump. Benson pressed his hands into the bed and scooted forward, meeting me halfway. And once my cock was in reach of his tongue, there was no looking back.

I sometimes think there might be such a thing as overenthusiastic cocksucking, and if there is, Al Benson was guilty of it that night. He set about my dick like a starving man presented with a steak. He licked it, he rolled it over his face, he kissed it, and when he finally got it in his mouth he seemed determined to devour it.

"Easy, fella. We've got all night."

He wiped his mouth on the back of his hand. "Sorry, Dan. It's been a long time."

"Well, you'd better start making up for it then. Do the job properly." I lay back on the bed, propping my head up with pillows, and spread my legs. Benson lay between them, freeing his feet with some furious paddling. His pants and shorts lay tangled and inside out on the floor.

Once he recovered from his initial excitement, Al Benson made a very serviceable cocksucker. Far from perfect; there were times when I had to remind him to cover his teeth, and a couple of awkward gagging moments that made his eyes water. But he got into a rhythm, he took almost all of me, and he knew exactly how to make me feel good, breaking off to lick and suck my balls. And judging from the state of his own dick—fully hard, pumping sticky fluid onto his hairy stomach—he was enjoying it. Some guys will suck cock because they think it's expected of them. Others do it because they love it, because it turns them on. You can always tell by sneaking a peek between their legs. If they're hard, you're in for fun. I reached down and rubbed Benson's prick with the sole of my foot. He said, "mmmmmfff" and took me way into the back of his throat. Careful, Dan. Don't let him come. Don't come yourself, for that matter. Every few seconds it hit me that this wasn't just some married man satisfying his taste for cock—this was Red Benson, a man I'd served with, looked up to, jerked off over.

My mind wandered, as it often does at these times, to that last operation we'd been on together. The Iraqi surveillance station, that sadistic bastard Harry Armitage, me and Benson and—who else? A handful of us, that was all. Special ops. Off the radar. The US military says there are no such things as black ops, so what was this? Very dark gray? All part of the chaos that surrounded Operation Desert Fox, the short, sharp destruction of strategic targets that was aimed to shut down Iraq's WMD capability. We all know what came of that—but at the time, we thought it would work. We had the intelligence, we had the plans, and we followed orders. Captain Armitage took us ashore with one clear objective: capture the station and shoot on sight. Take no prisoners, leave no witnesses. There would be three, maximum four personnel inside, all of them armed, all of them dangerous. We outnumbered them, we were trained, we had weapons. It was a classic get-in-do-it-get-out job. Or so we thought.

But it was a fucking mess. Too many people, too few of them armed, and Armitage screaming, "Fire at will! Fire at will!" as bullets sprayed into walls and machines and flesh and bone. The deafening reports, the screams, the stink of blood and shit...

"What's the matter? Am I doing it wrong?"

Great job, Dan; you've gone soft in his mouth. Now, that, in my book, is one serious fucking breach of sexual etiquette. Stop thinking about the past; move on and enjoy the present. That's what Jody's always saying.

Jesus. Jody. Another reason to feel bad about myself, to screw up a nice night with an old buddy. Because that's what this was, right? Two veterans indulging in a little mutual therapy, salving the wounds of posttraumatic stress with a little hotel-room loving.

"No, Al. You're doing just fine. C'mere."

I pulled him up toward me, put my arms around him, and drew him close. "Now kiss me." Benson was a better kisser than he was a cocksucker. His lips were soft, his tongue firm, and there was enough stubble on his face to get some agreeable friction going. Within seconds I was back at full erection. Benson grabbed me, I grabbed Benson, and we kissed and stroked each other like a couple of horny teenagers in the back row of the movies.

Now, this was more like it. I don't mind sex without affection—sometimes, like fast food, it's just what you need. But if I like a guy, I want to go all the way with him, even if it's just for one night. And that's exactly what I thought this would be—one night of hot sex, and then we'd go back to our normal lives. So let's make some memories.

I kissed Benson on the chin, the throat, down his chest, sucking his tits. Maybe he thought he was going to get a little more head, but I quickly dispelled that notion. I reached around under his big ball sac. The hair was thick here, and I had to prod around a couple of times until I found what I was looking for: his hole.

For all I knew, Benson was still a virgin. There were plenty of guys in the USMC who would fuck all the ass they could get, who would even suck dick, but suggest they might like to take it themselves and fists started flying. I was on that spectrum myself, and though I will open up to the right guy, he's got to earn it. Dick Coburn might have settled for that, might have preferred it. I struggled to remember what he was like. Any telltale signs that he liked to get fucked? Jesus, I couldn't even remember his face, let alone anything else.

But Benson didn't yelp when I started pressing on his ring. In fact, he sounded pretty damn pleased with the prospect. He drew his legs up and held on to his knees. That's the kind of body language that even a dunce like me can understand.

I started moving my finger around in little circles, warming him up, waiting until he was ready for more. It didn't take long. He said, "Yes," and that was all the consent I needed. I spat on my fingers and stuck one in him, enough to show him who's boss. Benson winced and drew in his breath, but that was all. Pause, proceed. Once you're in past the second knuckle, you're good to go.

If you're familiar with my MO, you'll remember that I always try to have condoms and lube on hand—standard operational procedure, even if sometimes you don't use them for days, weeks, or months at a time. And I was about to get back to my jacket pocket when Benson said, "I've got some rubbers on the dressing table. In that bag." So: he was prepared. He'd been to Walgreens. Good man. Good marine.

I couldn't resist a little jibe. "You were planning on getting fucked, then?"

"There's more than one condom in there, Dan. We can take turns."

"Yeah, right." I tried to sound macho and dismissive, but hell, if he had the stamina for it, so did I. But first things first. I rolled one down my dick and got it slicked up. "You ready for this?"

"Ready as I'll ever be. Go easy, buddy. It's been a long time, and that thing is fucking big."

"Relax. I know what I'm doing."

He felt my slippery fingers pushing the cool gel up his ass, and he pulled his knees right up to his chest. "I sure hope so."

It was tempting to shove it in and see the married man suffer, but I'm not really the vindictive type. Besides, the idea of a return match was appealing. Go back to my youth and live out a few fantasies. But first things first. Alan Benson, Head of Software Design, was about to experience some of Dan Stagg's hardware. His asshole was pink and crinkled, surrounded by white flesh and red fur, shiny with lube.

I knelt between his legs and placed my cock against the target. He shuddered, and his nipples stood out even further. I pinched one and Benson moaned and pressed forward, engaging my head with his sphincter. It fit snugly, and I had enough self-control to let it stay there for a while. Men who don't get fucked often, myself included, need to get used to it physically and psychologically. It doesn't take long. Couple of deep breaths to relax the muscles and calm the conscience, and you're away.

"Fuck me, Dan."

From the look in Benson's eyes, he'd been wanting to say those words for quite some time. I proceeded slowly, watching his face for signs of pain. There were brief flickers, narrowing the eyes, biting the lower lip, but he never said stop. I inched forward—halfway—three-quarters—and then, at last, I was fully in. The muscles of my lower abdomen made contact with the underside of his thighs. Like a good marine, he held his ground in the face of assault.

Benson's cock, which had been bouncing about and drooling like an excited puppy before I entered, had softened and shrunk, the skin concertinaed behind the head. We'd have to do something about that. I take it very personally if the guy I'm fucking isn't enjoying himself. Moving gently inside him, I took hold of his dick and stroked. "How does it feel, Al?"

"Mmmm..."

"You've got a cock inside you now."

"Yeah." He started to grow.

"A big." I pushed. "Hard." Push. "Cock."

"Oh..." He kept looking right into my eyes. "Go on."

"It's what you need, isn't it? What you dream about."

"Yes." He was half hard now, and I didn't have to stroke anymore. His prick inched up toward his navel like a snake approaching a watering hole.

Once I've established my claim on an ass, I like to work it from several different angles. I pushed forward, rocking Benson onto his spine, so that I could drive downward into him; he supported himself with outstretched arms, which made me wonder if he did yoga in his spare time. One of the advantages of this position is that you can make your partner come in his own face, a little trick that I've enjoyed more than once, but perhaps not appropriate for now. I pulled out.

"Turn over. On your knees."

He didn't need to be told twice. Was it coincidence that placed him with his head toward the full-length wardrobe mirror, in which he could watch himself getting fucked? I think not. A marine takes in every detail of his environment, and uses them to his advantage. Good man, Benson. You may have been invaded, but you're still thinking strategically.

I slid straight in this time, ramming into his prostate. Benson pressed his cock back toward me so that I could see, between thrusts, how hard he was. I kept a close eye on it: I didn't want him to come yet. When I thought his hand was starting to move a little too fast, I pulled out.

He looked over his shoulder, kind of disappointed. "What made you stop?"

"I want you on top, baby. I want you to ride me."

That way he'd be doing all the work—showing me, with every effort, just how badly he wanted to be fucked. It's a great way of reminding guys that this isn't just something that's being done to them. When you're bouncing up and down on a stiff prick, forcing it to fuck you, there's nowhere left to hide.

I lay on my back. Benson threw a leg across me as if he was mounting a horse, took hold of my dick, and guided it into place. This was not his first rodeo. When he was ready, he sat.

I braced myself, pushing my hips upward, tensing my abs, letting him set the pace. With one hand he felt my dick going into him, with the other he stroked his slick shaft. We both knew that this wasn't going to take long.

Benson came first, milking out three huge irregular white splats onto my stomach and chest. The rest ran down his knuckles. As he collapsed forward, his red face close to mine, I grabbed his hips to keep him firmly in place and pumped hard inside him, using maximum force. I wanted him to remember this feeling.

When I'd finished, and only then, I let him climb off. His legs were shaking, the veins in his neck and forehead were standing out, and a flush spread from the roots of his hair right down his chest. He rolled over and lay beside me, an arm across his forehead, his chest rising and falling in time with mine. I took his free hand in mine and placed it on my stomach, just to make sure he was aware of how much, and how far, he'd shot.

We must have fallen asleep soon after that. First of all we showered, kissing under the hot water, soaping each other's backs, brushing our teeth. We went to bed fully intending to continue fucking all night long—and I was more than ready to give it up to Benson—but the cool clean sheets got the better of us, and when I woke it was light outside. Benson was naked beside me, warm, fuzzy. I was hard, as I usually am when I wake up, and I turned toward him, pressing into his thigh. He stirred, and I rubbed my scratchy chin against his arm.

That was a tactical error. He was sober now, and perhaps a little hungover, and I shouldn't have reminded him quite so abruptly that he was with a man who'd just fucked him.

"What time is it? I need to piss." He stumbled to the bathroom, his half-hard dick swinging around in front of him. I waited. And waited.

When Benson came back, he was half dressed—torn boxers, shirt, one sock, and a frown.

"Where's the other fucking sock?"

I said nothing, just watched him stomping around the room, carefully avoiding my eyes. Every time he bent over to look under the bed or under the chair I remembered how different he was last night.

He found what he was looking for and pulled it onto his foot. There was a ripping noise. "Shit."

"In a hurry?"

"Yeah." He stepped into his pants. "I have a meeting at nine."

"Oh, right." I pulled the sheet back; I was naked and hard. "Mustn't keep them waiting."

"Don't, Dan."

"Don't what?"

"Don't...make an issue."

"An issue?" I wagged my dick at him. "Is that what it is?"

"You know what I mean."

I knew all right. It was the morning after. Sore head, sore ass, sore conscience. Jiminy Cricket was biting back. He was thinking of Brenda and Al Junior and precious Jeleen.

"Okay." I put the sheet back. My cock went down fast. And despite myself I felt a terrible sinking around my heart. Last night I thought I'd done something meaningful—made a connection with my past, laid some ghosts to rest, even laid the foundations for an important friendship. Yes, I'd cheated on Jody, but this was something bigger than that. I'd rediscovered a part of myself that had been buried for years now. My past. My youth.

I thought Benson felt the same way. Married as he was, unavailable as we both were, we could have talked and fucked and worked things out. I might have spanned the gulf between what I am now and what I was then, instead of spending the rest of my life pretending that "then" never happened. There are times when I think the only good thing I took from my years in the Marine Corps is the ability to kill and wound people with my bare hands.

And now, as Benson tied the shoelaces I'd undone just a few hours before, the bridge to the past was cut away, the gulf was wider than ever.

"I'll see you, then," he said.

"Will you?"

"Sure." He still wouldn't look me in the eye. "Call you in a couple of days. I've got a lot of work stuff to do, but I'll be free again on—" He didn't commit to a day. "I'll call you."

"You do that."

No mention of Dick Coburn.

I dressed quickly, without even bothering to shower. I wanted to talk, to sort this out, but even more I wanted to get out of room 249 and pretend that the last twelve hours hadn't happened. I put on my jacket, stepped into my shoes. The last thing I saw, as I scanned the room to make sure I was leaving nothing behind, was a now-empty Walgreens bag.

04

So why was I in New York City two days later?
To pay a surprise call on Jody, that was the official
reason—and it was partly true. I wanted some loving,
and I wanted to check up on him. Nothing like guilt to
make you suspicious of your partner, is there?

And while I'm there, I said to myself as I drove down
the interstate, I could swing by Queens and ask a few
questions. Poor old Dick Coburn. He deserved better.
Kidding myself, you see, that I actually remembered
Dick Coburn, let alone gave a damn what happened to
him. It's terrible what happens to veterans. The government should do more to look after them. But it's up to
individuals to take care of their buddies, and that's why I
was crossing the bridge into Queens. There was plenty of
time to get to Brooklyn, and Jody. "Guess what?" I'd say,
as I arrived with a bunch of roses in one hand and my
dick in the other. "I couldn't wait till spring break." He'd
be delighted, of course. Or I'd catch him with his pants
down, in which case I'd give him and his little friend the
ass-whupping of a lifetime. Either option was fine.

And in the meantime, there was a trail to follow.

I have friends in the NYPD, the guys who helped me put Julian Marshall's ugly face behind bars. A couple of calls got me the basic information: Richard Coburn deceased November in a house fire in South Jamaica, suspected arson, no arrest. That much was in the newspapers. What wasn't reported was that the address was familiar to the police as a crack house, and had been busted the previous month. Coburn was known too: homeless, living in hostels and squats, one of the thousands of regular users who drifted from dealer to dealer. Nothing unusual about him, said my sources. Just another junkie. And he wasn't the only one who got a little too hot on that cold November night: three bodies were recovered from the fire, one of them so badly charred it could not be identified. Doused in gasoline, according to the forensic reports. Used as living fire starters.

I'm not squeamish about dead bodies. I've put so many people out of their misery over the years that I've lost the ability to be shocked by death. But even I was upset by the callousness of the crime—part of an ongoing turf war between rival gangs, according to the cops, one narcotics ring trying to put another out of business, destroying premises and markets in one strike.

What nobody in the NYPD seemed to know was that one of those burned-up junkies was a member of the United States Marine Corps, a highly trained professional killer who had got so fucked up on drugs that he couldn't even stop some small-time hood putting a match to him.

Nothing I could do would bring him back, but at

least I could find out how Coburn sank so low. Stop it happening to someone else, that's what I told myself. Get involved in some of the veterans' support programs. Make something good come out of all this bad. Great job, Dan, pat on the back and polish your medals.

What I really wanted was some news to take back to Al Benson. A reason to see him again.

The house on 161st Street was still standing, its black, windowless facade covered in scaffolding and tacky plastic sheeting. The rest of the street looked respectable enough—far from the hellhole of legend. Two-story red-brick houses with steps up to the door, small front yards, cars parked by the sidewalk. Some of them were empty, but most of them looked lived-in. I walked up and down a few times; some curtains twitched, and a guy washing his car gave me a dirty look. I just said, "Hey," smiled, and kept going.

It didn't take long to see the other side of the street life—the shabby, shadowy characters who congregated briefly on certain corners, hands in pockets, feet shuffling. Users, waiting for the delivery man. A guy on a pushbike comes around the corner and off they go, all in the same direction, hurrying along with that characteristic speedy walk. Get me to the gear, and get it quick.

I watched it happen twice before someone started getting jumpy.

"What you want, man?"

A gray face, sunken cheeks, the skin weirdly smooth and hairless. Probably younger than me, but looked about a thousand. Filthy gray hood over a baseball cap.

"Just hanging out. Remembering a friend."

"You a cop?"

"Do I look like a cop?"

"Yes."

I reached into my pocket, and he flinched—expecting a badge, or a knife, who knows. "Want twenty?"

A shaky hand shot out of his pocket, but I was quicker.

"Uh-uh! Not so fast, buddy. I need information."

"Fuck you."

"Okay." I pocketed the bill. "Have a nice day." I looked across the street at nothing. Twenty bucks is good money when you're living from one fix to the next. Smack and crack are cheap.

He spat on the street; I took good care to avoid it. "What do you want to know?"

"Remember a guy named Dick Coburn?" I jerked my thumb over my shoulder toward the burned-out house. "Died in there a few months back."

"A lot of people died in there."

Bull's-eye. Someone with a little local knowledge. "Three, to be exact."

"So fuckin' what?"

"So, one of them was a friend of mine."

He sneered. "Sorry for your loss." Jesus, I could crush his scrawny windpipe with my finger and thumb.

"Okay. Thanks." I started walking away.

"Wait. I knew him. He was an asshole. He owed me money."

I stopped. "Go on."

"Everyone fucking hated him. He was always trying to cop without paying for it. Borrowing money that he couldn't pay back. Fucking lowlife."

"Everything's relative, I guess."

"He had it coming, man." His eyes darted up and down the street, waiting for his connection. "Come on. Give me the cash."

"How much did he owe you?"

"I don't know. I don't keep accounts."

That word—accounts—gave me pause. This guy, this shaking, stinking ghost, had a job once. A life, a future. Went to school. Learned about stuff like accounts. Buried somewhere deep inside was a code of conduct and a set of values. You don't rip people off. You pay for what you buy. What was his story? Was he another one like Coburn who had fallen through the safety net?

"If I give you fifty bucks, will you get off the street and go see a doctor?"

"Fuck you, man."

"A hundred?"

"What's your game, asshole?"

"Okay." He was starting to look really crazy. "Calm down. Here's your twenty. Don't kill yourself with it."

He mumbled "Thanks," and scrunched the bill up in his fist, too frightened to let go.

"You know anything else about Coburn?"

"The dealers hated him. He owed money all around."

"Is that why they killed him?"

He shrugged. "I don't know. I didn't talk to him in a long time." He came closer, afraid of being overheard. The sweet dirty smell was stomach-turning, but I've smelled worse. "He disappeared for a long time. People do that. They come and they go. Thought he was dead already."

"When was this?"

"Before the fire."

"Yeah. I figured that out for myself."

"Maybe six months? Three months?" He sighed. "I don't know. Time goes by so fast."

"Did he say where he was going?"

"He said a lot of shit. Always told me he was going to clean up. Get off the streets. Get a job." He spat again; this time I had to jump back to avoid it. "Bullshit. Every junkie says that." He scowled, probably thinking, *Even me*.

"And what do you think? Did he clean up?"

"I don't know, man, and I don't fucking care. He went away, he came back, he died."

"You saw him on the street again?"

He shrugged. There was movement on the corner, the dealer was coming, and my window was closing.

"You saw him?"

"No. I don't know. I can't remember."

He walked away. I called out, "What's your name?" but he was gone, reabsorbed into the pack, his habit overwhelming him.

I needed to get away. I'm not easily frightened, but that house scared me. Dick Coburn scared me. *It could have been me.* That's what I kept saying to myself as I got in the car and drove back to the bridge. I might have been the one who fell through the net—an inch at a time, coming home with a broken heart and discharge papers in my pocket, desperate to silence the screaming in my head, the pain in my guts, taking whatever gave me relief. Scotch. Dope. Smack. Crack. Little by little, puff by puff, smoking my way to the streets. There were times after Will's death when I thought about ending it. I'd have taken a quicker way out: a bullet through the top of the mouth, fast and effective if not clean. Dick Coburn opted for the long, slow suicide of drugs, wallowing so deep in self-hatred he couldn't even end it himself. Had to wait for some bastard with a can of gas to do it for him.

Coburn chose a path I could have easily followed. Many had.

Al Benson chose another. The married man, keeping it secret, checking his every move, his every look, going quietly crazy in a respectable life with a wife and kids, trying to be what people expected him to be. A marine hero. A regular guy. A son to be proud of, a father to look up to. Could I have done it too? Pretended that nothing had happened, taken my honorable discharge and walked into a decent civilian life with my head held high? Nobody had to know what really happened. We all do crazy stuff in wartime.

And which path had I taken? I was stuck in the middle, still trying to find out who the fuck I was.

One thing was for sure. As my junkie pal put it, Dick Coburn had it coming. He played with fire so long he got burned. You don't screw around with the dealers on those streets. So whether it was a turf war or an organized hit from a pissed-off supplier or some lowlife with empty pockets, Dick Coburn was dead. Nothing Al Benson or I could have done, even if we'd been standing there with buckets of water to put him out. It would have happened sooner or later. Someone would have got to him, he would have overdosed or fallen in the river or just frozen to death in the winter streets. Coburn was a dead man walking for months before he died.

Except... For months before he died, he disappeared. Talked about cleaning up his act and then, hey, presto, he's off the streets. Coincidence? Probably. Found a different source, moved to a different neighborhood where nobody knew him. Pissed them off, and came back to South Jamaica just in time to meet his maker.

Typical drug chaos.

But a little voice in my head kept saying, *The man was a marine. A marine never acts without purpose.*

Ridiculous. Coburn hadn't been a marine for a long time. Look what happened: he let them set fire to him without a struggle.

But it might not be that way. He might have straightened himself out. Maybe he was getting his life back together again, far away from everyone who knew him. Trying to forget Al Benson. Trying to kick the crack or the smack or whatever his particular demon was.

And then, someone got to him. Murdered him and disposed of the body where it would attract the least suspicion.

Why? I had no motive, no suspects, barely more than a shred of suspicion backed up by guilt and shame and lust.

My shoulders shivered as I drove back across the bridge, that feeling of someone walking over your grave. Once I reached the Bronx it all seemed much simpler. Dick Coburn was just another dead junkie, Al Benson was a closet case with a sob story. That's all.

Time to concentrate on the important stuff. I had a visit to make. An ass to fuck.

* * *

I didn't call Jody to warn him I was coming. I planned to turn up unannounced, and if he got angry I would tell him it was just a late Valentine's surprise. Jody's never angry at me for long. I've got what it takes to calm him down.

I reached Pratt around 1800, when the chances of finding Jody at home were pretty high. If he was studying, he'd be fixing himself something to eat before getting down to work. If he was partying, he'd be having a nap before showering and starting his getting-ready regime, a ritual of potions and lotions that I try to ignore. I can go from battleground to parade ground in half an hour, and that includes wiping off mud and blood and getting a proper shine on my shoes. Jody takes up to two hours to achieve the casual look. I've learned to live with it. He makes up for it in other ways, and I was thinking of some of them while I parked the car.

The contrast with South Jamaica was kind of striking. Tall, clean buildings surrounded by well-kept lawns, a few spring flowers showing through the grass, clean, healthy young people strolling around with portfolios and book bags. Safe, friendly, nice. Not the kind of place you get burned to death in. Jody lived on the fifth floor of one of these blocks: they looked like housing projects for middle-class kids. I knew my way up, even recognized a couple of the guys in the lobby. One of them smiled and said, "How you doing?" I guess they all know who I am: Jody Miller's older boyfriend, the one who comes to Brooklyn every few weeks and bangs his pretty ass. Maybe they laugh at me behind my back. Maybe they'd like to give ol' Dan a try. It was an appealing thought. As a boy, I used to dream about being locked in a candy store overnight.

I took the elevator to the fifth floor: a carpeted corridor with doors to left and right, like a budget hotel. Jody and his roomie were in apartment 5C, a tiny floor space into which were crammed two bedrooms, plus a shower and a kitchen that were barely more than cupboards with running water. But it was secure and warm and dry, and I liked to think of him in there while I was sharing my bed with the bugs in Lowell.

My heart was beating fast as I walked down the corridor. This used to freak me out, when Jody and I were first dating. Jesus, just the idea of dating freaked me out. I was a love-'em-and-leave-'em guy, except with Will Laurence, and we all know how that ended up: a sniper's bullet, a body bag, a fucked-up career, and a mess of a life. Now I've got used to it. Your heart's beating fast because you're looking forward to seeing someone. A man. A man you like. Love, even. It's normal, it's natural, it's what every other human being on the planet does apart from those fools who entered the military machine in their teens and had their emotions drilled out of them. A few deep breaths and then ring-a-ding on the doorbell of 5C.

"Hold on."

Not Jody's voice. His roommate. Shit, what was his name? Lance? Larry? Something with an L. Lloyd, that was it.

The door opened. "Hey, Lloyd."

"Er... Hi."

"Jody home?"

"Oh! Hi! Dan! Sorry, for a moment I didn't... Yeah,

Dan." We shook hands. He was a cute little thing, if you like 'em slim and geeky. A scrappy beard and glasses, a band T-shirt with the arms cut off.

"Jody?"

"Oh, he's not here."

"Where is he? Studying in the library?"

This was meant to be a joke, but Lloyd said, "Yeah, yeah," a little too quickly to be believed.

"Right." I stood on the threshold, not really knowing what to do. "Can I come in and wait?"

"Oh." He looked nervous. Was Jody in there with someone else? "I… I guess. It's a mess."

I walked in. "I don't mind. I won't bother you. I'll wait in Jody's room."

"No!" Again, too quick. "I mean, really, the place is a pigsty. Come into the kitchen. Want coffee? A beer?"

"When's he likely to be back?"

"I don't know."

"Does he spend a lot of time in the library?"

"Jody?" He looked incredulous, but caught himself, and fiddled around at the sink, his back to me. "Oh, yeah. Quite a bit. They work us pretty hard."

I rolled my eyes. Hard work, my ass. Making dresses? I'm sure those scissors and pins and sewing machines are real bastards. Lloyd gabbed on, and I had time to survey his long, slender back, his gray stretch-cotton pants and unlaced sneakers. I could push his fuzzy face into the dirty wash water, lube him up with soap, and—

He turned around, as if he'd read my mind. "So: coffee? I'm having some."

"Sure, why not? I'm in no hurry." I sat back in a chair, spread my legs. Lloyd's eyes darted up and down.

Easy prey. Unsporting. Geeky fashion student, husky ex-marine. Even as a scenario for a porn flick it might seem hackneyed. Well, I never claimed to be original.

He blushed and turned back to the sink, jangling around so much he was bound to break something. A cup of brown liquid appeared on the table. "There you go."

"Thanks."

"You don't say much."

"Nope." I spread my legs a little wider. Lloyd hung on to the edge of the sink, as if to restrain himself.

"Anyway, I'm sure Jody will be back soon." He looked at his watch, perhaps calculating if we had time for anything. The sound of a key in the lock put an end to that train of thought.

"Yo!"

I closed my legs, and Lloyd sprang back a foot. "Jody! You have a visitor!"

Thud, thud, as shoes were kicked off, slam of the bathroom door.

A muffled "What?" and the sound of pissing. These little student apartments didn't afford much privacy.

"I said you have a visitor."

Jody started singing at the top of his voice—I was familiar with his bathroom habits—something by Beyoncé or Miley or one of his other idols. Lloyd rolled his eyes.

"That's my little songbird," I said. Lloyd was looking increasingly nervous as Jody approached the kitchen.

"So who's this—" He appeared in the doorway, clocked me, stopped in mid-breath. "Oh."

I didn't get up. "Jody."

"What are you doing here?"

"Nice to see you too. Lloyd was just telling me you've been in the library. Good to hear you're working hard."

Jody frowned, paused, then smiled. I know him too well to be fooled by his actorish smiles. "We've got an assignment to finish before spring break."

"That's three weeks off."

"I know." A slightly defensive tone. "I want to get a good grade."

"I'm pleased to know my money's being put to such good use." This was a shitty thing to say, especially in front of company, and I regretted it. But I was pissed off by the coolness of my welcome. I'd hoped for at least a kiss and a hug.

Lloyd said, "I gotta go. Nice to see you, Dan," and beat a hasty retreat. Jody turned his back on me, taking his roommate's place at the sink. This time I didn't have to restrain myself. I stood up, placed my groin against his ass and put my arms around his waist, pulling him in. "Come here."

Jody remained tense. "Dan..." He pushed my arm away with a wet hand. "Not now."

I kissed the back of his neck, suddenly intoxicated by the touch and smell of him. My dick surged. I had to fuck him. "C'mon."

Jody squirmed, but I had him pinned. "No, Dan."

I whispered in his ear, scratching his face with my stubble. "Why not? Huh?"

"Jesus! I just said no."

I squeezed tighter, constricting his ribs. "You never said no in your life."

"Fuck off!" Now, that was loud enough to alert the

whole building, and I let him go. "What the fuck is the matter with you, Dan? Are you a rapist now?"

I took a deep breath to clear my head, and went to the other side of the table. Better to get some furniture between us. "I'm sorry. It's been a long time." This was bullshit, obviously, since I'd been banging Al Benson and Lee at the gym in the last few days, but that was not the point.

"Yeah, well."

"Don't you want it?"

"Not right now, no."

"I see." My stomach tightened, and I felt sick. "You getting it elsewhere?"

"Is that what this is about? You're checking up on me?"

"No."

"Then why the fuck didn't you call?"

"I wanted to surprise you." It sounded lame, and from the look on Jody's face I guess it was.

"Well, mission accomplished. I'm surprised. I thought you had more respect for me. I actually thought you trusted me, but I was obviously wrong."

"So this is the thanks I get for driving all the way to Brooklyn just to see you, is it?" Again, bullshit, but he didn't need to know about my detour to Queens. "I'm glad you made that clear. I won't bother again."

"Please don't."

"And perhaps I shouldn't bother to pay any more money into your account. How about that?"

Jody shrugged, sipped a glass of water. His face was calm and pale. "Fine by me. I can always find ways of paying the bills."

Oh, this was turning into a bad one, all right. Whenever Jody flaunted his past as a hustler I knew we were in trouble. It hurts me, and he knows it. I felt like walking out of that shitty little kitchen and never coming back. Running away—tactical retreat—that's my default for emotional scenes. I must be evolving, because this time I stayed and counted to ten before I spoke.

"Okay. I'm sorry. It was a stupid thing to do. I wasn't checking up on you, but you know I can't help being jealous. You're too fucking beautiful, and there's a lot of horny college professors out there."

Jody smiled and looked up at me. "Don't I know it."

My fists were bunching behind my back, itching to lay into whatever prick in a sports jacket dared to lay a finger on my boy, but I kept them out of sight. "You mad at me?"

He waggled a hand. "Maybe."

"Anything I can do to make it better?"

"Maybe."

I unzipped my fly, hooked my cock out with my finger. "Like this?"

Jody licked his lips. OK, he could have been fucked by every single member of the Pratt faculty, but at least he still wanted me. He moved around the table.

"Get me hard."

"Lloyd's still here. He's in his room."

"So what?"

He stepped closer. "He'll hear."

I took his wrist. "I don't think that's a problem, do you?"

"Dan…"

I placed his hand on my cock. He sighed, all the fight

gone out of him, and started stroking. Within seconds we had fallen into a familiar rhythm, his hand moving to meet the thrust of my hips. We were still OK. We still loved each other. I was quickly hard, and judging from the way he moaned when I grabbed his ass he wanted this as much as I did.

I spun him around, unbuttoned his pants, and fished in my pocket for the ever-present condoms and lube. It was tempting to use nothing but spit, but I've trained myself to resist that temptation. If Jody and I ever find ourselves on a desert island with nothing else to fuck, then I'll give up using condoms. Until then, while I'm unable to stop screwing around, I'll go in protected.

I was rubbered up and pushing into him within thirty seconds. Jody was impatient now, pressing back against me. He braced himself against the kitchen wall. One good push and he'd have gone through to the next room.

"Now, fucking take it." Jody responds well to orders, and I know how to give them. He spread his legs as wide as he could, pushed up on the balls of his toes and took every inch. I slapped his ass hard, then gripped his narrow hips and ploughed into him. This wouldn't take long. Any concern he'd had for privacy or noise had evaporated.

"Oh, yeah, Dan. Fuck me. Fuck me hard."

I can take orders too. I thrust up into him, my balls bouncing against his thighs. Jody's arm pumped as he jerked, his cock, biceps, and deltoids bunching. We weren't going to last long.

Something caught the corner of my eye—a slight movement—and I saw, through a narrow crack between the kitchen door and the frame, the glint of Lloyd's glasses as he watched Jody getting fucked. And that was enough to make me come. I thrust hard as Jody shot a load over the kitchen floor.

We went out for pizza, had a couple of beers, and then went to bed. We talked about—oh, I don't know. Nothing. Trivial shit. Nothing about the future, about us, where we were at. Jody was bright and cheerful—a little too bright, as if it was for everyone else's benefit, not mine. As if he was trying to avoid something. And I'm not good with all that stuff—I don't know how to have relationship discussions. They didn't teach that at Naval College. I can kill a man with barely a second thought, but I can't love him.

So we went to bed, we made love again, slower this time, with more care, and we slept. Correction: Jody slept. I dozed once in a while, but mostly lay awake in that narrow bed, pushed to the edge by Jody's strange positions, listening to every noise, wondering where the fuck my life was going. Sure, Jody and I had done what we do, and it was great. We still clicked, and it still felt right having him in my arms. But why was he so pissed off when I arrived? What did he really think about our future? How did a career in fashion, a new beginning in life, fit in with a miserable ex-marine who was knocking on forty and only had one thing to offer—his dick? How long before he found someone richer and younger who could fuck him just as well as I could? I know I'm good at it, but I'm not stupid enough to think I'm the only one who can feed Jody's ass. Why was he so uncommunicative over dinner? Was he hiding something? An affair? Did he plan to leave me? Was he waiting till spring break to let me down? Had I preempted his plans?

I caught myself getting angry and upset, and then I thought about Al Benson and Lee at the gym and the others, and I felt even shittier.

And then it got light.

05

I don't like getting stuck in traffic on the interstate, so at 0500 I showered and dressed and kissed Jody goodbye. He woke just enough to return the kiss, then rolled over and went back to sleep.

It was cold outside. I turned up the collar of my jacket and tried to find my way back to the car. One block of student residences looks much like another, and I went around a couple of times before I figured out where the hell I was. My mind was elsewhere—thinking about Jody, his coldness and evasions, his roommate's nervous lies—when I heard footsteps close behind me. My first thought, for maybe a tenth of a second, was that Jody had come to drag me back to bed, in which case I wouldn't put up much resistance. And then the military training kicked in.

I turned in time to block an arm that was about to grab me. A man of about my height, in a black jacket, black hat. I aimed a kick at his balls, but he was quick, and turned just in time to parry the strike with his leg. That hurts too, but it doesn't disable you. He knew what he was doing. He was combat-trained. Well, so am I, and unless the odds were really against me I was a better fighter than your average martial arts musclehead. While he was still recovering from the blow I smashed my elbow up under his jaw, and heard the familiar and oh-so-satisfying ker-CHAK of teeth blasting together. If I was lucky, he bit his tongue. I was about to deliver the knockout blow when there was a swish and a thud behind me, and a bolt of pain shot up my spine. I staggered around in time to see a baseball bat being raised in the air, ready to come down on my skull. I sidestepped just enough to take the impact on my shoulder. One more like that and I'd be down on the floor with two assailants, at least one of them armed. And I wasn't carrying.

Once my vision had cleared a little, I could see that the guy with the baseball bat was dressed the same—black jacket, black hat, a nice little mugger's uniform. But why were combat-trained muggers roaming the Pratt campus at five o'clock in the morning? Looking for drunk students to roll for maybe twenty, forty bucks? It was hardly rich pickings.

That question could wait for later. At the moment I was busy disarming the guy with the bat—grab the shaft about halfway down, give one hard up-and-down jerk, then a rapid clockwise twist—enough to focus all the pain on his rotator cuff and, with luck, tear the muscles. It's a move you usually employ to remove an automatic weapon, but it works well with your common household and sports implements too. He screamed and fell to his knees. With both of them down, it was a relatively simple matter of smashing their faces into the gritty asphalt sidewalk, one after the other—an effective way of deterring pursuit, not least because your opponent is blinded by blood. The forehead bleeds easily.

I jogged back to the car, all senses on the alert for further attacks. Now that the screaming had stopped, the campus was quiet. My shoulder and back hurt like fuck, but nothing was broken. I could breathe without too much pain, and if I can breathe I can drive.

First priority: get out of the area.

Second: check that Jody is OK. He wasn't pleased to be woken up, but I felt better knowing that this was a random attack, and nothing to do with him. I see conspiracy everywhere, I'm aware of that. Jody calls it paranoia.

Third: call the cops. I don't want homicidal muggers at large in an area where my boyfriend lives. Someone might get killed.

The desk sergeant I got through to didn't sound too interested: yeah, you were mugged, you were walking around in the small hours in Brooklyn, this stuff happens, come down to the precinct and we'll take a description.

I caught the night officer at the end of his shift, even more tired and cynical than New York cops usually are. He took one look at me—a strong, relatively young man with no obvious injuries—and sighed. "Sir?"

"I've been mugged."

"Yes, sir." He opened his notebook. "Name?"

I gave him the information he needed, the who-what-when-and-where of my attack.

"And what did they take?"

"Nothing."

"They took nothing?"

"That's right. I fought them off."

"Okay. And where are they now?"

"Isn't that kind of your job?"

Another deep sigh. "Can you give me a description?"

"Two white males, black caps, black jackets, about five-ten, six feet tall."

"Okay. That narrows it down."

I don't appreciate sarcasm at the best of times, but I find it particularly distasteful in a public servant. "Oh, and perhaps I should mention they'll have blood all over their faces. That might give you a clue."

He put his pen down. "I'll file a report, sir."

"Good."

"Is that all?"

"Oh, excuse me, am I in the way? Would you prefer me to make an appointment for my next attack? Or perhaps I just shouldn't report it, and then you'll have less paperwork."

He looked at his notes. "Mister Stagg—"

"That's Major Stagg to you, officer."

That made him sit up a little straighter. "Obviously we'll be doing everything—"

"Get one thing straight. There are two maniacs out there who would have killed me if I hadn't known how to fight them off. My boyfriend lives about a hundred yards from where the attack took place."

His mouth hung open at the word *boyfriend*. This wasn't turning out quite how he expected.

"And if I find that there are further attacks in that area, and you people haven't launched a very full investigation, you are going to find yourself all over the goddamn *New York Times*. How's that going to affect your promotion prospects?"

He was starting to look nervous now, possibly wondering if he had a psychopath on his hands. "Okay, sir. Do you need to talk to a counselor? We have people—"

"No, thank you." Jesus, I survived war zones around the world and the death of my lover without seeing a counselor, I don't intend to start now. "I'll take an aspirin."

The cop looked me in the eye and eventually smiled. "I'm sorry, Major Stagg. It's been a long night. A woman got murdered and we still can't find her kid. I didn't mean to...you know."

"It's okay, officer. I'm a little shaken up, is all."

"The thing is, it's dangerous to walk around the streets at night."

"Up at Pratt? It looks pretty safe to me."

"Everywhere is dangerous these days, believe me. There are people out there who will kill you for twenty bucks if they need a fix."

"These weren't addicts. They were combat-trained. Believe me, I know the difference."

"Okay. So they were street fighters. Gang members, probably. They send them to gangster boot camp these days. You should see the weapons we seize. There's a war going on out there."

"I thought I'd left that behind in Afghanistan."

"Hey," he said, "welcome to New York City."

I picked up a big strong coffee and hit the road. It was nearly eight by now, but most of the traffic was coming into the city rather than leaving. I put on a rock station and drove.

Street fighters. Gang members. Okay, I know the streets of every large American city are teeming with lunatics, but I still don't buy it. What did they attack me for? There was no attempt to rob me. Motiveless violence? A thrill kill? Possibly, but why go for someone who could fight back? If killing is your aim, go for an easy target. A woman, an old person, a fashion student. A junkie like Dick Coburn, even. Junkies don't fight back. They just roll over and let you strike the match.

The only conclusion I could draw was that they were after me specifically. They knew who I was, they knew where I was, and for some reason they wanted to hurt me. Kill me, maybe. Now, that opened up all sorts of interesting possibilities. First, there was someone out there who did not wish me well. I can deal with it, but it makes me curious. Second, they had been tracking my movements. They followed me to Brooklyn, they waited till I came out of Jody's building in the early morning with no witnesses, and they attacked. They must have been following me for some time.

Who knew that I was in New York? Nobody, apart from Jody and his roommate and the bums down in Queens.

And Al Benson, maybe. He sent me there.

Now, unless Jody was much more angry at my surprise visit than I imagined, or he had an extremely jealous boyfriend with powerful criminal connections, the type who could rustle up a couple of hit men at short notice, I thought I could rule him out. As for the Queens connection, the only thing they were following was their addiction. Perhaps someone had been talking, and someone didn't like what they were hearing—a man asking questions on the street about Dick Coburn and the fire. Opening up closed cases. Yeah, possible—but they'd have to be pretty fucking tricky to get on my tail so quickly. Homing device? Unlikely.

And that left Al Benson. What possible motive could he have for hurting me? I've met some guilty closet cases in my time, but I've yet to meet one who would murder a man for fucking him. There's a first time for everything, but Benson would have to be a rare psycho to pull that one off. "Colleagues at the Pittsburgh Medical Center said Benson was a friendly, respected worker who never showed any signs of being a raving homosexual homicidal maniac." Stranger things have happened, but not much.

I got home a little before midday, tired and hungry, my back and shoulder hurting like fuck. There was no time to sleep: I had to be at work by four o'clock for the evening shift. I took a shower, surveyed the damage in the mirror—some big fucking bruises, but nothing too serious—and phoned Jody. Sounded like he just got out of bed: so much for getting that assignment finished on time. Oh, well, let him get his beauty sleep. He didn't get much last night, not while I had my dick inside him. He sounded happy, contented, pleased to hear my voice.

"How was the drive?"

"Quiet. You okay?"

"Yeah. My ass is sore."

"Good."

"I love you, Dan."

That's what I wanted to hear. "Love you too." See? I can say it sometimes.

* * *

Days went by, and the whole New York episode started to fade away. I was never going to get to the bottom of Dick Coburn's death—it was sad, it sucked, but it meant nothing to me. If it mattered to Al Benson, let him hang around the shitty streets of South Jamaica. I'm not so desperate that I'll do other people's dirty work for them—unless the money is really good. At the moment, I'm content with my pathetic life in Lowell, picking up towels in the gym, fixing my parents' leaky gutters, living with a house full of little six-legged buddies. At least I know that things can only get better. Perhaps my folks will wake up one day and think, Hey, you know what? Dan is our son, we love him, and we need to make it all better. Maybe I'll get a decent job at a better gym, qualify as a personal trainer, earn enough to get a place with Jody and even—yeah, why not?—go join him in the city. In the meantime I can fool around with Lee to keep myself in practice. He's ready to graduate to the next stage. His ass is as good as mine. Maybe take him out for that beer I promised him, and then we can continue his education.

Forget New York, and all that happened there.

Just one loose end to tie up. I'd promised Al Benson to let him know if I found anything out, and I'd keep that promise. He said he'd call me, but what do you know? That hadn't happened.

His number was stored in my phone. I dialed: no reply. I left a message.

This went on for a week. "Hey, Al. It's Dan Stagg. Call me back, okay? I've got some news."

Nothing. Just the suspicion that Benson knew I was

in New York. He knew Jody was at Pratt. He sent me there.

And that's where it should have ended, except for one thing. I couldn't get rid of the suspicion that somehow the death of Dick Coburn and the attack on me were connected. Okay, there are probably a few people out there who would like to see me dead—I've made enemies here and there, and there's always a few crazies who have a personal grudge against members of the armed forces. I've killed a lot of Muslims: that usually puts a price on your head. And I'm a gay ex-marine: perhaps this was a hit squad sent out by one of those crazy queer-hatin' churches.

But me *and* Dick Coburn? Both members of an undercover operation way back when. Both former comrades of Al Benson. Both lovers of Al Benson. We knew something about that surveillance station, and we knew something about Benson.

Was that the link? Was I making something out of nothing?

I wanted to forget, but I couldn't. At night, fiddling around on the Internet, I started searching for Al Benson. Found his home address in Pittsburgh, his land-line. Even found photos of his wife and kids: it's so easy.

And if he wasn't going to pick up his cell, maybe I should call him at home, leave a message with his wife. And then he'd really have a reason to hate me.

06

Time passed. Nothing happened. And no, to answer your question, I didn't fuck Lee. I didn't want to. Dan Stagg, the hard-hearted, hard-dicked ex-marine, who never turned down a tight hole, was losing his edge. Lee was nervous and moody at work, because he wasn't getting what he wanted. Friendship, love, dick, whatever it was, he wasn't getting it. I was always "too busy" or "seeing my family." I didn't even take the poor homesick kid out for a beer, which he needed more than my cock rearranging his rectum.

I worked as many hours as the boss would give me, and when I wasn't working at the gym I worked out there, and if there was any more time to kill I sat at home alone with a takeout and TV. Pathetic, yes. But I was tired. I was disappointed. I was… I'm struggling not to say I was depressed, because guys like me don't get depressed, they soldier on and make the most of a bad situation. Hell, there are guys my age, younger, with missing limbs, no dicks, guys who wake up screaming every night, fighting off imaginary enemies. What the fuck have I got to complain about? I'm healthy, I have a roof over my head, and I have a boyfriend a ways down the road. So why didn't I want to see anyone? Why did I lie in bed at night listening to the cars going past, counting the headlights as they moved across my window, feeling like nobody would give a shit if I didn't get up again?

It's at times like this I'm glad I've never been much of a drinker, and I can't stand drugs. Because one sip would have led to another until I was coming home with quarts of cheap bourbon, losing my job, and ending up traveling the Dick Coburn Expressway to oblivion.

Instead of drinking I spent my time thinking, which also leaves you with a headache in the morning but tends not to get you fired. I sat at my yellow Formica kitchen table, one of those spindly-legged things that probably looked pretty cool in the early sixties, making notes on the backs of envelopes and trying to figure out what was wrong with me. The old tactical approach. Evaluate the threat, analyze the options, and you'll be left with the most effective available means of neutralizing it.

I came to three conclusions.

I was missing Jody and afraid that I was losing him, based on the lukewarm reception I got at Pratt.

I thought I was about to embark on an exciting adventure, viz. tracking down the killers of Dick Coburn, and when it was taken away from me I was confronted with the dreariness of a dead-end job and a family that doesn't want me.

I had fallen in love with Al Benson, for whatever reason—nostalgia for our youth, real fellow feeling, his ass—and now I felt guilty and frustrated.

* * *

Of the three, it was the last that was hardest to accept. Men like me don't fall in love with men like Benson, the same age, the same background; we have nice young guys who we can boss around, like Lee. Whatever my relationship with Jody, it certainly wasn't one of equals. And men like me don't fall in love after just one fuck. I'm not the impulsive type. It took me months and several near-death experiences to figure out that I loved Jody, and even longer to admit my feelings for Will Laurence. I'm slow. I was a late starter. And now—this? One night with Al Benson in a hotel room and suddenly I'm playing tragic violins? It didn't make sense, but however much I stared at that list, however much I doodled and tried to obliterate the truth, it kept coming back to me that number three was the real reason I was feeling so low.

And to make matters worse, I had this nagging suspicion that Benson was up to no good. The longer the radio silence, the bigger that suspicion grew. He knew something about Coburn's death, and he knew something about the attack on me in Brooklyn. And there's nothing more likely to get a guy down in the dumps than thinking the man he's falling in love with is trying to bump him off. If I want rejection on that kind of scale, I can get it from my parents.

It wasn't just Benson I was thinking about, though. It was that whole stinking chain that led from him back into the past—all the shit that I was trying to get away from. Twenty years of pretending to be something I wasn't, screwing guys and running away, hiding my feelings, biting my lip when the jokes and put-downs started flying. Killing for a living, and if that wasn't enough to turn you into a heartless bastard, lying about love and sex, the only things that made it bearable. And then Will Laurence—falling in love in the desert, stealing time together in seedy hotels in dangerous cities, daring to think for a moment that we might have a future together—and look where it left me. Will Laurence—all roads lead back to Will. Whatever happens in the rest of my life, he will always be the big love story. The only one. Yeah, because he died young and pretty, and because I never had time to get bored with him. We never sat around bickering, we never went to IKEA to choose furniture—every touch, every kiss, every fuck was magic.

Benson reopened that door, the bastard, and I was back in a sea of grief without a fucking lifejacket. And the fact that things were getting screwed up with Jody, whatever he said to the contrary, and I was bored and restless and didn't have a clue what to do with the rest of my life, a life I'm probably not even halfway through...

You get the picture. Sitting alone at a kitchen table. Probably the best thing for me.

And then, to make matters worse, I had a call from Jody. Spring break was off. Two days before he was due to come home, and I was setting myself a deadline for cleaning up the house and getting my head together, he rang and told me that he was too busy with that famous assignment, that he was going to stay at Pratt for the whole week and "get as much work done as I can." He hoped I'd understand, he was really missing me, but he wanted to do the best he could in the course that I was paying for, it was the only way he could show me how much he appreciated my generosity, blah blah blah.

When I put the phone down I had the sure feeling that he was seeing someone else.

Well, I thought, two can play at that game.

"Hey, Lee. It's Dan."

"Dan! All right, mate?"

"Good. You closing up tonight?"

"Yeah. Why?"

"Thought I might come down and do a little training."

"Oh. Right." He sounded disappointed. That was what I wanted to hear.

"Although actually, what the hell, I'm supposed to be buying you a beer one of these days, right?"

"Yeah."

"Is it busy?"

"No. It's fucking dead."

It was nine-thiry. The gym was supposed to close at ten, but latecomers could keep you waiting till ten-thirty. "Start clearing up. I'll pick you up in half an hour."

"Great. See you then."

"Oh, and Lee?"

"Yeah?"

"Bring a toothbrush." I put the phone down, imagining the blush on his white English skin.

He was waiting outside the gym when I got there, leaning against the door, one leg crooked up, fiddling around with his phone. It was a mild night, and he was still in his uniform—tight black T-shirt, black sweatpants, sneakers. His gym bag was slung over one shoulder. He hadn't seen or heard me, so I snuck up on him, hugging the wall, moving quietly, as if going in for the kill. Which I suppose I was.

I got close enough to read what was on his screen—a sports website of some sort, predictably—before I sprang out right in front of him, feet apart, hands raised as if to attack. He yelled, dropped his phone, and almost got into a defensive position in time—but almost is as good as never. I had a forearm against his throat, exactly where I'd put it if I was planning to crush his windpipe. But I kept it gentle and friendly. Our noses were almost touching.

"Evening, Lee."

"Christ, Dan, you scared the fucking life out of me."

I didn't move. "You should pay more attention."

"Yeah, I would if I was in a war zone. God, you're a psycho." But he was laughing and not attempting to get out of my grip. Our legs were pressed together, mine between his.

I let him go. "Pick up your phone."

He crouched down, checking over his shoulder to make sure I wasn't going to jump him again. "Lucky for you it ain't broken." He looked up at me, his deep-set eyes shaded from the overhead streetlights, his cheek-bones casting deep shadows.

"Now, while you're down there..." I put a hand over my cock and squeezed.

"Fuck off!" He laughed and stood up. "You're mental."

"I'm horny."

"Yeah." He stood up. "Me too." There was my night already planned: it only remained to decide where, and how far, we would go.

There's a bar in the downtown area where the gym staff go to unwind—big-screen TVs permanently tuned to the sports channel, beer by the jug, crappy food cooked somewhere out back. Not the sort of place I'd normally go, but it would do. We took a table near the back. Lee frowned at the screen. "Basketball. I still don't get it," he said. "It's not a proper sport."

"It's a national obsession."

He looked disgusted. "I only watch football at home."

"You're not at home now."

"Don't I know it. What's up with people in this town? They're so bloody unfriendly."

I looked around the bar at the fat slobs eating burgers and swilling beer, the loners and the groups. "You're going to the wrong kind of places, kid."

"Well, where should I be going?"

"Fuck, don't ask me. I'm an old man. A gay man too, for that matter." Lee looked into his beer glass. "What about the guys at college? Where do they go?"

"I dunno. Clubs in Boston. House parties. I can't afford the clubs and I don't get invited to the parties."

"What about movies? Doesn't anyone go to the pictures anymore?"

That cheered him up. "I love movies. Go on my own sometimes. That big place down on Reiss Avenue. The Showcase."

"And what sort of movies do you like, Lee?"

"Action stuff. Stallone. Jason Statham." He pronounced it *Staffum*. "That sort of shit. You look a little like him."

"Jason Statham? Well, we're both bald."

"He's from Kent. Shit county. I'm from Essex." He took a long drink. "Statham's got a really good body."

"He sure has."

He wiped his lips on the back of his hand. "So have you."

"Thanks. Want to see a little more of it?"

Lee looked me directly in the eye, and frowned. "Yeah, but…"

"What?"

"I don't know. What's it mean?"

"Does it have to mean anything?"

"I had girlfriends at home."

"I had girlfriends when I was your age."

"Yeah, but I'm not… Well, I don't think I'm…"

"Gay?"

"Yeah. Am I?"

"Not yet." I reached under the table and grabbed his thigh. "Tomorrow morning, I'm not so sure."

"Right." He swallowed. I didn't move my hand.

"Ever sucked a cock, Lee?"

"Well, yeah. Once. A mate at home, rugby team, we were pissed."

"And?"

"It was all right."

"Ever been fucked?"

"What? No way."

"Thought about it?"

"Suppose so."

"You liked it when I got my finger inside you."

His face was getting very red now, which turned me on. He cleared his throat. "That was weird."

"It's even weirder with a dick."

He gave me that troubled James Dean look again, then laughed. "Fuck, man, I said you were mental."

I reached a little further under the table and pressed my knuckles into his crotch. It wasn't hard to figure out that he was getting hard. There was nothing to be gained by getting thrown out of the bar, however, so I sat up and put my hands where everyone could see them. Let him steam awhile. He finished his beer.

"I need a piss." He stood up, and his sweatpants confirmed what my hand had felt.

"Me too. Let's go."

He had the good sense to hold his gym bag in front of himself as we crossed the bar to the bathroom.

It was one of those old-fashioned facilities that looked like it was last fixed up sometime in the seventies—a long ceramic wall with occasional greenish faucets to flush the piss away, a handful of strong-smelling disinfectant cubes thrown into the trough to keep the smell down, one tiny washbasin, and a towel dispenser that needed filling. There were two cubicles with busted locks, toilet paper strewn on the wet floor, and a dirty mirror. I'm used to digging a hole in the ground if I need a shit, so I'm not that bothered about toilet luxury, but this place was rough.

Lee turned his nose up. "Good job I only need a piss." He hoisted his gym bag over his shoulder, stood at the urinal, and pulled his waistband down. His cock flopped out, half hard. He took it between large thumb and forefinger, and pushed his hips forward.

I positioned myself next to him, my feet apart, shoe touching his. No point in being demure. I unbuttoned and we looked down at each other.

Lee cleared his throat, sniffed, and started pissing, a slightly broken stream at first, jetting off in two different directions, splashing over toward me. It quickly resolved itself into a thick, steady line. I started too, and deliberately aimed my jet to cross with his, causing a little burst of yellow drops.

"Hey! My trousers!" He retaliated by turning thirty degrees toward me, the still strong stream of piss coming dangerously close to my legs. This is the kind of swordplay I can enjoy all day, but our bladders were emptying and if it went on much longer I'd be far too hard to piss anyway.

Lee finished first, and took his time shaking off the last drops. He was in no hurry to put his cock away, despite the fact that anyone could walk in at any moment. He rested it in the palm of his hand as if judging the weight.

I was fully hard now. I put my hands on my hips and let it swing from side to side. Lee watched, coughed again, licked his lips. "That thing really goes up an arse?"

"Yeah, with a lot of lube and a little determination."

"Doesn't it hurt?"

"Of course it fucking hurts. Feel your hole."

"What?"

"Stick a finger down the back of your pants and feel your asshole. Go on."

He did as he was told, his cheeks flushing red, eyes glancing to the door.

"How big is it, Lee?"

"Small."

"Now." I took his forearm, pulled it over. "Feel this." I placed his hand on my dick. He hesitated at first, then grasped it, fingers wrapping around. "How big is that?"

He nodded, eyes wide. "It's big. It's fucking thick."

"Yeah. Damn right. But you're not the first boy I've broken in."

"You'll be careful, right?"

"Don't worry. You're not going to end up in the ER. I know what I'm doing."

He started stroking me, his thumb catching the last drop of piss and rubbing it over the head.

"So what are we waiting for?"

His cock was as hard as mine now, and it was tempting to grab ahold. But a clunk from the door alerted us just in time to the arrival of another bladder full of beer. We both reacted quickly, stuffing our hard pricks away as best we could. I don't think the guy was fooled for a moment, and even if he hadn't noticed, Lee's crazy laughter as we left the bathroom might have given him a clue.

He was a good fuck. As good as any I've had. Cocksucking left a lot to be desired, but I kind of like that: I know if I have him again he'll do better. But once I was inside his ass, and in control, he took it like a man.

We went back to my place—hardly my idea of a great location, but it was either that or having to be very quiet so as not to disturb Lee's roommates. At least in my uncle's old place we could yell the place down and nobody would notice. The sheets were clean, and there was a bathroom that we clean up in, or fuck in. A couch that would just about take the weight of two men. Various tables and chairs that we could reduce to matchwood and it wouldn't matter. A plentiful supply of condoms and lube. And if he stayed over, he could borrow clean underwear.

I never really understand what goes on in straight guys' minds that gets them from the "no way is that going in me!" stage to the "cram it right up to my guts" stage, but it's a mental process I'm familiar with. I guess that first touch of the prostate, the first finger slipped past the sphincter, releases some kind of hormone that works its way up the body to the brain with a simple message: MORE. Lee had had plenty of time since our first encounter in the gym showers. Now he was ready to get fucked good and hard.

I didn't want this to be over too soon, though: once he unloaded, he might run back to his apartment with a sore ass and a head full of regrets. I needed to keep him eager until it was way too late for him to go home, and he was so tired he'd fall asleep in my arms. That way I ensured breakfast. We were both on early shift tomorrow, opening up. But before that, Lee had a little opening up of his own to do.

He kicked off his sneakers as soon as we were inside the house and threw his gym bag down the hall. "Where do we go?"

"You come here." I put one hand on the back of his neck, the other on his ass, and pulled him in. His buttocks were big and round, soft and fleshy on the outside around a core of dense muscle. I kissed him on the mouth. He stiffened a little—perhaps he thought he was going to get through this without actually having to kiss another man—but then relaxed and opened his mouth. Whether it was loneliness or lust that persuaded him I don't know; the results were the same. His eyes were half closed, eyelashes fluttering over blue irises, and he kissed with all the passion that he'd give to a woman, of that I'm sure. I slipped my hand inside his pants and felt that smooth white butt. Virgin: for now. My index finger found the groove that began at his coccyx, and followed it down. It was smooth, and slightly damp with sweat. He would have showered at the gym. This was going to taste good. I like to rim before I fuck, if the circumstances allow. I'm an officer and a gentleman.

Lee was grinding his groin into mine; he was taller than me, so he was pressing into my lower belly while I was stabbing him in the balls. One hand was up inside my shirt, rubbing my hairy stomach and chest, the other was on my back, making sure I didn't escape.

I found his hole and started rubbing my finger around it; he kissed me harder. I was ready to push him to his knees right there and ram into him; if this was Jody, that's exactly what I'd do, a quick, rough, dirty fuck. But this was Lee's cherry, and I wanted to pluck it responsibly. First of all, I wanted to see his lips around my cock.

I yanked his pants down, then pulled his shirt up over his head. He raised his arms and let me undress him. His cock stood out at ninety degrees to his body, and he was already dripping. I was tempted to start sucking again, but this time it was Lee's turn to get to his knees.

"Undo me."

He didn't need to be told twice. Sitting back on his heels, he got to work on my fly buttons and soon had my cock free.

"Suck it."

He took hold of me, looked up and said, "I don't know if I'm any good."

"I'll tell you what to do. Just don't bite me."

He took a deep breath, focused on my piss slit, and licked cautiously, taking my precum into his mouth. "Nice," he said, and then took the head. He licked a little, grazed me slightly with his teeth but hastily corrected himself, looking up for instructions. His dick was still jutting up between his massive rugby player's thighs.

"Okay, now take your time. Make sure you have plenty of saliva. Get it nice and wet, and slide down as far as you can."

He managed maybe a couple of inches before he gagged and stopped.

"That's okay. Back off. Take it easy."

He wiped tears from his eyes. "It looks so easy in porn."

"Practice makes perfect. Try again. Open wide."

This time he got more than halfway, and stopped just before he had to. His tongue was running up and down the underside of my cock, and he was still fully erect—always a good sign. I rubbed his head. "A little further. You're doing well."

Lee responded well to encouragement; he'd make an excellent soldier. His lips moved down, stretching over the widest part, until my bush was tickling his nose.

"Now, up and down. You know what to do."

Like I said, he wasn't great at it, but for a first-timer he could have been a lot worse. And a little dryness and a few scrapes were nothing compared to the look in his eyes, the sight of his fist working his cock. There was sweat on his forehead, and a flush spread right down his neck and shoulders and over his chest, where that red rose bloomed.

I gently fucked his mouth—nothing too rough, I didn't want him to throw up, just in and out half an inch or so to get him used to the sensation. He was nice and wet by now, spit spilling out of his mouth and making his lips and chin glisten. This was getting too hot for comfort, so I stopped moving and waited for Lee to come up for air. He released me after a minute or two.

"Come on," I said. "Time to get naked." I took his hand and we hobbled toward the bedroom, trying to kick off our pants as we went. The bed wasn't far away, and we fell onto it. Lee threw one hefty leg across me, straddling my hips. He pushed my shirt up, leaned forward, and started kissing my chest. My cock was squashed in an uncomfortable position, and he weighed something like 210 pounds, but it was worth it. He found my left tit and started sucking. I let him explore; I was hard and hairy, very different from the girlfriends he'd been fucking back home. Maybe this was one of the reasons he left home. Maybe he wanted to find out what he really was, away from the judging eyes of friends and family. A lot of us did that. I sometimes wondered if that's why I joined the military. Killing was a great cover-up for fucking guys.

After a while I really had to shift that weight off me, so I pushed up and rolled him onto his back. I pulled my shirt off, and we were both naked, side by side. Time to get serious.

We kissed for a long time, hands everywhere, jerking each other off but both conscious of how quickly this could all end if we weren't careful. Neither of us spoke, apart from occasional swearing. Lee said "Oh, mate" a lot.

Finally I said, "Are you ready?" He propped himself up on his elbows. His face was red from kissing and stubble, his dick was hard and wet, and his tits were sticking up like little mushrooms.

"Take it easy, won't you?"

"Relax. You're in good hands."

As I tore the condom package open and started rolling it onto my rock-hard dick, I remembered for the first time that I was cheating on Jody. Well, *remembered* is probably the wrong word; it was just that the familiar routine of stroking the latex down over my head and shaft evoked him so clearly it was like he was in the room. *Yeah,* said a voice in my head, *but he's the one who isn't coming home for spring break. He's the one who broke your date.* So what: I just fuck the first available ass and pretend I'm the injured party? And it gets worse: I'm leading Lee on, making him fall in love with me, doing everything I can to make this so fucking good that he comes back for more. Then what am I going to do? Mention that I have a boyfriend and that he was only ever a fuck on the side? Yeah, pal, I took your cherry, I looked into your beautiful blue eyes as I slid my dick into your ass, the first dick you had ever taken, I kissed you as I fucked you but you were never more than a distraction, a revenge fuck.

I'm very good at blocking out unwelcome thoughts: you have to be when you're in a combat situation. You can't run around bleating, "Oh, the humanity!" when you're clearing up rotting corpses or bursting into a terrorist rat hole with guns blaring. You block your frequencies and go ahead. And that's just what I did: I rolled on the rubber, I lubed myself up, and I started prepping Lee's hole. He squirmed at the touch of my fingers, moaning, eyes half closed, dick drooling. I concentrated on the job, on the feel of his tight ass, the sight of his beautiful flesh, and I didn't hesitate. Didn't even lose one percent of my erection. That's how disconnected I can get.

"You ready?"

"Ready as I'll ever be. Take it easy, for Christ's sake."

"Okay. Now lie on your side."

I positioned him right side down, legs crooked up, and put my arms around him, rubbing my sheathed prick against his lubed ass. I kissed his neck and jaw, pinched his pink tits. He reached around and positioned my cock at his ring. I grabbed his hip and pushed gently. I was in.

He hissed his breath in and bit his lower lip, pressing a hand against my stomach to prevent any further progress. "Fuck," he said, "that really hurts."

I stroked him gently from his ribs over his hips to his thigh. "It's okay, baby. Take it easy. Just get used to it."

"I can't. It feels like it's burning me. Take it out."

"Okay." I withdrew. Some virgins need several attempts. He didn't move away.

"I'm not sure if I can do this, Dan."

"Sure you can. Just take a few deep breaths and we'll try again." I reached around and found his cock, still huge and hard. "If you want to."

He collected himself, twisted his head around to kiss me on the mouth, then said, "Right. Give it another go."

I pushed in again, and this time there was less resistance. I waited, barely moving, then pressed forward again. With one loud groan Lee yielded, opening himself up to me, and I slid in nearly all the way to the base of my cock.

"Fucking hell," he said, half laughing. "What the fuck is that?"

"That's my cock inside you, Lee." Sometimes with these guys you have to state the obvious. "And now I'm going to fuck you."

"Oh, my god." He grabbed his cock and started jerking; I could feel tightness building inside him.

"Okay, hands off. I don't want this to be over before it's begun. Just let me do the work. You concentrate on taking my cock."

He did as he was told, grabbed my hand and squeezed. I increased my pace until I was really fucking him, all the way out, all the way in, no restraint. Veins stood out in his neck and forehead. His lips were parted and he grunted with each thrust. Time for a change of position. I pulled out.

"On your hands and knees."

He rolled over quickly and presented himself to me. His hole was wet and open, and I shoved myself back in. Lee rested his forehead on his forearms, displaying the huge spread of his back and shoulders tapering down to his waist, a rippling triangle of white skin. I was glad he only had that single tattoo: it would be criminal to spoil this with ink. I grabbed his hips and fucked, slapping against him with my balls. Rhythmic grunting had given way to a continuous undulating moan. I reached around and felt his dick, pressed up hard against the curve of his stomach, sticky with precum. A couple of quick strokes was enough; he was close.

I wanted to finish on top, so, without withdrawing, I

carefully turned him over, corkscrewing him around my cock, until he was on his back, my hands on the back of his thighs.

"You ready for this?"

"Yeah. Just fuck me, Dan. I want it."

He looked so serious I almost laughed. I raised my knees off the bed and started ploughing into him with all my strength. I was going to come soon. I grabbed his hand and placed it on his dick.

"Come on."

It didn't take long. One huge jet of white semen shot out of his cock and landed on his chin and neck. That was enough: I spewed a load up his ass, feeling his rectum gripping me tight with every spasm of his orgasm.

When it was over I withdrew slowly, lowered his legs to the bed, and lay beside him. His chest was rising and falling, the skin glistening with sweat. He didn't speak for a while. I put an arm out and drew him in, resting his head on my chest. He moved closer, pressing against me.

"That was fucking incredible, Dan."

I kissed him.

"I wanna do it again."

"Right now?"

"Yeah." He took my hand and placed it on his cock; it was still hard. Oh, to be twenty-one again.

"You'll have to give me a while. I'm an old man."

"I'll get you hard again," he said, and moved down. My dick was still sticky and tasted of rubber from the discarded condom, but Lee didn't seem to mind. He started sucking, and kept going until he got what he wanted.

07

Lee kept me busy and happy all through spring break. He was cute, he learned fast, and even though he still looked at girls on the street, and flirted with the women who used the gym, for the time being he was mine. It was nice to spend time with someone easy and straightforward. Okay, he was straight—nothing straightforward about that, you might think—but I've had some of my happiest times with guys who are taking a little holiday over on my end of the beach. Lee liked eating, drinking, movies, sports, and fucking, not necessarily in that order. He wasn't the world's most stimulating conversationalist, but who cares? He had the body that only a twenty-one-year-old athlete can have, he had that English accent that made the most throwaway remarks sound cute, and he had stamina. On a few occasions we went straight to the gym from a night of fucking, with very little sleep.

But try as I might, I couldn't turn my brain off completely. I couldn't ignore the texts and emails from Jody, and I had to make sure that I could perform for our regular Skype jerk-off sessions. Well, I thought, Lee will get tired of this quickly, he'll go back to girls, or to the UK, and I can focus on Jody again. Nobody will be any the wiser.

It was harder to dismiss the enigma of Al Benson. His disappearance pissed me off at first—who the hell did he think he was, reeling me in with some sob story about a dead buddy, getting me all wired up about the injustice and tragedy of Dick Coburn's death—just a cheap excuse to get his ass plowed, with one hell of a good alibi. But then I started to worry. Someone killed Coburn, someone tried to kill me in Brooklyn, and now Al Benson had disappeared. At first I suspected that he was somehow to blame for the attacks—then I began to worry that he was another victim. Suppose he was dead? Nobody would think to tell me. I Googled his name and found nothing, just a professional profile and a couple of mentions in articles. No news of his death or disappearance—and surely the death of an upstanding citizen like Alan Benson would make the headlines?

I went round and round in circles, puzzling over Benson's whereabouts when I should have been sleeping or concentrating on fucking Lee's ass. Even then—when I had the most beautiful twenty-one-year-old bucking away beneath me—I thought of Benson, his furry body, no longer the slender athlete I'd known and jerked off over, thick around the waist, red in the face, taking every inch of my dick and begging for more. Fuck this! You've got a boy who wants you right here and now, you've got another one in Brooklyn who loves you, and you're fretting over some middle-aged jerkoff who sweet-talked you out of your pants and up his ass? Get a fucking grip, Dan Stagg. Get your priorities right.

So, of course, my resolve snapped and I called the Benson residence. This time I got a response.

"Hello."

"Hi. Is that—" What was her name? Benson had mentioned her often enough. Brenda. That was it. Just in time. "Is that Brenda Benson?"

"Who is this?"

"My name's Dan Stagg. I was a—"

"Oh, hi, Dan. Al mentioned you. You served together in…where was it? Sorry, he was in so many different places."

"Iraq. Ninety-eight."

"That's it. Al said he looked you up in Boston."

That's one way of putting it, sister. "That's right. It was great to see him after so long. Is he there, Brenda?"

"No, I'm sorry. He's away again. We no sooner got home from vacation and he was off at another confer-ence. I mean, I ask him, what does he do at these confer-ences? Is it just the drinks and the cute little secretaries running around?" She allowed herself an indulgent laugh. I rolled my eyes and wondered if this was Benson's MO—four or five conferences a year, and a cock up his ass each time. Ex-comrades, guys in the steam room, escorts, who knows?

"But he's okay."

"Yeah, he's fine. We had a great time visiting with friends in Florida. Certainly a change from Pittsburgh. Do you ever come out this way, Dan? You should visit. I know how much Al enjoys seeing his old buddies."

No, you don't.

"Sure, sure. Well, listen, just tell him I called, okay? I have some news for him. He has my number."

"Okay, Dan. It's a pleasure talking to you. Take care, now."

What did she think I was? One of Benson's lame ducks? One of the guys who never adjusted to civilian life, needed a helping hand, and Al was there, always the hero.

"Goodbye, Brenda."

My first feeling was relief: at least he wasn't dead in a ditch somewhere, or fighting for his life in a hospital. And then, anger. A fucking vacation in Florida, while I was interrogating junkies and nearly getting killed on his behalf? Okay, I had no proof that the attack in Brooklyn was connected, but suspicion and obsession had provided the link. Whatever the truth of the matter, Benson should have been around. He should have cared. And he was in the Everglades or Miami Beach or fucking Disney World. Bastard.

He'd really gotten under my skin.

Time to calm down and let reason take control. Benson was a married closet case who spun me a line to get my dick. It was a great fuck, I fell in love with a memory, and it was over. The attack in Brooklyn: they were muggers, or gangsters, maybe as an outside guess something to do with Julian Marshall. Nothing to do with Coburn. I was in the wrong place at the wrong time, just like the cops said. Brooklyn is dangerous, even the nice parts. Period, dead end, back to reality.

Work, family, Lee, Jody. That was enough shit to handle without cooking up a fresh batch.

But... But...

Even when I had my tongue up Lee's ass, or tasted my dick when I kissed him on the mouth, that goddamn *but* kept getting in the way. What had happened to my concentration, my focus? If I'd been this distracted when I was a marine, I wouldn't have left under a cloud. I'd have left in a coffin. When a conflict has an unsatisfactory outcome you evaluate and learn from your mistakes. You don't keep playing "what if?" Every check is an opportunity. Use it or die.

A memory was coming into focus in my mind. Me—Al Benson—Dick Coburn—Iraq '98—Operation Desert Fox. Under the leadership of Harry Armitage, then a captain, now a general and, according to Benson, soon to be more. Tapped for a job in the West Wing. And there was another guy, surely. Five of us who went ashore that night. Four plus a leader, Armitage. Me—Benson—Coburn—another. Who was it? Jesus, who was it? It started to matter.

We were stationed on an assault ship in the Gulf, one of many vessels mustered for the bombing campaign that, according to our orders and intelligence, would take out military and security targets in Iraq and effectively disarm their WMD capacity. The bombardment began in the middle of December, and lasted for four days and nights; our little unit was sent ashore twenty-four hours before the first official raids to take out a specific target, quickly and quietly. Why a landing party, when everything else was being targeted from the air? Why the tiny "need to know" briefings, the sequestration from other personnel on board the ship? I never questioned it. Don't Ask, Don't Tell applied to a lot more than sexuality. Captain Armitage received his orders directly from above, and his was the only authority we accepted.

Harry Armitage. Christ, he was a bastard. That was the first thing you learned about him, and the last thing that stayed with you. Even now I can summon up a lot of rage and hatred thinking about Armitage—the same way you might still hate a bullying schoolteacher or a violent father even thirty, forty years later. Armitage inspired extreme loyalty from those who enjoyed being under the thumb of a psychopath—and there are plenty of them. The rest of us treated him with uncomplaining respect, because we knew damn well that if we stepped out of line we'd be in the shit. There were many legends concerning Harry Armitage, and I guess they had some foundation in truth. The young lieutenant who committed suicide after Armitage reported him for cowardice and desertion. The USAF pilot who got into a fight with Armitage in a bar and ended up blind in one eye. The others—five? Ten? More?—who quietly disappeared, either AWOL or discharged, because they couldn't stand his bullying. Whatever the truth, you didn't fuck around under Armitage's command. If you were ambitious and didn't mind kissing ass, you could pretty much guarantee promotion: the Corps was full of officers who had done his bidding and been rewarded for it. It's a clever strategy, one that carried Armitage all the way to the rank of general. Surround yourself with yes-men, make them grateful and scared enough to be loyal, play on their weakness and vanity, and you'll just keep on floating upward. Like shit.

Armitage was a thickset man, the same width from shoulders to hips. He had a broad face accentuated by jowls; at times he looked like one of those alpha male orangutans. Very pale blue eyes, tiny pupils, a small, wet mouth. What color was his hair? Hard to say. It was always cut to within a millimeter of his skull. His eyebrows and eyelashes were pale, as I recall. His uniform was immaculate and a little too small for him. He looked like he was about to burst.

I could see him clearly—and as I summoned up that hated face, I felt my mouth turning down in a grimace of disgust. Fuck, why had Al Benson reminded me of that pig? I've met some bad men during my career, but Armitage was the worst. And I'd managed to forget him, just about: must have been years since I'd even thought about him. One of the things I left behind when I left the Corps. But no—he was still in there, lurking around my memory, waiting to spring out and piss me off.

Me—Benson—Coburn—Armitage and... Oh, shit, so close. The comms specialist. A geeky little guy, glasses, underweight. I could see him. We called him Woody, for Woody Allen. Stuck to Armitage like a shadow. Worshipped him—many did, like you might worship a destructive god. Five of us embarked under cover of darkness and landed in a quiet bay, then up to an unguarded coast road, not much more than a track, wheel ruts that might have been centuries old, across scrubland to a perimeter fence. It was exactly what we expected from briefings: the boundary to a surveillance station that was monitoring the precise location of our fleet. If we could take out the target quietly and efficiently, then the Allied ops of the next few days would meet considerably less resistance: none at all, in theory. That's how naive and trusting we were: we believed that the entire Iraqi security operation hinged on one badly guarded surveillance station, and if we simply went in and killed the personnel then the bombing could proceed unchecked. Maximum shock and awe, the whole thing over in days, Saddam likely to be toppled once his WMD capacity was wiped out, job done, pat on the back, thanks, boys. We didn't expect much public recognition: it had been made very clear that this little job was off the radar in terms of press and public. But we'd get our reward in more tangible ways: promotion, opportunities, the chance to be part of Armitage's army. He was charismatic enough to get that kind of loyalty. We also knew that if we screwed things up, or questioned him, our career trajectory would go the other way.

We got through the perimeter easily: no alarms, no obvious guards. That's when I started to feel uneasy. If the target was as important as we'd been told, why the fuck wasn't it surrounded by Republican Guards? Why wasn't there a mesh of laser beams, razor wire, and land mines between the fence and the installation? How come we could just breeze up to the door as if we were coming around for coffee?

Armitage stationed two of us at the front entrance, two at the back. It was a squat concrete building, not much more than a bunker, probably slapped up sometime in the last five years and already falling to pieces. The flat roof was bristling with aerials, wires slung loosely down to generators that throbbed in the back. Judging from the smell there was no proper sanitation, just a hole dug somewhere nearby and regularly filled with sand. We could hear voices and what sounded like a radio or CD player. Music. This was Saddam's most strategically important base and they were listening to Michael Jackson? I exchanged a glance with the guy I was positioned with—Coburn, was it? No—Douglas, that's it. Jerry Douglas, alias Woody, the comms guy who had been monitoring radio output from the station. He shrugged.

Armitage gave the signal and we stormed the place, one, two, three, kicking down the doors with weapons at the ready. Douglas and me at the back door, Benson and Coburn at the front, and as soon as Benson yelled "target secure" Armitage came in behind them.

And this is where it started to go wrong.

Instead of a bunch of soldiers and signal operators, all armed to the teeth and ready to offer resistance, we saw a group of seven civilians sitting around tables, some in Western dress, talking and smoking, drinking Coke and listening to the radio. There were newspapers—some Arabic, some English—I'm pretty sure I saw the *Herald Tribune*. The guys looked surprised when we burst in, faces smeared with camouflage, weapons primed. They didn't scream or panic. A couple of them got up from their chairs; one of them, a man of forty-five, fifty, in Western dress, shirtsleeves rolled up, slacks and sandals, steel-rimmed glasses, untidy hair, made a placatory gesture with his hands and actually smiled. "Gentlemen," he said, but he got no further.

"At my command," screamed Armitage, one beefy arm raised. "Fire!"

His hand came down, and death spewed out of five automatic weapons. I was familiar enough with the effect of bullets at close quarters not to be shocked by the way the bodies jerked and jumped, the way blood and brains splattered out of heads and guts. Even the smell didn't bother me much; I'd smelled it before, I'd smell it again, too many times.

The blast of gunfire lasted ten seconds, no more. When the reverberation died down there was a moment of silence broken only by the gasping, squelching sounds of dying men, before Armitage raised his gun to the ceiling and let out a rebel yell.

"Woooo-hooooh! We fucking did it!"

Benson, Coburn and I glanced at each other—we dared do no more—a look that said, *Yeah, we did it, but what the fuck did we do?* Douglas was too busy punching the air and saying "All right! All right!" to notice. He had that look of the true believer that I've seen on the faces of fanatics all over the world.

"Let's get out," said Benson, but Armitage scowled.

"All in good time. I want a souvenir."

"What?"

"Pile the bodies up over there, boys." He pointed to a corner of the room where there was a pitiful collection of clothes, books, and food, now spattered with blood and guts and chunks of smashed cinder block. "Make a nice big hill."

Douglas pitched in right away, grabbing one corpse under the arms and dragging it across the floor. The rest of us stood dumbfounded.

"Did you hear me? Move the fucking bodies."

Nobody questioned him, though we all knew where this kind of thing could lead. The political repercussions of abusing the enemy were deadly. Armitage was putting his career in our hands—if this got out, Washington would destroy him. But if we disobeyed... We didn't disobey. We were marines.

It took five minutes to stack the bodies in a pile stable enough for Armitage to stand on. He mounted a chair, steadied himself with one hand on the wall and stood on top of the corpses, one leg crooked, the boot on top of a head. The guy with the glasses—smashed now, the lenses missing, the skull broken open—Armitage's boot pressing down, distorting what was left of his mouth into a grotesque parody of a kiss.

"Douglas, quick. Take the fucking picture."

A picture? Jesus Christ. Coburn, Benson and I shrank against the opposite wall. Armitage didn't notice, too busy preening and posing on his victory mound. Douglas had a compact digital camera, the kind of thing you might take on vacation. Flash, flash, flash. "That's great, sir! One more, you blinked. Okay, that's fantastic. Woo-hoooh!"

And then, dazed and sick, we crept back the way we had come, through the breached perimeter, down the rutted track to the transport waiting at the beach.

I don't think any of us discussed what happened. Nightmares, maybe, of those piled corpses, of Douglas and Armitage's sadistic glee. And then there was another horror to drive out the last one, and another, and the memories faded into the general background of a soldier's past. But now, dug up by Al Benson and the mystery of Dick Coburn's death, it came back with vivid horror. The smile on the guy's face as he came toward us, hands out in a gesture of peace... The English-language newspapers, the clothes, the cans of Coke... and above all, Michael fucking Jackson on the radio, silenced by gunfire. Armitage crowing on a mound of carrion. Douglas's eager, fanatic gaze. The camera. It was all as clear to me as a photograph.

I needed to talk to someone who would understand—but who? Jody? He tried to listen to my stories of active service, but I never got far before he started sucking my dick. My parents? Forget it, they were only interested in the reflected glory, and when that was tarnished they just dismissed the whole sorry subject. Lee? Poor kid, he had problems enough of his own, and, besides, it was nice to have some uncomplicated company without darkening it with my nightmares. And Al Benson, the man who started this whole chain of memory, was off the radar, hiding out until his ass needed filling again.

That left one person: Jerry Douglas. The crazy little shit who took the photographs. Armitage's number one fan. Maybe he could tell me something about what happened after that operation, when the team was disbanded and we were all assigned to different jobs. Maybe he even knew something about Dick Coburn. He was the sort of guy who'd follow the details of everyone's career—the nerd with the scrapbooks full of newspaper clippings. He'd love to talk about the good old days. All I had to do was find him.

If you'd asked me to find an old buddy a couple of years ago, I'd have started looking in the phone book, then called information, and if that didn't work I'd hire a private detective. Now I know that you can find almost anyone on the Internet, though nine times out of ten I haven't got a clue how to go about it. I can just about switch it on, position the webcam, and turn on Skype, which is how I keep Jody happy. If I am keeping him happy, which I begin to doubt. Beyond that is enemy territory. Jody has explained it to me in the same way you'd teach a moderately bright four-year-old: you move the mouse until the little arrow points to the box, and then you put in the letters that make the word that you want to find. After a couple of days and a lot of shouting from both of us, he taught me how to use the Google search engine. So that's what I did. "Jerry Douglas." Lots of results, most of them relating to a highly successful guitarist and record producer. I screwed up my eyes and scrutinized the face. Could be him, I guess, with a new haircut and a beard... Was that the face I saw grinning at a pile of corpses? No way. Wrong Jerry Douglas. I kept searching. There were thousands of them: doctors, lawyers, ordinary guys, fat guys, thin guys, but nobody I could recognize as my partner in crime from '98. I was about to give up and go down to the public library to use the phone book, when I remembered something Jody had said to me about one hundred times a day for the last two years.

Use Facebook.

Fucking Facebook. The hours Jody wasted on that thing when he could have been—I don't know, cleaning his room, reading a book, studying, sucking my dick. I hate Facebook. I'd do almost anything in this world to avoid letting people know my private business, and here was a way in which people happily gave away their privacy without even charging for it.

But everyone's on Facebook, Dan. Everyone!

Not me. Never. But Jerry Douglas? Yeah, he might be there.

And so—slowly, painfully, two steps forward one step back—I signed up to Facebook and created my own profile. I put next to no information on it, and I sure as hell didn't add a photograph, but there it was. Dan Stagg. And within a few moments, I had received a kind offer of marriage from a nice young woman in Guatemala.

Now what?

Search for people, places, and things.

Sounds about right. Jerry Douglas.

So many Jerry Douglases. None of them mine. And then—flash! Inspiration.

Woody Douglas.

There was only one of them. I was right. He clung on to those memories, even keeping the nickname that was given as an insult.

Message.

Hi, Woody. Dan Stagg here. Don't know if you remember me...

08

I was right: Jerry Douglas was the sort of guy who is desperate to talk about the old days. We've all met them: the high school jock who went fat, boring the pants off his old buddies about the glory days. The failed musician who once did a gig in a club the week after someone more famous played there. The uncles and aunts who talk about long-ago summer vacations as if they were the happiest times of their lives. It's one of the reasons I don't go to reunions and I avoid parties as much as possible. That and the fact that, according to Jody, I'm a miserable bastard.

Douglas was still in the Corps, pushing paper in DC. A really exciting job, he said, in the education branch, helping marines work their way up the promotion ladder and giving them a real advantage in civilian life as well. He made it sound like his own personal crusade, but in fact he was part of the bursar's office, dealing with administration, and never set foot in a classroom from one year to the next. But he was there in DC, close to power if not part of it, based in the old marine barracks on 8th Street. An impressive building, full of history, with Jerry Douglas tucked away in a tiny office on the top floor, baking in summer and freezing in winter, handling the application forms of people younger, smarter, and more successful than himself.

This much I learned from the eager correspondence we entered into on Facebook. Left unchecked, he'd keep messaging me for an hour plus. I asked him nothing about Coburn and Armitage; I didn't want to scare him off. "Remember taking those photos? Yeah? And you're *still* not in prison?"

Instead I told him that I was passing through DC on business—Benson wasn't the only one who could invent business trips—and took time off work to make the trip. Despite everything it represents, I actually like the capital. I still get a kick out of wandering around the national monuments and government buildings. I feel proud that I served my country. What my country did to me in return is a different matter. Times have changed, and I'm trying to change with them. A trip to Washington might be a good chance to make peace with the past. They threw me out, but time moves on.

It was hot in the city, one of those early blasts of summer that make we want to head for the mountains. DC wasn't yet the humid hell it would become—you could still walk around the streets without having to change your shirt every other block—but it was warm enough to get the guys into T-shirts and shorts. I dropped my gym bag at the YMCA and walked downtown, my head swiveling at so much beauty on the streets. Perhaps later I'd find a bar, or just hit the Y gym.

Douglas wanted me to come to his office, of

course—he would do anything for the illusion of rank and status. He was still a serving USMC officer, and I was just a civilian, and it would have been unkind to remind him that I'd risen to the rank of major while he was still just a first lieutenant, unpromoted in all those years. I reported to security and was given a pass. Was it my imagination, or did the guy on the desk smile when he said, "Lieutenant Douglas is expecting you, sir?" Perhaps Douglas gave a lot of people a guided tour of his little empire. Perhaps he was one of those joke characters; every office has one.

He met me at the elevator door. Five-five, and almost as wide. Time and a desk job had not been kind. He was bald apart from a gray-black band above the ears. Glasses perched on the end of a blobby nose. Shirt too tight, wet with sweat. He pushed his glasses up his nose and grinned; his teeth were discolored.

"The Stag!"

I don't recall anyone ever calling me this, but I said, "Woody!" and clapped him on the back. He hugged me back like a long-lost friend.

"Come in, come in. This is where it all happens." A tiny room, ten feet square, with two walls entirely taken up with box files. His desk was a chaos of paper, with an antique-looking computer hogging most of the space. Post-It notes stuck to every surface, cold cups of coffee congealing and half-eaten donuts leaving grease marks on documents. The single window had not been opened for weeks, judging by the stale smell.

"Thanks." I wanted to back out with my hand over my mouth, but I braved it. "I can see you're a very busy man."

"Yeah." He gestured around, proud of the chaos. "I think you can say I'm pretty busy. Every single application passes across my desk. I have to keep everything in order. I tell you, Danny, the whole operation would fall to pieces without me."

"You were always organized, Woody."

"You gotta be."

"Impressive setup."

If he registered any sarcasm, he didn't show it. "Thanks!" He sounded really pleased. "Means a lot. It's a long way from the front line, but I think I found something I'm really good at. I miss the action, of course. And I'm a little out of shape." He patted his belly, which wobbled. "But hell, we had some times, right? Jesus. Wooh!"

A chill ran down my spine, and I heard that "Wooh!" echoing off the bullet-riddled concrete walls of the surveillance station.

"Oh, yeah. We had some times."

"So how's life treating you, Dan? You doing okay?" He had that look of concern on his face that always tells me someone knows my history. Pity and contempt cloaked with care. Fuck you, Woody, I wanted to say, I made it to major and I would have been a general if the fucking Neanderthals in the White House had pulled their fingers out of their asses a few years earlier.

"I'm doing fine, thanks. Busy. Loving it."

"What is it you do, exactly?"

I was damned if I was going to say, *I pick up wet towels in a fourth-rate gym.* "I'm a personal trainer. Still kicking asses."

"That's awesome. Maybe I should book myself in for

a couple of sessions. What do you think, Dan? Help me shift some of my happy fat?"

The only thing that was going to shift Douglas's belly was a forklift, but I said, "Sure, if you ever come up to Massachusetts. But you've got access to better training right here in the Corps."

"If only I had time," said Douglas. "I'm so busy. That's the problem when you move over to the executive side."

"Right."

"Anyway, let's get out of here." He looked at his watch. "I've got an hour. Important meetings this afternoon, but"—he held up his hands in a what-can-you-do? gesture—"I'll have to wing it. Come on. Let's eat."

"Where would you suggest?"

He patted his briefcase. "We're having a picnic."

We walked down to the river and found a bench. Douglas spread a paper napkin between us and produced packets of sandwiches wrapped in foil.

"Your wife makes you lunch every day? Lucky guy."

He snickered through his nose. "Not my wife, Dan. My mother." He patted his stomach. "Good old home cooking."

"Lucky guy." It didn't surprise me. I could imagine Douglas's mother, a female edition of her son, short and round, bossing him around the house, sending him off to work with a packed lunch and a pat on the head. But the food was good—some kind of sausage between great chunks of white bread, oozing with mustard and mayonnaise. Little wonder Douglas was heavy.

"You in touch with any of the gang, Dan?"

"Not really. I ran into Al Benson a couple of weeks back."

"Al Benson? Jesus! How's he doing? Lives in Pittsburgh, right? We kept in touch for a few years—Christmas cards, you know—but then I guess we were just too busy. Red Benson. He was a great guy. Married with kids now, right?"

Douglas had the lowdown on everyone; I imagined him spending his leisure time hunting around online.

"Yep." And if he knew that much about Benson, he knew plenty about me.

"Send him my best. What a great guy. Tell him Woody Douglas still owes him twenty bucks! He'll understand, long story. We were real good buddies back in the day. I mean, he had my back, I had his, you know what I mean? Tight."

Not nearly as tight as Benson's asshole when I shoved my cock into it, I thought, but that was one little detail that Douglas didn't need to know.

"Apart from that, though, I kind of lost touch. You know how it is." I didn't want to tell him too much—and I certainly didn't want to tell him that I was investigating Dick Coburn's death. Not yet.

"Well, you stayed in active service, didn't you? I saw your name popping up here and there. Guess you saw a lot of exciting stuff."

"They sent me to all the major shitholes."

"I got an injury." He rubbed his shin. "It was bad for a while, but I'm lucky to be alive. And you know, they look after you." He grimaced as if in pain. "Up to a point."

"Still, you've got a job."

"Yeah, yeah, I'm not complaining." He spoke a little too fast, obviously realizing that he was on thin ice. "I'll retire from this job, I guess. Not much of a career, but... Well, certain people made sure of that."

"What do you mean?"

"There are some nasty people up there." He nodded in the direction of the Pentagon.

"You're telling me."

He brushed the crumbs off his jacket and stared out at the river. "Do you remember Harry Armitage, Dan?"

Douglas and Benson, both dwelling on Armitage. "Captain Armitage? Of course. He was a mean moth-erfucker."

"Still is." He picked his nails; they were chewed down to the quick. "Still is."

"I read about him in the papers. He's a big shot now, right?"

"Those journalists don't know what they're talking about. Harry Armitage went a long way by being a bully and a liar, but he's never going to make it to the West Wing."

"Why not?"

"Because..." He stared out at the river again. "Politicians come under so much scrutiny."

"What's he got to hide?"

Douglas glanced at me and quickly looked away. We both knew: Iraq, a pile of corpses, a photograph taken in a moment of madness.

We sat in silence.

"Everywhere I went," Douglas said at last, "Armitage was there. Every posting. And now he's in Washington."

"That's where generals usually end up."

"And I'm still a lousy lieutenant." He took a big, angry bite of Mom's sandwich, tearing the bread with his teeth. "He hates me."

"You think he remembers you?" I must have sounded incredulous, because Douglas scowled at me, mayonnaise glistening on his chin.

"Of course he fucking does. He always—" He checked himself and wiped his face with a handkerchief. A couple of people passed along the Riverwalk. Douglas waited till they were out of earshot.

"It's all because of Quiller."

The name meant nothing to me.

"Come on, Dan. Quiller. Don't you remember?"

"I don't know what you're—"

"In the surveillance station. The guy we killed."

"They were just radio operators or something. Surveillance guys."

"Peter Quiller was a UN weapons inspector." Douglas spoke in a low monotone. "Remember the guy in the glasses? The guy who tried to—"

"Talk to us. Yes."

"Peter Quiller. That's who we were sent to kill that night."

"Come on, Douglas. You can't be serious. We didn't kill UN inspectors."

"How do you know?"

"Because—no way, man. That's just ridiculous."

The Riverwalk was getting busy; it was a beautiful afternoon. "We can't talk here. Meet me tonight, six o'clock. There's a bar near my house." He gave me an address in Friendship Heights. "It's quiet. Military personnel don't go there. More of a family place."

At least he didn't invite me home to try Mom's meat loaf.

"Talk to no one, Dan. No one. If we've been seen…"

He scuttled back to his office. I sat in the sun for a while, watching the guys; one or two of them turned back to pass me again. It would be easy to pick someone up and take him back to the Y, forget all about Jerry Douglas and his crazy theories. But something stopped me. Suspicion. Discipline, perhaps. I was turning back into a marine.

The bar looked like an airport lounge, ugly and soulless, all gray and blue with too much metal. Douglas thought it was classy. Half a bottle of beer was enough to loosen his tongue.

"You don't believe me, do you, Dan? I'm disappointed."

"I didn't say that. It's just…"

"What?" Douglas's cheeks were flushed, his pupils dilated. What kind of crazy pills was he on? "You think I'm making this stuff up? You think I'm one of those conspiracy theory guys who believe any shit they like?"

That's exactly what I thought he was, but I said, "No, of course not. But come on—a weapons inspector? The UN had withdrawn all the weapons inspectors before Desert Fox started."

"Not Peter Quiller."

"And we didn't kill our own people. We were on the same side, remember?"

"Were we?"

"They were looking for WMDs, same as us."

"They didn't find a thing, and you know it. Everyone knows it. Jesus, Dan, are you the last person who still believes this crap?"

"I don't know what I believe anymore." That would have shut most people up. I looked across the bar, half turning my back on Douglas. He was undeterred.

"We were lied to, Dan."

I said nothing, just shrugged.

"Armitage lied to us."

"Armitage was nuts."

"Ah! You do believe that, then."

I turned back to him. "Yes. I remember enough to believe that. He was a bastard among thousands of bastards. The Corps is full of them, from the bottom right up to the top. It's not news, Woody. You've been around long enough to know that. And you know what? I think you were the smart one. You took a desk job and kept your head down. Took Uncle Sam's money and stayed safe."

Wrong move, Dan. Douglas's face went purple, then abruptly white. He half stood. "You think I'm proud of that?" He was shouting in earnest now, and the barman shot warning glances at us. "You think I took the coward's way out?"

"I didn't say that."

"I know what you mean, Major Stagg. Oh, it's so easy for you, traveling around the world and kicking ass and getting decorated and promoted for it." Douglas seemed to have forgotten how I was rewarded for my efforts. "Everybody loved you. The big fucking hero. It all came easy, didn't it? They handed you a promotion on a plate. But some of us struggled and got overlooked every time. How do you think that feels, knowing that younger men are laughing at you? Knowing that every single time you put in for promotion someone's marking your card? I never had a chance." He sounded like an aggrieved five-year-old. "They always hated me."

"They?"

"Armitage's people."

"Right." How soon could I leave?

"I'm serious. He's destroyed me."

"Yeah. You said."

"It's true." His voice cracked and went high. He took a sip of beer. "And we both know why."

"Enlighten me."

"Because of Iraq."

"Ah." Here we go.

"Don't say you don't remember the photo."

I played dumb, and looked as if I was drawing a blank.

"Come on, Dan. All of us on that mission—we've all suffered. You were thrown out. Benson was thrown out."

"He quit."

"That what he's saying? Okay. He jumped before he was pushed. And then there's Dick Coburn."

"Who?" As if I didn't know.

"Did it really mean that little to you, Dan? I remember it all so clearly." He put his hand over his eyes for a moment. "Every fucking thing."

"Okay—yeah, Coburn. Was that his name? What happened to him?"

"I don't know. He disappeared. But he was kicked out too."

He didn't know Coburn was dead, then. I wasn't going to tell him. It would be like throwing gasoline on a fire. "What are you saying?"

"He screwed us all."

"Woody, listen. I was thrown out of the Marines because I fell in love with another man. I got caught, and I didn't deny it. Okay? That's the beginning and end of it."

"Oh, no, no. There were thousands of guys like you. Did they all get discharged?"

"Plenty did."

"Yeah. And plenty didn't. Why you?"

I was getting angry; my past, my pain, my business. "I broke the rules. And now, thank god, the rules have changed."

"Too late for you, though."

"Yeah. Right." I finished my beer and got up to leave.

"They'd have got you for something else."

"Forget it, Douglas."

"And I'm next."

Why didn't I just walk out? "What?"

"They're getting rid of me. They call it restructuring. I call it the sack."

"They can't fire you. They have to redeploy you."

"Oh, they're clever, Dan. Very clever. They know all about me—my mother's health care, just how much that costs. They've kept me on the breadline for all these years." A first lieutenant's pay isn't great, but it's not the breadline. "And now she needs surgery or she's going to die. They waited and watched, Dan. They bided their time. And now you know what they're offering me?"

"Go on."

"Severance pay of one hundred grand."

"That sounds pretty generous to me. It's a lot more than I got. What's your problem?"

"It's exactly what I need for my mother's treatment."

"Next you'll be telling me that they poisoned your mother to make her ill."

"Don't think I haven't wondered."

I sat down and tried to change the subject. "Well, that's a great opportunity, Douglas. You can do a lot with that money. Make a fresh start. We're young enough to—"

"Just exactly at the time when Harry Armitage is about to become National Security Advisor."

"I thought you said that couldn't happen."

"It won't, if people like you and me stand up to be counted."

"Why us?"

"You know why."

I nodded. "The photo."

"You know what would happen if that got out?"

"Armitage's career would be over. He'd be convicted of war crimes."

"Exactly." Douglas folded his arms across his belly and looked very pleased with himself.

"What happened to the photo, Douglas?"

He shrugged and smiled.

"You think someone's got it?"

Silence.

"Do you still have it?"

He started to look nervous. Perhaps I wasn't one of the good guys, after all. Perhaps coming to an empty bar with me and sharing his conspiracy theories wasn't such a great idea. Maybe I was one of Armitage's army, deep deep undercover—the DADT story a smokescreen for the blackest of black ops. That's what I'd think, if I was in Douglas's shoes. I'd be frightened, and not without reason.

He started babbling. "All I want is justice. There are men who fought for their country, dammit, who gave their lives and never got a thing, and he's all the way up at the top of the tree looking down, and if he thinks he can just do this to me without... Without..."

"What, Douglas?"

"It's not right." The sulky five-year-old was back. "I'm frightened."

"Why?"

"I'm being followed."

I was about to dismiss this as paranoia, until I remembered that someone had followed me too—all the way to the Pratt Campus in Brooklyn, with a baseball bat. Like someone followed Dick Coburn, with a can of gas and a lighter.

"What makes you say that?"

"I went through the same training you did, Dan. Don't insult me."

"Tell me what happened."

"At night. Early in the morning. If I go out for a walk. I think the house is being watched. My mom said there have been some callers."

"Who?"

"They said they were selling insurance."

"Okay." There might be a grain of truth in what Douglas was saying. I wasn't about to tell him my worst suspicions, but perhaps he wasn't as crazy as I suspected. "Look, if you get worried about stuff, you give me a call, right? We can look out for each other."

"I knew you had the right stuff, Dan." He looked relieved and pleased. "I'm not making this up, you know."

"No," I said, "I don't believe you are."

09

Another victim of the Marine machine. Another one driven crazy—not by death and danger, not by lies and secrecy, but by the slow drip-drip-drip of disappointment. Some of us get screwed because of who we sleep with. Some can't handle civilian life, and end up dying on the street. Others stay inside and get crushed. Maybe Al Benson was the smart one: he got out and made a life for himself. Okay, it's not one hundred percent honest, but it works. If he has to sneak off once in a while and get a dick up his ass, so what? He has a family and a future.

And you know what Al Benson doesn't need? A fuckup like me making waves. Yes, he used me. He spun me a line and I took the bait. He got his money's worth out of that trip to Walgreens, and now he's home with his wife and kids enjoying the life he was meant to have.

What life was I meant to have? Jody—and a future I never believed could be mine? Or was I going to waste my time in a bug-infested shack, trying to please a family who hated me, screwing some poor confused kid who was already falling in love with me? What would I say to Lee when I no longer needed him? Sorry, buddy, I got bored waiting for my boyfriend to come on a visit, and yours was the nicest ass I could find. Now leave me alone.

I needed to do some serious thinking. That much, at least, I worked out on the way home from DC.

Travel makes me miserable. I don't like the feeling of impermanence and rootlessness, which is kind of stupid for someone who spent most of his adult life going wherever the Marine Corps sent him, most of them places you'd want to get out of as quickly as possible. But that was then. I was young and dumb and too scared to stand still. How many kids join the military so they don't have to think about themselves? It's so much easier to be, and do, what you're told. If someone sat me down at the age of eighteen and said, "Listen, Dan—things are about to change. All the things that make you feel sad and wrong are going to be okay"—well, maybe I'd have made different choices. Plenty did—the guys in the front line of liberation, who fought the battles that mattered. I just traveled the world killing foreigners. Now I want a home and permanence and a family. I want it so bad I'm almost begging. And yet, the closer I get to it, the more determined I am to fuck it up. I've allowed myself to believe that Jody's pushing me away, that I'm alone and unlovable.

See? I really should never take the train.

At the same time as I was wallowing in self-pity and self-reproach, I was going over what Jerry Douglas told me. Peter Quiller, a UN weapons inspector who somehow stayed behind in Iraq after the withdrawal, long enough to get himself killed in a targeted assassination. Could that really be true? And if so, who gave the order? Who were the other guys in the room—the mixture of Arabs and Westerners, all of them listening to Michael Jackson? It looked like a Friday night poker party—not the sort of thing the Pentagon would send a mad bastard like Harry Armitage to break up. What kind of threat could they possibly pose? And who was threatened?

I got home late, but my mind was buzzing and I couldn't sleep. I switched on my laptop and started searching. Peter Quiller—WMD—UNSCOM—Desert Fox—Iraq—death. Nothing at first. Dig deeper. Search the blogs. I'd been listening when Jody taught me the basics of Google. And there. Just three. Three little mentions of Peter Quiller in the right place at the right time and very, very dead.

"Friendly fire," said one of them. "Accidental death," said another. The other reported his "disappearance." I clicked through and read on. Two were sketchy in the extreme, little more than third-hand gossip. "People in the know" does not cut it for me. Neither does "Washington sources" or "ex-military personnel." But there was one blog, the least sensational of the three, that had something useful to say. Peter Quiller, who was forty-nine when he disappeared, was one of the most vocal critics of the WMD theory inside the UN. He had announced to the press when he was sent to Iraq that he would be looking for "substantial, verifiable proof" of Saddam's WMD capability before he was willing to sanction any kind of military action. During the inspections, he consistently dismissed stories that were being reported in American newspapers as fact. "Until a thing has been seen, we cannot be sure that it exists," he said during a press call; it was not widely reported, nothing he said was widely reported, and the blogger's one and only concession to speculation was that Quiller had been sidelined from the inspection, if not absolutely gagged. Was he an opponent of US military involvement in Iraq? Did he challenge the legality of the attacks? Perhaps, but not on record. Other, less dependable writers were prepared to make him out to be some kind of hero—but it's easy to create heroes after the event. At the time, nobody could have known whether he was right or wrong. It was only his disappearance that made him a martyr.

If it was Peter Quiller who we killed in that undefended surveillance station, then maybe Douglas was on to something. The single photograph that all three blogs reproduced looked unfamiliar. Was that the man I saw coming toward my gun with his hands out in greeting and a smile on his face? Or was Quiller one of the others—perhaps the body that ended up at the bottom of Armitage's victory mound?

I needed more information. Why? Because I suddenly cared about justice and peace? My ass. I wanted something to take back to Al Benson. Because at the back of my mind, like a noise that won't go away, was the nagging desire to see him again. To do something, anything, to please him. That was the driving force— far stronger than my desire to settle down and have a family, to work things out with Jody, even to fuck the relatively convenient ass just down the road in Lowell.

I emailed the blogger, who went under the name of

Newsbuster. Nothing too definite. *I'm an ex-marine, and I was wondering if you could help me with a few details about the 1998 Desert Fox campaign.*

That should get a response.

It did.

At three o'clock in the morning, which is presumably the time when bloggers, like coyotes and cockroaches, are at their most active, my inbox made the irritating little pinging sound that I haven't yet figured out how to turn off.

Hi, Dan, it read. *Always happy to hear from military personnel, serving or otherwise. What can I help you with? Best, Nas.*

At the bottom it said, *Naseer Khan, editor in chief, Newsbuster.*

How much should I give away? Was I playing with fire? What the fuck. After a lifetime on the frontlines I tend to shoot first and deal with the consequences as they come. I wrote back.

I was interested in your piece about Peter Quiller. I served under General Armitage during Operation Desert Fox.

If there was any substance to Jerry Douglas's theories, that should be enough to hook him.

The reply came right back.

You have friends in high places. We're just getting confirmation of Armitage's appointment as National Security Advisor.

I felt a shudder across my shoulders, that feeling you sometimes get when an unseen person walks behind you. Armitage is in the West Wing. Nobody and nothing can stop him. What had Douglas said? *He'll never make it. Too much to hide.* Hints that someone—Douglas himself?—knew the whereabouts of the Desert Fox photo. Armitage crowing on a heap of corpses, his boot smashing into a face that might or might not be Peter Quiller's.

And now he'd made it. Douglas's ideas evaporated like morning mist. There was nothing on Harry Armitage—or if there was, he knew how to take care of it.

Who knew? Four witnesses, and one of them was dead. That left Benson, Douglas, and me.

And if Armitage was in the White House, he now had unlimited resources with which to make damn sure that he stayed there. Baseball bats. Strange callers at Douglas's home.

Good for Armitage, I wrote back. *Always knew he'd go far. Can we meet?*

Sure, man. I'm in DC. Where are you?

Damn it. Why didn't I do the research before I got on the train?

I'm down that way often, I lied. *I'll be in touch.*

It was my father's seventy-fifth birthday that weekend, and against my better judgement I agreed to go to the party. You know the kind of thing: they invite you, hoping you'll say no. You say yes, because you don't want to upset them, but all the time you're looking for a way out. It gets so complicated with everyone saying the opposite of what they mean that you end up going just to spite them. My sister would be there with her husband and kids; my brother would be there, possibly with his latest girlfriend. I can just about manage a conversation with my ten-year-old niece; the rest of them stare over my shoulder and talk about the weather. If it got too bad I could always disappear to the cellar and start ripping out some of the rotting woodwork. It got damaged in the floods a few years back and badly needs replacing. There's always something to do if you want to escape a party badly enough.

Of one thing I was sure: nobody would ask a single question about me—at least, not to my face. "How ya doin'?" maybe, but that doesn't require an answer.

I dressed in jeans and a polo shirt—that's pretty much my uniform these days—and checked my face in the mirror. There wasn't much left of the bruising I got in Brooklyn, so I wasn't going to scare the kids. My hair (what's left of it) was tidy, and I'd shaved. I didn't look psychotic, and I didn't look gay. My brother-in-law dresses better than me, and unless there's a big skeleton in that family closet he's strictly a ladies' man.

I lasted an hour and a half—not bad, considering that for much of that time I stood at the edge of the group hardly speaking. My parents had invited all their neighbors, but I wasn't introduced to a single one. I cleared up empty glasses and bottles. I ran the barbecue for a while—it was a warm day, and they'd thrown caution to the winds and moved the party out into the garden. Still nobody talked to me. Had they been warned? Did they think they could catch something from me? I gave the kids a hug and a few bucks each, and then slipped away. Happy fucking birthday, Dad.

I walked home to clear my head. I was angry and restless, and there's only one way to deal with that, right? But Lee wasn't picking up his phone. Shit. I'd turn on Skype when I got home, and have a booty call with Jody, if he was home. Better than nothing.

One of the military habits I find impossible to break is the basic security routine that you deploy on your own quarters. It's important to know if someone's waiting for you before you enter your room; once you're inside, it's too late. So even in civilian life I leave something on my door that will show whether it's been disturbed in my absence: a piece of tape, a cigarette paper, cotton. I rotate the position and the materials regularly, without much thought. Why? There's nothing to steal, and nobody's looking for me. Are they?

Perhaps they are. The cigarette paper that I'd gummed to the top of the door, between the frame and panel, was gone. I looked around the porch: no sign. It's possible it had blown away, though it was a still evening. Quickly and quietly, making sure the old boards didn't creak, I examined the rest of the door. Scratch marks in the grime and dust around the lock; someone's been fooling around with a credit card and popped the lock. It's not difficult. Anyone with a basic knowledge of housebreaking could get in.

I crept around the back of the house, into the overgrown yard. There's a screened-off bathroom window that doesn't close properly; I've been meaning to fix it for a while, but now I was glad I hadn't. I climbed up onto the windowsill, opened it, and dropped to the floor. The bathroom was dark. I stopped and listened. Nothing. Someone's been here and left, maybe. Realized there was nothing worth stealing and left the way they came. I opened the door and froze.

There was a light in the kitchen.

I never leave lights on.

A dim light—not the overhead fluorescents, something soft and bluish. The open fridge door? Maybe. A cellphone screen?

There was a firearm locked in a strongbox underneath a floorboard in the bedroom. Not an option. But I have my hands.

I moved swiftly, silently.

The door was open. A figure sitting in a chair, the table in front of him, the door behind him.

Bad mistake. If Armitage is sending out hit men as stupid as this, he deserves to fail.

One explosive jump, a forearm around the windpipe, and we crashed to the ground with all my weight on top. The breath went out of him, and the phone, still bright, skittered across the kitchen floor and under the fridge.

We were in the dark.

When the struggling stopped—it didn't take long, since he couldn't breathe—I eased my arm off. I didn't want a corpse on my hands. I rolled him over, taking care to pin his biceps with my knees. That's the kind of pain that prevents too much resistance.

"What the fuck do you want?"

There was a groan and a spluttering, choking sound. "Dan..."

My eyes were adjusting to the dark. I looked down at a pale face in the gloom.

"Benson?" I moved quickly off his arms. "What the fuck?"

"Is that the kind of welcome you always give your guests?" he said, then started coughing. I helped him sit up.

"Yeah, if they come uninvited. What's the idea? I might have killed you. You should know that."

Benson sat heavily in a chair and rubbed his throat. "I need a place."

"Brenda throw you out?"

"Very funny."

"Then what?" I turned on the light; Benson looked bad, his face pale and greenish, dark circles under his eyes and a nice bruise coming up on his neck.

"I think someone's following me." He coughed again, and his mouth filled with saliva.

"Here. You better come into the bathroom."

I was ashamed of the filth and dereliction of my home—but we'd both been billeted in worse. Benson hawked and spat over the toilet bowl.

"Any chance of a bath?" He looked at the cracked enamel tub, the antiquated faucet that supplied an unreliable source of hot water.

"Sure." I set it running. "It takes about twenty minutes to fill. So why don't you tell me what's going on? Why are you here?"

"Do I need a reason to see you?"

This was the kind of stuff I'd been dreaming about hearing, but I wasn't ready to lower my guard yet. I had enough suspicions about Benson—everything from him being part of a covert conspiracy to destroy the evidence of war crimes right down to just being an asshole with a dishonest sex life—to make me wary.

"You came all the way from Pittsburgh for the pleasure of my company? I'm a good fuck, Al, but I'm not that good."

That made him nervous; he licked his lips and couldn't look me in the eye.

"Okay," I said, "let me ask some questions. You said you were being followed."

"Yes. Maybe."

"Are you, or aren't you?"

"I don't know."

"Bullshit. You can figure that stuff out."

"Weird things have been happening. People calling the house."

"That was probably me."

"I know about you. I got your messages..." He trailed off.

"You didn't call me back."

He looked at the floor. Steam was rising from the tub and the room was getting hot. "I'm sorry. You know what it's like."

"I have a pretty good idea. You wanted to forget what happened."

"No!" Now he was looking me straight in the eye. The old Al Benson was back, the senior officer, accustomed to obedience. "Never say that."

"What, then?"

"I... I don't know. I freaked out a little. It was all too much. I hadn't...since Dick. And with you it all came back."

"You seriously expect me to believe I'm the only guy you've slept with since Dick Coburn? Come on, man."

Benson shrugged. "Believe what you like."

"I'm sorry. Go on. About the calls."

"Probably just my imagination."

"You're a marine, for Christ's sake. You've been in combat situations all over the world. Don't talk to me about imagination."

"Okay. It started a week after I saw you. There were these guys in a car—every morning when I left for work, every evening when I came home, just sitting across the road, watching."

"Did you challenge them?"

"Sure. I asked them what they were doing and they said they were cops on a stakeout."

"They show you ID?"

"No."

"Great."

"A couple of days later I saw one of them outside my office. He gave me the slip."

"Who do you think it was?"

"How the hell should I know? Nobody's got any reason to—" He stopped again. What secrets did Benson have? What was he hedging around? "Can I get into that bath now?"

"Give it a few more minutes. Did you see them again?"

"No. But Brenda came home one day and said she'd been chatting with a guy I used to know in the Marines. Said a name that meant nothing to me—Tommy something, I think. He met her outside the school gates when she was picking up Jeleen."

"What's your point, Al?"

"They know where I live. They know where I work. They know where my kids go to school."

"Who's *they?* There is no *they.*"

Again, that morose face, the shifting eyes. "Someone's trying to frighten me."

"They've succeeded, by the sound of it. Is it still going on?"

"I'm not sure."

"You were sure enough to come here."

"You don't understand…"

"So tell me."

"I'm a coward, I know. I ran away."

"From me?"

"From everything."

Neither of us said anything. We leaned closer to each other. We both knew what was going to happen. But I had one more question.

"And today?"

"I needed to see you."

"Just like that."

"I…" He stopped, and rubbed his face. "Dan, do you mind if we just get in the tub now? I'm kind of done talking."

I stood up and pulled my shirt over my head. Suddenly, everything seemed urgent. He was here—Al Benson—here in flesh and blood, in my house, in my bathroom, and now, right now, in my arms, his body pressed against mine. We kissed with a kind of desperation, both knowing that whatever we had, whatever was growing between us, could never flourish. We were trapped, surrounded, outnumbered.

And yeah, that was hot. Just like being in the Marines, breaking all the rules.

As you know, I don't give it up very often. I'm usually the one on top. But when I decide to take the other part—I want it. I really fucking want it. And this was one of those times. I wanted to give myself to Benson, to make love to every part of his body, to worship his cock and balls and to take him deep inside my ass. All the frustration and doubt of the last few weeks, the crap I'd been through with my family, with Jody, with strangers swinging baseball bats, all those doubts and suspicions were focused on one, simple need: to be fucked, and fucked hard, by Al Benson.

I got his clothes off quickly. The shirt up over the head, the belt unbuckled while he kicked off his shoes, the pants and shorts down in one swift movement over his thick, hairy legs. That just left the socks. I didn't care about the socks.

His cock was hard already, and all I had to do was kneel. I put my hands on his thighs, feeling the muscles tensing, and started kissing up the underside of his shaft, over the head, the balls. Benson sighed and held still, letting me do the work. After what I had in mind, there would be no more question of top and bottom. We'd be equal.

I opened my mouth and took him. A quarter, halfway down, caressing his balls with my left hand. I wanted every inch; I wanted to gag and choke and take more, right down my throat. I did my best, breathing slowly to keep from gagging, letting him see how badly I wanted him inside me. Benson understood: he'd have had to be fucking blind and stupid not to get the message. He put his hands on the back of my head and started slowly fucking.

After a while he said, "Hey, Dan. The bath's getting cold."

I stripped off quickly, just as if I was washing after a training session. Shirt, pants, socks, underpants, all on the floor within ten seconds. My dick was rock hard and oozing. Benson stared at it, licked his lips—but this wasn't about my dick. This was all about him—giving myself to him. I wanted him to know that I was his.

Crazy, maybe, but try telling that to a man who has just decided that he is going to get fucked, come what may. Reason doesn't enter into it.

Benson got in the bath first, lying back in the hot water, his cock breaching the surface, red hair floating around it like seaweed. I climbed in.

Whoever built the shack I live in never planned on having two grown men in the tub at the same time—a lack of foresight in my opinion, but there you go—and it was no easy feat to get my legs around Benson's and then lower my body in without flooding the floor. But I made it, thigh to hairy thigh, feet against the side of our heads, cocks close enough to touch. We lay together for a while, reveling in the feeling of slippery skin, warmth, and wetness, but then it was too much. Benson shifted himself into a sitting position, slopping water over the side, and pulled me up.

"Come here."

He held my head in his hands and started kissing—not the insane hungry kiss of a few moments ago, but deep, slow kisses, our tongues exploring our mouths, tasting and touching. I reached down and held his cock, gently stroking it in the water.

"I want you," I said, when we stopped kissing for long enough to speak. "I want you to fuck me."

He smiled. "Seriously?"

"Very seriously."

"Jesus." His cock pulsed in my hand. "Dan Stagg, the tough guy, wants to give it up?"

"Yeah. To you."

"Okay." Now it was his turn to reach between my legs, under my balls, a finger probing into the wet hair of my ass. "You've got it." He found my hole, and pressed. "I'm going to fuck you"—he kissed me again, and he started fingering me—"so hard"—another kiss, another press—"that you're going to be begging for mercy. Got it?"

I opened up, let him in to the knuckle. It hurt, to be honest, because nothing much goes up there, and he must have seen it in my face. He didn't pull out.

"Sure you want it?"

"Mmm-hmmm."

"Okay. But first of all, you're going to suck me."

Benson taking charge, Benson being the man I am with my lovers, with Jody, with Lee. Benson putting me in my place—on my knees, on my back.

I tried to get him in my mouth while we were still in the bath, but after swallowing a lot of water and not much dick, I got out. He followed, and we dried off without saying much. Our cocks were both hard, swaying wildly as we dried our backs.

Benson sat on the edge of the bath, his hands by his side, knuckles facing forward. He opened his thighs, the golden hair standing up fresh and damp.

I dropped a towel on the splintery floorboards, and got to my knees.

I sucked Al Benson's cock until I thought there was a real danger of him coming in my mouth. Now, if this had been Lee or Jody, I wouldn't have worried—take a load, take a rest, and in half an hour they'd be ready to go again. But Benson and I weren't kids anymore, and I was damned if I was going to miss out on my fucking for the sake of a badly timed blowjob. I knew Benson too well: he was quite capable of getting cold feet after he came, and running for the hills.

I stopped sucking and looked him in the face, wiping my mouth with the back of my hand. He was smiling.

"Ready for your punishment?"

I got condoms and lube from the drawer, threw them to him. "Yes."

"On your knees, soldier. I'm coming in from behind."

He took me by storm—judging, rightly, that I was in no mood for gentle, considerate treatment. I needed to be fucked, and fucked is what I got. He placed his head against my hole, and pushed.

It hurt like hell, and I hollered.

"Fucking take it, Dan."

That's what I wanted to hear. Not a considerate "Oh, are you okay? I'll stop if you want." I wanted Benson to understand what I needed. He kept on pushing till he was all the way in, and I was gasping. Stars were bursting in front of my eyes, and I had to dig my fingers into the towel to stop myself from wrestling him off.

Benson was experienced enough to know that you have to wait a while before proceeding: if you try to fuck an ass that's clamped around you in pain, nobody's going to have fun. He stayed inside long enough to feel the first relaxation of my sphincter and then—not a moment later—he started thrusting. The pain subsided. My ass was on fire, and my dick, which went down quickly with the first blast of pain, was coming swiftly back to full erection. Benson picked up the pace, and I started pushing back to meet each thrust. One hand was on my shoulder, pressing me down to the floor; the other was kneading and pulling at my ass, stretching me wider so he could see himself disappearing inside me.

This was good, but even if I craned my head around

I couldn't see much—and I like to see, whatever I'm doing. I wanted to watch Benson fucking me, and I wanted him to see how turned on I was. I wanted him to see me come—which I was going to do soon enough, however much I tried to hold it back.

I pushed myself up and forward; Benson's cock shot out of my ass.

"What the fuck?"

I didn't leave him in doubt for long. I lay back on the floor and lifted my legs. "Come on."

"All right." He had a lascivious look on his face—a wolf about to devour a lamb. He was back inside me in seconds, holding my ankles in his hands, pivoting forward to press into me. I reached around and felt his cock stretching my ass lips wide. I knew if I touched myself now, I would come within seconds. Benson sensed it too.

"I'm close, Dan," he said, after a couple of minutes.

"I want to come first."

I grabbed my dick. Benson picked up the pace of his fucking until he was slamming into me, putting the whole weight of his hefty body through his hard cock. I felt like he was splitting me open, and the hard muscle of his thighs, the bones of his pelvis, were bruising me. And that was enough: I started coming, squirting huge jets of the stuff all over my belly. Benson bellowed "fuck" and started jackhammering into me, fighting against the muscle spasms in my ass to stay deep inside me. The effort and the tightness sent him over the edge, and soon he was filling the condom.

When we'd both finished he stayed inside until the discomfort was intolerable, then carefully withdrew.

The emptiness he left felt like a vacuum, and for a moment I thought I was going to empty my guts over the bathroom floor.

We were both sweating. The bathroom smelled of men.

We lay together on the floor for a while, side by side. Benson gently rubbed the cum into my stomach and chest, slicking down the hair. We needed another bath, really, but there seemed little point.

"Can we go to bed?"

"Yeah."

Benson got to his feet and pulled me to mine; my legs were shaky. We kissed, got into bed, and slept.

I awoke two hours later—Benson was still there. And so were the questions, so many questions, that were only silenced when his cock was inside me. Why was he here? What drove him? What did he know, what was he hiding?

And what the fuck were we doing?

10

I woke at nine, after maybe four hours' sleep. Benson was already sitting up in bed, arms folded. I said, "Good morning," but he didn't respond.

Here goes, I thought. End of round two. At least he stayed all night this time. Now for the sheepish excuses, the sullen departure. Then silence for weeks, months.

I stopped, rolled back onto my pillow and put an arm across my eyes. I couldn't face it again—the desertion, the guilt on his face, and then the clawing hunger inside as I tried to forget him.

"Go, if you're going."

He said nothing.

"They'll be wondering where you are." I stopped short of saying the names—Brenda, Al Junior, Jeleen. I didn't want to be bitchy, even if I felt it.

More silence. Well, two can play at that game. I went to the kitchen and started the coffee.

"Dan."

I didn't respond.

"Dan!" Nearer this time. He was standing in the

doorway, naked. My heart soared, then plunged. I wanted him so badly, and I could never have him. Not without hurting everyone I cared about—including myself. Not without tearing his marriage to pieces. A wife. Two kids. The whole fucking social fabric, and for what?

"Jesus, Dan, talk to me."

I faced him, as naked as he was.

"Okay, I'm talking. What do you want me to say?"

"Come back to bed." He stepped toward me, put a hand on my arm. "Please. We need to work this out."

Work what out? "All right. But not without coffee."

He kissed me. "Well, hurry up."

I fixed coffee as fast as I could and jumped back into bed. "Go on."

"After the last time—I mean the first time—I went away."

"Uh-huh."

"Took the family on vacation. A surprise. We flew down to Miami. It cost me a fortune but—you know. It was worth it."

Nothing about strangers accosting his wife at the school gates now. No sinister men in parked cars.

"How was the weather?"

Benson was absent-mindedly stroking my chest. "It was good," he said. "We had a nice time."

"Great. Happy families."

"That was the idea." He seemed lost in thought.

"What happened?"

"Oh, nothing. That was the trouble. Nothing." His hand was moving down to my stomach, fingers weaving in the fur. "I thought that if we... That we could..."

"What?"

"Be normal again. I could put it all behind me."

I had a flashback to his assault from the rear last night, and laughed. "You certainly did that."

Benson wasn't in the mood for jokes. He withdrew his hand.

"I'm sorry. Go on."

"It's gone, Dan. It's over."

God forgive me, I felt a surge of triumph. "What is?"

"My marriage. My family. Everything."

"Why?"

"You know why."

"Me?"

"You. Me. The way I am. The things I want."

"You're gay."

He sniffed, and looked away, out the window. There was nothing to see. He was crying.

"Jesus, Al, what's the matter?" Stupid fucking question. I put my arms around him, held him while his body shook. After a couple of minutes he calmed down. I handed him a tissue.

Benson sat up and took a deep breath. His eyes were red, his hair messy. He looked older.

"I'm going to tell you the truth."

As opposed to the pack of lies he told me last night, perhaps? "Okay."

"Please just listen and—don't be mad."

"I won't be." I put my arm around his shoulder, and he flinched.

"It'll be a lot easier if you don't touch me. When you touch me I—" He rubbed his eyes, leaving tiny folds and lines in the skin. I removed my arm.

Another deep breath.

"I told you I was being followed."

"Yes."

"I didn't tell you why."

I sat back and waited. If I kept quiet, it might be easier for Al to spill his guts.

"All that stuff I said was true. There were two guys in a parked car, and someone talking to my wife at the school gates. And that was one of the reasons why I packed up and took the family on vacation. I wanted to get away from it all. I was—I really was frightened."

What was this? Something to do with Dick Coburn? The same kind of fear that plagued Jerry Douglas? If we could put the pieces together, if it all led back to Iraq...

"I should never have contacted you in the first place. It started it all over again. The feelings I thought I'd left behind when I married Brenda. You fool yourself, right? You put those thoughts into a locked drawer and you throw away the key. Then suddenly, one day, you find it again. You can't resist opening it up and taking things out and having a look, though you know it's wrong."

I can't say I'd ever experienced this, even when I was deep in the closet. I knew what I wanted.

"It started when I heard about what happened to you. Why you left the Marines. At first I thought, Poor guy, then I thought, There but for the grace of god... And then it hit me. Jesus fucking Christ, why didn't I know? Why did I waste all that time? Another man, another marine who was like me. You, me, Dick Coburn—how many others, hiding from the truth? From each other? Together we could have... I don't know."

Fucked each other's brains out, most probably. Then fucked each other up, like you did Dick Coburn.

"And I couldn't stop thinking about it. What it would have been like if we could have just told each other, talked about stuff. We would have been strong together. We were such fucking cowards."

I bridled at this, but of course he was right. It was left to braver, younger guys than us to challenge the military status quo.

"I had to talk to someone. About Dick. About my feelings. So I found you on that website. It took me weeks to pluck up the courage to write. I couldn't stop looking at your profile, Googling you the whole time, and that's how I picked up that bit of news about your involvement in the Julian Marshall case."

"Not something I'm particularly proud of."

"You should be."

I shrugged.

"I told myself that nothing was going to happen. We'd have dinner and talk about old times and if I thought you were really an okay guy—well, then I'd tell you about myself. But when I met you—Christ, Dan. I don't know. Something happened to me. I wanted you so much I—" He caught his breath, unable to trust himself to speak further.

"And all that stuff about Dick Coburn? Paying me to find out what happened? Was that just an excuse?" I still hadn't told him what I'd found, about my trips to Queens and DC.

"No. I don't know. I was sincere. I want to know. I do. But—"

"You wanted something else more."

"Yeah." He turned and looked me in the eye. "You."

I was happy about that, of course. Who wouldn't be? Even so, I resented being sent on a wild goose chase to justify Benson's real feelings. And what about the stuff I'd found out? A chain of circumstance and coincidence and a beating with a baseball bat?

"I got home and I could hardly stand for Brenda to touch me. It just seemed wrong. I felt dirty and ashamed, and to bring that into the family home, with my kids..."

Thanks, pal. Fucking charming.

"So we went on vacation. I told her I'd been over-worked and stressed out, and I tried, I really tried to get it together again in Florida. Every night in the hotel room... But it was hopeless. Once, maybe twice, I managed to keep it together for long enough to satisfy her. But only by thinking about you."

I was starting to get hard again. I hoped this confession wasn't going to go on for too long. I wanted to fuck him before we parted, send him home with a sore ass.

"When we got home, I was desperate. I knew you'd been calling—I got your messages and I just got scared. That same feeling you used to get before combat. But this time, I ran away. Just pretended it wasn't happening. I blocked everything out—you, Dick Coburn, even the fact that I was being followed. Because that started again as soon as I got home. Brenda told me you called, you even spoke to her, right?"

"Yeah."

"And I still didn't get back in touch. I went away on business."

"She said."

"Boston again."

"You came to Boston, and you didn't call me?"

"I wanted to, but I was frightened."

"Jesus, Al."

"I nearly did it. I dialed your number, even. And then I thought—if I take this step, that's it. A double life. Divorce. The kids. The whole fucking thing."

"I know. It's not easy."

"But if I let myself see you again, I'd never be able to stop. I had to do something to relieve myself."

"Oh."

"So I went to this place." I waited, pretty sure what kind of place *this* was. "A bathhouse."

"Right." I swallowed hard, jealous in spite of myself.

"And I... Well, I got laid."

"I see."

"I'm sorry."

"Jesus, Al, you don't have to apologize." Why was my voice shaking, damn it? "We're not..."

"Aren't we?"

This time I was the one having trouble. "I don't know. I really don't know."

"Anyway, I'm sorry I lied to you. I told you there hadn't been any others. There have. A couple of times. I thought I could keep it in control that way. Just a safety valve."

"Doesn't work though, does it? In my experience, the more you have, the more you want."

"Absolutely." He smiled. "And now I want it all the fucking time."

"I noticed." I squeezed my cock.

"Please, Dan, not yet. Let me finish."

"Then I'm going to fuck you."

He nodded in a businesslike fashion. "Okay. I still haven't told you why I came here."

"I thought that was pretty obvious."

"In a way. But something else happened."

"Oh. What?"

"You know I said I was being followed? That wasn't all bullshit. Even after that time in Boston, coming out of the baths, I was sure someone was there, watching me."

"That's just a guilty conscience."

"That's what I told myself. Then the other day... Oh, shit."

"What?"

"I was away on business again, this time in Albany."

"And don't tell me. You sniffed out the action in Albany."

"It's not difficult. It's all online."

"'Course it is."

"So I went to another bathhouse. I was familiar with the routine now—felt a little more comfortable about it. I let my guard down, I guess. I got blasé. Because I was getting together with this guy and then—"

He buried his face in his hands.

"What happened?"

"Someone started taking photos. I had this feeling I was being followed all day. And then—"

"It turned out you really were."

"So someone took a little amateur porn. So what?"

"I'm being blackmailed."

"Seriously?"

"Think I'm imagining it?"

"No. But how?"

"The usual way. A copy of the photo was sent to my work email. Cropped. Nothing pornographic. Just a nice little message saying that the complete image would be sent to my wife and employer unless I did what I was told."

"How much did they ask for?"

"They didn't ask for money."

"Then what?"

"They said they'd contact me again."

"And have they?"

"Not yet. I ran. You're the only person in the world I can tell. I guess I just panicked. Left a note for Brenda, broke into your place..."

There was a minute's silence.

"Any idea who's doing this?"

"No," said Benson. "It could be anyone, couldn't it? They see a guy like me, plenty of money, a nice house, a lot to lose. And they find my weakness."

"But not asking for money."

"They're just waiting. When they're ready, they'll bleed me dry. Why else would you blackmail someone?"

I could think of a few reasons, but I wasn't ready to share them.

We bought food at the supermarket and went down to the Esplanade to eat in the sun.

"I've got something to tell you too, Al."

"I know you're not free."

"I didn't mean that." But shame on me; surely Jody should have been my priority. Even Lee had a prior claim.

"Then what?"

"It's about Dick Coburn."

"Oh." Benson frowned. "What did you do?"

"I went to Queens." I told him about the sad streets of South Jamaica, the army of ghosts, and the stories I had heard about our former comrade, his dead lover. His bad rep among dealers and users, the money he owed, his disappearance for months before he died.

Benson was distressed. If we hadn't been in public, he'd have cried.

"I'm sorry, Al. But there's nothing we could have done."

"That's not true. It's my fault. I should have looked after him. I drove him to it."

"Hey, don't take all the credit. Plenty of guys make a mess of their lives without any help from you."

"You don't understand."

"I understand very well. I've done exactly what you've done, more times than I care to remember. I screwed people over, and people screwed me over. The only time I tried to do the right thing by the man I loved, he ended up with a bullet in his head."

"That wasn't your fault either."

"Exactly."

"Okay." Benson picked at a piece of bread and salami, folding them up, tearing them to pieces. Some nearby pigeons looked interested.

"And then he came back." I took a deep breath. "And died."

He nodded, wiped his eyes. "Dick was in the wrong place at the wrong time."

"I guess."

"What do you mean?"

"I don't know. Why did he disappear for so long, then come back just in time for the fire?"

"Bad luck."

"Maybe."

"What's your theory, Dan?"

"There's another reading of the facts. Coburn cleaned up, got himself off the streets, and started over. But someone wanted him dead. His body was found in the one place where it would cause the least suspicion. The streets where he was known as a crackhead. Just another victim."

"Who would want to kill Dick Coburn? Poor bastard. He never hurt a fly."

"Now I'm going to tell you something else. I went up to Brooklyn after that, to see Jody. When I was coming home, early in the morning, I got jumped. Two guys, one of them with a baseball bat. They beat the crap out of me."

"I bet you got the better of them."

"Yeah, I did, don't you worry. I can take care of myself."

Benson gripped my arm and squeezed.

"Did you report it?"

"Of course. The cops pretty much ignored me. Said I was in the wrong place at the wrong time. Brooklyn's a dangerous place, they said."

"Around the college?"

"Everywhere, according to the NYPD. They took a statement, issued a description, gave me a crime number. That's it."

"Did they take your money?"

"No. They didn't even try to rob me."

"Then why not just shoot you?"

"They wanted to scare me. Or warn me off."

"Warn you off what?"

"While you were dragging your ass around the bathhouses of the eastern United States, I was thinking about the weird things that happened to all the men who served on a particular undercover operation in Iraq in 1998, just before Desert Fox."

"Go on."

"And I tracked down Woody Douglas."

"Jesus! That geek."

"You thought he was geeky then? You should see him now."

"Oh, I know. He used to pester me all the time. Phone calls, Christmas cards, trying to come visit. In the end I had to drop him. He was too much."

"Woody told me some interesting stuff, in among all the bullshit."

"About Dick?"

"About a lot of things. Mostly Harry Armitage."

"Christ."

"You're not the only one who's worried about an incriminating photo, it seems." I told him what Douglas had said about Armitage's trophy picture, the catastrophic threat it posed to his advancement in the West Wing.

"And does Douglas have the photo?"

"He says not."

"Do you believe him?"

"I don't know what to believe. You know the other really insane thing he said?"

"What?"

"He thinks he's being watched. Followed. Spied on."
I let that one sink in. "Crazy, yes?"

Benson was quiet for a while, then said, "Okay. Go
on. Give me the whole story."

I told him about Peter Quiller, the UN weapons
inspector who, according to Douglas, was one of the
men we killed that night in Iraq. I told him what I'd
learned from Naseer Khan—there was at the very least
a mystery surrounding Quiller's death and his possible
readiness to speak out about WMDs. Evidence of war
crimes—if it still existed—hadn't stopped Armitage's
appointment as National Security Advisor, a post he'd
lose in disgrace if the truth ever got out.

And then, counting off on my fingers, I told Benson
what had happened to the members of that landing party.

"Dick Coburn's dead. Could be a routine drug
death, could be a targeted hit disguised to look like a
drug death. Jerry Douglas is convinced that Armitage
has blocked his promotion and sabotaged his career,
and now thinks he's being followed and threatened. You
think the same—and now you're being blackmailed by
people with the resources to know exactly where you
are and what you're doing."

"And then there's you."

"Exactly. Someone tracked me to Brooklyn—
someone who knew exactly how to do it without being
discovered. I was attacked by combat-trained assailants—again, points to someone with money and power
who can hire the best. Clever people, like the ones who
killed Coburn, the ones who are blackmailing you, the
ones who are threatening Douglas. Money does not
appear to be the motive."

"You think it's Armitage."

"What else do we have in common?"

"You, me, and Dick Coburn are all gay."

That made me raise my eyebrows. Benson laughed. "Okay, bi. Whatever."

"Do you think that's relevant?"

"Might not be. Might just be a big old coincidence. But if Armitage was looking for people he could control when he put that operation together, it would make sense to recruit people with something to hide."

"Where does Woody fit in?"

"Who knows. Perhaps Armitage had something on him too."

"How could he have known about you?"

"Okay. It's not much of a theory. But it seems weird, don't you think that at least three out of the four of us...?"

"I don't know, Al. There's so much about my time in the Marines that doesn't make sense. Sometimes the whole fucking Corps seems like a conspiracy of silence. How much do you really remember about that night in Iraq?"

"It's a long time ago." He counted. "Seventeen, eighteen years. Other stuff happened."

"Do you remember the photo being taken?"

"I guess."

"If Douglas is right, then anyone who remembers that night is in trouble, whether there's a photo or not. We're all potential threats."

"Then why blackmail me?" said Benson. "Why not just kill me—and you and Douglas?"

"Too obvious. Someone like Nas Khan would figure

out the connection and trace it back to Armitage. But to kill one and scare the others into silence…"

"What do you think these blackmailers are going to ask me when they get back in contact?"

"They want your silence. Armitage is about to reach the White House. He's looking over his shoulder."

"Does Armitage know that you and I are talking to each other?"

"He seems to know everything else," I said, "and it drives him crazy with fear. People know too much about him."

"And yet," said Benson, "here he is in the White House."

"Perhaps he has leverage with the administration. If that really was Peter Quiller that we killed that night—one of our own, a UN inspector—then Armitage was receiving his orders from somewhere. He hadn't gone rogue. He had been briefed by someone very high up. Above the generals."

"The president?"

"Or someone close to him. If it ever got out that the White House ordered the assassination of a UN inspector in order to precipitate war…"

"So Armitage gets rewarded for his silence."

"And we get silenced to protect his position."

A shadow passed across the sun, and suddenly the Esplanade seemed dangerous, full of spying eyes and listening ears. How much danger were we in? They tracked us before—were they tracking us now?

Benson didn't disappear. He called his wife, told her that business was keeping him in Boston for the rest of the week, and that was that. He moved into my place, bugs and all—once or twice he suggested we relocate to a hotel, but then thought better of it. In my house we could fuck all day if we wanted to—and we did. Our only constraints were my working hours, and Benson even turned that to his advantage by getting a short-term membership to the gym and working out every day. To my colleagues, even to Lee, he was an old USMC buddy who was up on a visit. He visited my parents, and charmed them with tales of Al Junior, Jeleen, and their wonderful life in Pittsburgh. "Dan's a great, great guy," he said to my father, while my mother actually blushed with pride. "He was the best marine I ever served with, and he's a true-blue friend." They didn't need to know that the true-blue friend was sticking his cock up Al Benson's rose-pink ass every chance he got. They wouldn't have believed it even if they'd seen it.

He barely mentioned his family, and I didn't ask. Once in a while he checked his email for contact from the blackmailers, but there was nothing. Maybe we were safe. If Benson stayed for a week, maybe we could figure out what's going on between us. If we have a future—a future good enough to leave Brenda and the kids in Pittsburgh, and Jody in Brooklyn, and start a life together.

Could anything be worth that sacrifice? Easy for me, maybe: I already thought that Jody and I were growing apart, and whatever we had was running its natural course. But for Al Benson—a family man, a father, a pillar of his community, suddenly to run off with another guy? The sex was great—but you'd have to love someone to do that.

Did Al Benson love me?

I thought so, for a few days. I believed it when we stared into each other's eyes as we fucked, when there seemed to be no barrier between us, when our bodies said what couldn't be put into words.

Yes, I thought, this could sustain us through any amount of misery and betrayal. It's worth it.

And then one day, out of the blue, Al Benson said to me over breakfast, "Hey, Dan. That guy you work with—what's his name?"

"Lee."

"Yeah. Lee. He's fucking hot."

11

He was right, of course. Lee is hot. Anyone—male, female, young, old—would find Lee hot. But this wasn't just stating the obvious. This was a request.

"Yeah," I said. "He is."

"You should get him over."

"What for?" I hadn't told Benson about Lee and me.

"You know. Some mentoring. Like we did in the Marines."

"I don't know."

"Make the call."

"Seriously?"

"I'm sick of all this brain work. Let's have some fun before we die, why don't we?"

"I thought we were having fun."

"Come on. The kid's obviously interested. I see the way he looks at you. Hero worship." He squeezed my balls. "Can't say I blame him."

"And you think I should take advantage?"

"No. I think we should take advantage."

Should I tell him? It was going to be obvious anyway,

unless I just said, *No way, Benson, uh-uh, forget it*. And the more Benson squeezed my nuts, the more I wanted to do it.

"I already did."

His hand stopped.

"What?"

"Lee. I've… You know."

"Had him."

"Yeah."

One eyebrow twitched upward. "And how was he?"

I shrugged. "Good."

"You fuck him?"

"Yes."

"Okay." Was he jealous? "Think he could get two cocks up his ass at the same time?"

We met at the gym; I'd arranged to go for a beer with Lee, and mentioned that Benson would like to come along. Lee was pleased: much as he liked sex, it was the company that he really enjoyed, and the idea of having a couple of buddies to hang out with made him happy all through that Thursday afternoon. We were finishing at five; Benson came in for a workout at four. He wasted no time.

"Hi, Lee," he said, with a firm handshake. "Thanks for letting me crash the party."

"'S'alright."

"Dan tells me you play rugby."

Lee's face lit up; most Americans don't know what rugby is. "Yeah. That's my sport."

"Bet you miss it."

"I miss a lot of things about home."

"Rough game though, right? A lot of injuries."

"Oh, yeah." Lee reeled off a catalogue of broken collar bones, dislocated shoulders, chipped teeth. "And I get this neck thing." He squeezed the top of his shoulder where it joined the spine.

"From the scrums, I guess."

"Yeah. How'd you know that?"

"I played a little rugby in the Marines."

This was news to me, but I didn't interrupt.

"You'll understand, then."

"I still get a few twinges." Benson rubbed his own neck in sympathy. "Price you pay, right?"

"All sports are risky," said Lee. "We learn about that stuff at college. Anatomy, physio, all that. Look at Dan. He's got really tight hamstrings. I'm always telling him he needs to stretch more if he wants to avoid injury."

"We should all stretch more," said Benson, catching my eye.

"Hear that, Danno?" Lee winked. "Told you."

"Tell you what, Lee," said Benson as he headed to the changing rooms. "If you have a problem with that neck, I'll take a look at it. You have to be careful it doesn't start affecting your posture. I see a lot of that kind of problem in my field."

I had to chip in at this point. "In software design?"

"At the Pittsburgh Medical Center," said Benson. "There's a big specialized injuries unit."

"I bet."

Lee looked confused.

"Anyway, I'm going to have a workout before we hit the town. Catch you later." Benson sauntered off with a spring in his step.

"Great guy," said Lee, following Benson's retreat with stars in his eyes—a look I remembered well from parade grounds and mess halls back in the day, when everyone was in love with Red Benson. Whether Lee would still think he was great by the end of the evening remained to be seen.

An hour later, we were sitting at a table with the first beer of the evening. Lee was telling us in great detail about his sporting career, starting with under-twelve soccer, medals for swimming and gymnastics, and playing rugby for his county by the time he was seventeen. Benson took an interest, encouraged him, and generally played the benevolent uncle. After two more beers, a pizza, and a lot more tall tales, Benson suggested we make a move.

"Dan, let's get back to your place, shall we? I want to take a look at this neck injury of Lee's."

"That's really kind of you, Al," said Lee, eagerly drinking up.

"Yeah," I said. "Al's all heart. Aren't you, buddy?"

Benson licked his chops like a hungry wolf. "Think you might have some spinal rotation," he said. "You've got to be careful with that stuff."

We got to the house fast. "You okay?" Lee asked me as Benson went ahead to use the bathroom. "You've been very quiet all evening."

"I'm fine, Lee."

"He's a great bloke, your mate."

"He's just fine."

"Is he cool? With… You know."

"'Course he is."

Lee smiled, looked around and kissed me on the mouth. "I miss you, Dan. It's been ages."

I kissed him back, tasting the beer, and felt like a traitor. He had no idea what Benson had in mind, or if he did he was playing dumb exceptionally well.

Benson came back into the room and immediately set about massaging Lee's shoulders. "So, where's the pain exactly? Up here?" He rubbed the back of his neck, where the hair was clipped up into that absurd fin. Lee rolled his head forward. "Or down here?" Benson pressed his thumbs into the shoulder blades.

"Kind of all through, yeah," said Lee, his eyes closed, arms hanging by his sides.

"Don't you get regular sports massages?"

"Can't afford them."

"What about the other students? I thought you'd all be rubbing each other down."

"I don't do that course."

"Too bad. You're all knotted up."

I'm not a big consumer of porn, but I know that the "you need a massage" line is the oldest one in the book. There are whole websites dedicated to only that. Jody's shown me. We've acted it out often enough: Jody the young masseur, me the tired old soldier. He's good at it. He used to do it for a living, something I try not to think about too often.

"I've been training hard."

This was true: Lee spent much of his free time in the gym, when he wasn't working or studying. He was lonely, and he liked the environment. I wasn't complaining. His body was perfect, not too big, not too thin. I'd given him strict instructions not to turn into some zero-fat freak. I liked his ass just the way it was, with flesh on it.

"So," said Benson, "show me your stretching routine."

"Okay."

Lee brought one arm across his body, held it in a shoulder stretch. Benson starting prodding around.

"See? A lot of tension here." He pushed into the lats. "Now do the tricep."

Lee obeyed, crooking his elbow above his head and pulling his hand down his back. Benson squeezed and poked.

"Ouch!"

"Hurts?"

"Yeah."

"Thought it would. You've got some real tightness down there, boy." Benson caught my eye and smiled. "Want me to take a look?"

Lee said, "Okay."

"Take your shirt off, then."

Lee was wearing one of his many white polo shirts with the English rose embroidered on the chest, right over the tattoo. He grabbed the bottom hem and pulled it over his head. During the last couple of sunny weeks he'd developed a perfect farmboy tan—golden freckly arms and neck, still marble-white everywhere else, the pink nipples and red rose standing out like neon.

"Good. Tricep stretch again."

The hair in his deep armpit was slightly damp. I wanted to dive in with my tongue, or my dick. From the look on Benson's face, he was thinking the same.

Benson wasted no time. "You've been working hard on your chest." He grabbed the side of Lee's left pec and squeezed. "That's good."

"Thanks."

"And a nice tattoo. You're proud of your country."

"Yeah." Lee smiled.

"Got any others?"

"What?"

"Tattoos."

"Nah. Just that one. Right, Dan?"

Lee was smiling now. The light may not quite have come on yet, but it was imminent.

"I've never seen any," I said.

"You sure about that?"

"Pretty sure."

"I'm glad to hear it," said Benson. "Too many of these young guys today ruin their bodies with ink. Now this"—he brushed his fingers over Lee's rose, and touched his nipple—" is fine. It means something, and it looks great."

"Thanks," said Lee, looking down at his erect tit, which Benson was casually stroking with his index finger.

"But when they start tattooing their backs and their butts—it's crazy."

"I'm not going to do that. Fucking hurts too much, for starters."

"I bet. This one hurt much?" Benson was still playing with Lee's nipple, as if it was the most natural thing in the world.

"Yeah. Like hell."

"You don't want that kind of pain in your ass, right?"

Lee's eyebrows went up. "Not needles, no."

"Exactly." Benson's hand traveled south, and gave Lee a firm smack on the buttock. He was wearing tight jeans, and it made a sharp sound. "You should take care of that." He squeezed. "It's a very nice ass."

"Thanks, mate." Lee was smiling now, and I could see from the front of his pants that he was more than aware of what was going on.

"Promise me you won't deface it."

"I promise."

"And if you do, at least take a photo of it first. Just so we can all remember what it looked like."

"You can see if you want."

"Can I?"

"Yeah. Why not."

"Perhaps Dan could do the honors." Benson fiddled with his cellphone, switching it to camera mode. "I want a souvenir. Dan? Pull his pants down."

Any reservations I had about this situation were fast evaporating. Benson was my senior officer again, and we'd got our hands on a young private or lance corporal. Lee was breathing heavily as I stepped up to him and unbuttoned his fly. I could feel heat beating off his chest.

He was wearing a tiny pair of briefs, lime green and orange. I hadn't seen them before. Maybe he'd bought them for me to unwrap later. Maybe he'd hoped that something like this was going to happen. I pulled his pants down to his knees, while Lee rearranged his hard cock to lie up against his hip, just contained by the stretch fabric.

"Nice. Very nice," said Benson. "Hold still. I want to get a shot of this."

Lee gave Benson the rear view. The cellphone made its electronic click.

"Okay. Now, Dan, pull his underpants down. Let's see what we're talking about here."

I did as I was told, squatting in front of Lee. His dick bounced free, almost fully hard. He looked down at me, lips parted.

"That's a fine ass, boy," said Benson. "Stick it out."

Lee bent over slightly, curving his hips backward. Benson fired off a few shots. If he was really scared of blackmail, he was being reckless. I guess there's always the delete button.

"Dan? Hold his cheeks open. I want to see the hole."

Again, I obeyed, parting Lee's muscular buttocks, offering up that pink pucker that I'd eaten and fucked with so much pleasure.

"When did you last take a shower, boy?"

"When I left work."

"Taken a shit since then?"

"What? No!"

"No, *sir*."

"No, sir."

"Good boy." Benson smiled. "In that case, I'm going to have a taste. That okay with you, Dan?"

"Fine by me." I felt Benson's hands on mine, both of us holding Lee's ass open.

"Suck his cock, Dan."

"Yes, sir." We could play that game. It certainly seemed to be working for Lee. As Benson got to work with his tongue, Lee's dick throbbed up to maximum hardness.

"Oh, god," he said, and I wrapped my lips around his cockhead. Lee steadied himself with his hands on my head, and pushed back against Benson's mouth. We had him, both of us, devouring him. I knew from experience that Lee could come very quickly if you touched his ass. With Benson's tongue up there, and my mouth on his dick, things were going to happen fast.

Lee started pumping into me, and his breathing became rapid. Benson was eating him in earnest now, his face buried between Lee's cheeks, tongue-fucking him.

"I'm gonna come," said Lee, his voice high and shaky. "Oh, god, I'm coming."

He shot in my mouth, and I almost gagged, but I held on and took his load. Benson kept on lapping away, then stood up. Lee fell forward, his whole weight against me, hobbled at the knees by his pants. I held him, felt his heartbeat, tasted and swallowed his load.

"I haven't finished with you yet, boy." Benson was unbuttoning. "You're going to suck this, and you're going to suck Dan, and then we're both going to fuck you. Got it?"

Lee's voice was muffled into my shoulder as he said, "Yes, sir." The cum was still oozing out of his dick and he was ready to go again.

"Turn around, boy." Benson had his cock in his hand.

"Yes, sir."

"Get those fucking shoes off right now. I want you naked."

Lee did as he was told. I was painfully hard now. I can't say I liked the situation: Benson was taking away something I thought was mine, Lee was only too pleased to give it up, and I seemed to be losing both of them. But of course that made me want to do it more. My head was spinning. I felt drunk.

"Dan? You too. Strip."

It took me about ten seconds to get as naked as Lee was. Benson stood there stroking and watching.

"Is he a good cocksucker, Dan?"

"Pretty good."

"Dan been teaching you, boy?"

"Yes, sir."

"You like sucking his cock?"

"Yes, sir."

"Then show me. Suck him."

Lee got to his knees and did as he was told. He'd had plenty of practice since the first time, and now he was proficient, taking at least two thirds of me with no trouble. I could never get tired of seeing his lips around me, or his furrowed brow as he looked up to see if I was enjoying it.

"You're doing fine," I said, and stroked his hair. Benson was undressing.

"Now come here. Suck this." Lee started to get up. "No. On your knees." He snapped his fingers, pointed at the floor. Lee crawled over. "That's it. Show me what Dan taught you." Lee started sucking, and I could see that his dick, which hadn't gone down much in the first place, was soaring back to full erection. "Damn," said Benson. "That's pretty good. You got two guys twice your age fucking your face, boy. You like that?"

Lee nodded as he sucked, and made a noise that might have been taken for a yes.

"Come here, Dan." Benson beckoned me over. "Let's see what he can do with two."

I stepped close, positioning my cock next to Lee's head. He took me in his hand and started stroking, still sucking on Benson.

"Now his," said Benson.

Lee obeyed. His face was wet, saliva running down his chin.

"Lick his balls. Come on."

Lee started licking and sucking my nuts. Now that his mouth wasn't so full he could say "yes" and "god" more audibly. We kept taking turns with him, each time fucking his mouth a little harder. He gagged a few times, but didn't stop. Benson grabbed Lee's hair on top, where it was at its longest, pulling his head down. "Good boy," he said, pumping his hips into Lee's mouth. "Take it."

This could have gone on all night, but we all knew what was coming next. It was Benson, of course, who took the initiative.

"I'm going to fuck you now, Lee," he said, in a matter-of-fact kind of way. "And then Dan's going to fuck you. And then, if you think you can take it, we're both going to fuck you."

Lee looked puzzled. "What do you mean?"

"Two cocks up your ass at the same time." He pulled me toward him and pressed my cock against his, grasping them both in one hand, belly to belly. "Like this."

"Jesus," said Lee, but he couldn't take his eyes off our two pricks, wet and slippery with his spit, sliding together. He started kissing and licking the shafts. "I'll try."

"Even if it hurts?"

"I don't know."

"Good boy," said Benson yet again. It seemed to work. Lee looked like he'd do anything he was told just to get Benson's approval. I knew that feeling well—and

Benson knew his power. "Get on all fours. Dan—sit down. That's it. What are you waiting for, Lee? There's a cock there. Suck it. Show your daddies what you want."

I sat back and watched as Lee crawled over the floor to me, rested his big hands on my thighs and started sucking. Benson got himself rubbered up and positioned himself behind Lee. I hoped to god he was going to take care; I like role play as much as the next man, but I didn't want him hurt. Benson was always considerate when he was fucking me, waiting till I was up to speed before he started slamming into me—but then he knew that I could break his neck if he pissed me off.

"Ready?"

Lee looked over his shoulder for long enough to say, "Yes."

"Yes, what?"

"Yes, sir."

"Yes, what, sir?"

"Yes, please, sir. Fuck me, please, sir." The boy was quick on the uptake.

"That's better. Now get back to that cock."

Benson pressed his cock between Lee's buttocks and looked me in the eye. Neither of us smiled. I don't really know what passed between us: lust, of course, but what else? Contempt? Sorrow? He pushed forward, never breaking eye contact. Lee grunted, but kept sucking, and Benson slid inside him, slowly, inch by inch. When he was in, everything stopped for a while—my cock in Lee's mouth, Benson's dick up his ass, the calm before the storm.

"Now," said Benson, and started fucking. Slowly at

first, then faster, until he was pounding the whole length of it in and out of Lee's beautiful ass. I knew what that felt like—both to be fucked by Benson, and to fuck Lee.

We continued like this for a while, waiting for Benson to give the order.

"Okay, that's enough." He pulled out. "Your ass is too fucking hot, Lee. I don't want to come up there. Not yet. Now you ready to give it up to Dan?"

"I'm ready, sir."

"How do you want him to fuck you, Lee? On all fours, like a dog? How do you like to take it? Hmmm?" He caressed Lee's ass, and slipped a finger inside him. "You like to get fucked, don't you?"

"Yes, sir."

"So what's it to be? Show me." Lee pulled himself up onto the couch, lay back and pulled his knees up toward his chest. "All right. Dan? You ready?"

It was my turn to get a condom on.

"I got him nice and slippery for you, Dan. It's going to be a smooth ride."

I pushed my dick into Lee's wet hole. It was too much, and too hot, and I was too close, and I had to stop. Lee hadn't touched himself, but he was still hard.

"Okay, take a break," said Benson. "Who needs the bathroom?"

Lee cleared his throat and wiped his mouth on the back of his hand. "Me. I need to piss."

"Come on, then." Benson took Lee by the cock and led him into the hallway. Hypnotized, I followed.

Lee stood at the toilet, hands on hips, cock swinging frontward. "I'm too hard to piss," he said. "I need to come down a bit." His buttocks were red from the pounding they'd received, and a pink flush spread from his cheeks down his throat and across his chest, shading into the red of his rose tattoo.

I needed to piss too, and I was good and ready. I stood beside Lee, put an arm around his shoulder and pointed my dick toward the bowl. The stream had barely begun when Benson barked, in his best USMC officer voice, "Stop!"

I clenched, and the flow ended.

"I've got a better idea."

"What?" said Lee.

"Get in the tub."

"Me?"

"Yes, you. Get in the tub and kneel."

"Why?"

"Do as you're told."

Lee looked at me, a puzzled expression on his face. I kissed him on the mouth. "It's okay. Nothing bad's going to happen."

He climbed into the bath, giving us a generous view of his slippery pink asshole as he did so. He knelt, sitting back on his heels. "Like this?"

"Yeah," said Benson. "Now lean back."

Lee propped himself on his hands and tilted his torso backward, showing off the workings of his fine young abs. His cock stuck straight up at the ceiling.

"Now piss on him, Dan."

We were back in Naval College, hazing the new recruits. This was the kind of crap that the seniors liked to do—exercising their seniority, putting the grunts in their place. Sometimes it turned into sex, sometimes it didn't. I stood at the edge of the tub, pointed my cock toward Lee's stomach, and said, "You want it?"

He rubbed a hand over his belly and down to his dick. "Yeah."

"Do it, Dan. Piss on him."

I let go, and a strong stream of piss hit Lee just above the diaphragm, coursing down over his muscles and around his cock, dripping off his balls, running down his thighs. He played with it, rubbing it into his skin, stroking himself.

I aimed higher, pissing on his tits. Lee groaned, and his cock jumped.

Higher—there was still enough—his neck. Lee pushed himself forward and took the last jets in his face, eyes screwed shut, mouth open. There was no squeamishness or disgust. Perhaps this was something he'd dreamed of doing.

I was sorry to run out of piss: I could have watched it splashing into Lee's handsome face all day. But my time at the tub was over.

"My turn," said Benson, taking my place. Lee was stroking his cock, enjoying the wetness. "And I should warn you, boy, that if you come now it's going to make getting fucked afterward a lot harder. But we're going to do it anyway. Your choice."

Lee laughed, stopped stroking for a while and then said, "What the hell." He started playing with his cock again. He was perfectly capable of coming three times in a couple of hours.

"Good boy," said Benson. "Now get here and open that pretty mouth of yours. I've got something for you." He took Lee's wet chin between finger and thumb and steered him onto his cock. Lee didn't hesitate. He took

Benson's cock in his mouth and let the head rest on the tongue, keeping his lips open. Benson closed his eyes, took a few slow, deep breaths, and then said, "Here it comes."

At first, the piss gushed out around Benson's cock, cascading down Lee's chin. He caught some of it in his hand and plastered it over his hard dick, jerking himself in earnest now. Then he closed his mouth and started swallowing. I watched his throat working, his Adam's apple bobbing up and down as he drank.

"Jesus, Dan. Look at him. Swallowing a man's piss, and he fucking loves it. Look at him working that cock."

That was all it took to tip Lee over the edge for a second time. He started shooting over his wet thighs, the jizz slipping down into the tub. He went down to the base of Benson's cock, taking it deep in his throat. His face was flushed dark red, veins standing out in his neck, tears trickling from the corners of his closed eyes. He lay still in the tub for a while and then, when his cock was soft, added his piss to ours.

"That's all of it," said Benson. "Now it's time for your fucking. Stand up."

Lee got shakily to his feet. Piss and jizz dripped off him. I'd have suggested a shower, but Benson liked him just the way he was. I was going to feel bad about this in the morning—I was going to wonder what kind of person Benson was, underneath the bland mask of the family man, the head of software design—but right now all I could think of was Lee's shiny, pale skin, his tight ass, and the thought of my cock pressing against Benson's as we went in together.

Lust makes cowards of us all.

Lee climbed out of the bath and stood on the mat, hands hanging down by his side. Benson gave the order. "Dan? Get the condoms. Lee, bend over."

By the time I got back from my errand, Lee had one foot up on the sink and Benson's tongue up his chute. The smell of piss was strong in the steamy air. Lee looked over his shoulder at me and smiled. He was having a ball. He grabbed me around the back of the neck and kissed me, holding on to keep his balance. His other hand found my cock.

When Benson had eaten his fill, he started with the orders again.

"Okay, Dan. On your back." He snapped his fingers and pointed to the floor. "Lee, put a condom on him."

Lee rolled the rubber down and started applying the lube, as instructed.

"Now sit down on it, facing toward Dan. Nice and slow. Take it all."

Lee slid onto my dick. He was getting hard again, and pressed his dick into my stomach to make the point.

"Now raise your hips up, Dan. Nice and steady."

Lee braced himself with his thighs—it's a good thing he was strong; you need maximum fitness for this kind of exercise—and Benson came in from behind. I felt the rubbered-up end of his dick poking around my balls and then, after much shifting of position, he managed to line it up with Lee's hole. We'd used nearly a whole bottle of lube by now, and Benson's cock was like a steel bar. He slipped in, his head running up the underside of my cock, until we were both inside Lee. Lee was groaning loud and long, his face screwed up in what might have been pain. He sat up, reached around and felt the two shafts going into him. "Oh, Jesus. Oh, god. Fuck me. Fuck me hard."

This wasn't going to last long: the position was too precarious apart from anything else, and both Benson and I were close. We established a rhythm, me bucking my hips upward, Benson pushing in from the rear, and gave Lee what he was asking for, stretching his beautiful ass to the max. Juice was drooling out of his dick in sticky pools over my hairy belly.

We toppled, and Benson's cock slipped out.

"No!" shouted Lee. "Please! Get it in again! Quick! For fuck's sake!"

We regrouped, and Benson pushed in none too gently. Lee shouted "Oh! Fuck!" and started coming again. Benson and I stayed in as far as we could while his ass did its best to push us out with each spasming wave of his orgasm. Finally Lee collapsed forward onto me. His face and chest were covered in sweat. Benson pulled out, peeled his condom off and tossed it in the trash can. I was close to coming, but held back. I put my arms around Lee, pulled him down, and kissed him.

"Where do you want it, baby? Up your ass, or in your mouth?"

"Up my arse, Dan. Please. Fuck me."

The English pronunciation was the trigger, I think. It took a couple of upward thrusts, and I was filling the rubber inside him. Lee rode every last drop out of me.

"And you can take this," said Benson, standing beside us, "in your mouth."

Even now, multiply fucked at both ends, wet with piss and sweat and his own spunk, and with my dick still hard inside him, Lee could take more. He twisted his torso around, showing off the muscles in his back and sides, grabbed hold of Benson's cock and put it between his lips. We all know that the taste of rubber isn't pleasant, but it didn't stop Lee from sucking as if it was strawberry-flavored. Benson grabbed Lee's head like a football and fucked it. And then, just as he was about to come, he pulled out and unloaded all over Lee's face. It was a big load, jet after jet plastering him from forehead to chin.

Finally, we were finished. Lee climbed off me and I turned on the shower. We took turns to wash off, talking and drinking in the bathroom like old buddies who had just—what? Been to a football game? Taken a long hike together?

It was late, and we all needed sleep, three of us in my rickety bed, but we managed somehow. A couple of hours later, as dawn was breaking, Lee was sucking our dicks again.

12

So: great work, Dan. You've fallen in love with some kind of sadist, you've betrayed Jody, and you've fucked up a nice straightforward English boy so that now he's drinking piss and getting double-fucked.

I know what you're saying. I say it to myself in the small, sleepless hours. I don't have any excuse, except for the fact that from the age of eighteen onward I was in the military, which scrambles your sense of right and wrong. I can't live without conflict. War zones suited me well, so now I create as much conflict in my personal life as I possibly can.

Knowing something and acting on it are two very different things, though. I knew what kind of man Al Benson was now: dishonest, cruel, a user. Look what he did to Dick Coburn, and look what he was doing to me. Manipulating us to boost his ego, fucking us to satisfy his lust, and, in my case at least, using me as a pimp to procure fresh young flesh. And despite all that, or because of it, I was hooked. I couldn't stop thinking about him. I breathed, ate, and drank Al Benson. He controlled me. That's what I wanted—the control that I'd been missing since I left the Marines. Too much freedom; I had to enslave myself, and Benson was very happy to be my master. And he didn't just control my heart and my dick: he gave me a mission, which is what I need most. I can't exist without one. At heart I'm a mercenary, and if it's not Uncle Sam that's paying me, it might as well be anyone.

So we had our little mystery to solve: who's getting at the members of that secret task force, what does Harry Armitage know, and how much has it to do with the death of Quiller? My life, and Benson's marriage, had been threatened. But how real was the danger? Was it just an excuse for us to be together, to run away from our responsibilities?

The answers, if they were anywhere, were in DC. Armitage was there, right at the top of the pyramid, about to take up one of the most senior positions a serving officer can achieve. Woody Douglas was there—not so far away from Armitage as the crow flies, but in a different world, watching, forming his own theories. Naseer Khan was there, the blogger who might be able to tell us the truth about Peter Quiller. And there was another person who might be able to fill in some of the missing pieces of the jigsaw—someone who was close to Harry Armitage before, during and after Desert Fox: his ex-wife, Kim Evans. I remembered Evans well— maybe you do too, if you read the papers in any detail in the late '90s, because she was one of the first American women to fly combat missions as a US Navy fighter pilot. She was profiled in the newspapers and magazines, and had appeared on TV a few times, one of those people to whom war gives a brief fame. What the papers didn't mention at the time was that she was in a relationship with another rising star, Captain Harry Armitage USMC, but it was common knowledge among service personnel, and I certainly remember meeting her at the time of Desert Fox. By the time they married the spotlight had moved on, and now they were divorced. She'd have beans to spill.

"And why's she going to tell us anything?" I said to Benson as we were planning our trip to DC.

"She divorced him. She probably hates him. By all accounts the marriage was not a happy one."

"Which accounts would they be?"

Benson shrugged. "People talk."

"Gossip."

"If you like."

"So what are we going to do? Knock on her door and say, 'Hi, Ms. Evans, you don't know us but we were just wondering if you could tell us anything about your ex-husband's involvement in the murder of a UN weapons inspector?'"

"Something like that."

"Come on, Al. Even if she's not in the armed forces anymore—"

"She's not."

"She'll slam the door in our faces."

He smiled and grabbed the back of my neck, rubbing the stubble with his thumb. "Nobody slams the door in my face, Dan. Not even you."

"You're very sure of yourself."

He pushed my head downward. "Damn right."

"And what makes you think that's going to work on

Kim Evans?" We were fully clothed, it was two o'clock in the afternoon, but all I could think of was sucking his dick.

"It always did before."

I stopped dead. "What?"

"You heard."

I pushed back against his hand. "You mean you and her—"

"Yeah. Long time ago. When I was young and pretty. Remember?"

"Yes."

"She was my girlfriend."

"Oh."

"You're not jealous, are you? It was nearly twenty years ago."

"Of course I'm not fucking jealous. We're both with other people anyway, in case you'd forgotten."

Benson shrugged, still smiling, still rubbing my neck. "Are we?"

"Well, you are. You're married with kids."

"Thanks for reminding me, Dan." He let go of my head. "You really know how to make a guy feel special." He turned away. Now I felt bad; Al had a way of always making it your fault.

"Okay, I'm sorry. Tell me more about Kim Evans."

"All in good time. First you'd better suck this." He pulled his cock out of his fly. It was soft. "Get down on your knees and make me hard. Make me come."

I did as I was told. Benson lay back on the couch, staring up at the ceiling, occasionally stroking my head in an absent-minded way. It took about ten minutes of work before he came in my mouth.

* * *

If we were going to DC we had to think up a cover story. I don't know what kind of bullshit Benson was telling his wife; she surely didn't believe that he was that much in demand on the conference circuit. Perhaps she no longer cared, and was glad to get him out of the house. Perhaps she had interests of her own—girlfriends, boyfriends, whatever. I didn't ask, and Al didn't tell. Jody, however, was my responsibility. Since the disappointment of spring break we'd kept in touch with our usual Skype sessions, but they hadn't been the same. We used to do everything—the filthiest things that two men can do down a fiber-optic cable. Jody would fuck himself with inanimate objects, I'd jerk my cock, piss for him, come in my hands and lick it up—anything and every-thing that we knew would turn the other on. Recently, however, we'd talked about the weather. The fucking weather. We'd jerked off, but without enthusiasm; I even think Jody had faked it, and for me, given all the other demands on my balls, it was an effort. I was pretty sure he was tired of me, probably seeing someone else. I let myself believe that. It made me feel better.

But on this occasion I wanted to give him something to keep the peace—and, after sucking Benson's cock without once touching myself, I was more than ready to blow a load. Benson went downtown to buy himself a few things, and while he was out, I made the connection.

Jody looked tired and thin, with dark circles under his eyes.

We settled into our seats.

"Hey, Dan." He rubbed his eyes, mussed his hair. "How you doing, lover?"

"I'm fine. You look terrible."

"Gee, thanks." He scratched his face. He was unshaven, and it looked as if he hadn't been near a jar of moisturizer for weeks. This was not the Jody I knew— groomed and tweaked and plucked to perfection. It kind of suited him, to be honest—I prefer my men to look like men, and I always used to laugh at his beauty regime—but all the same, it worried me. "I just need to catch up on some sleep, that's all."

"Still burning the midnight oil?"

"Something like that."

"Are you eating properly?"

"What are you—my mother?" That was a joke, coming from Jody: his mother wouldn't have noticed if her son had died of starvation right in front of her.

"I'm the person who cares about you," I said, feeling like a piece of shit as I said it. I'd called him up in order to lie to him, and now I was trying to make the lie more plausible by pretending to be nice. But seeing him like that did make me care. If he asked me, I'd drop everything—Benson, the mission, the whole sorry farce—and go to him. At least that's what I felt for a few fleeting moments while Benson was away.

"Okay, okay. It's nearly done. Once this assignment's finished I'll get back to the gym and start eating properly."

"And come see me?"

"What's the matter, Dan? Don't you trust me?"

"Of course I trust you."

"Yeah, right. Like I trust you."

We knew each other too well to believe that we hadn't looked at another guy or sucked the occasional dick—but he hit on a sore spot, and it hurt. "Listen, Jody, you think it's easy for me being down here while you're up there?"

"No."

"Well, it isn't."

"Dan, we knew what we were getting into when we agreed I'd do this."

"Maybe you did."

"What do you mean?"

"What I thought we'd agreed to was that you'd come and see me whenever you can. Not cancel at the last minute. And when I come to see you, you could at least pretend to be happy."

"You took me by surprise, that's all."

"And now?"

"Look, Dan." He rubbed his face again; his eyes were bloodshot. "I'm not in the mood for an argument. I love you. Is that what you want to hear? I love you and I miss you."

"And whose fault is that?"

"Mine, obviously."

"Yeah." I wanted to stop behaving like this. I wanted to make it up to him. "I love you too," I said, but it sounded gruff and dismissive.

"That's all right then."

"When are you coming home?"

"Soon."

"Jody..."

"Yes?"

"If there was anything wrong, you would tell me, wouldn't you?"

"What kind of thing?"

"If you're...you know. Seeing someone else. In trouble. I don't fucking know. Anything. Would you tell me?"

"What do you think?"

"I don't know."

"Would you tell me?"

Shit: how much had he guessed? How much could he tell, just by looking at my face on a laptop screen? "Of course I would."

"There's your answer, then. I wish you were here, Dan. I'd show you how much I miss you."

"Yeah?"

"You know it." He licked his lips and rubbed his chest. "Like old times."

Oh, the old times: fucking him in the woods and car seats and motel rooms as we journeyed across New England, in washrooms and hotel beds and even in his Dad's house. Would we ever get that back? Would we ever be in love again as we were in those first dangerous days?

"I want you so fucking bad, Jody." And at that moment, I did. I wanted to feel his skin, the golden silk that covered his fine slender frame. I wanted to look into his eyes, to taste his lips as I slid into his tight ass. I wanted us to kiss away each other's pain as we knew how to do so well. Jesus, it was him I needed, not Al Benson—who turned my head around so that up was down, black was white, wrong was right. I was hard—instantly, painfully hard—and I had to come.

We had an effective routine. Jody fingered his hole and I jerked my dick and we talked dirty to each other. It worked. It didn't take long.

I wiped up. "Did you come, baby?"

"No."

Instantly, that stab of jealousy. "Why not?"

He pulled his pants up and laughed. "I have a head-ache."

It felt like a kick in the guts. Now that I'd come, I wanted this to be over. I just wanted to sleep. Oblivion. "Call you soon."

"You know where I am."

"Okay."

I hung up before either of us could tell any more lies.

Benson wasn't talking much when he came back, which suited me fine. He sat in front of the TV watching the news and drinking beer from the can; he'd bought a six-pack, and didn't offer me one. Something obviously happened when he was out. I suspected that he'd talked to his wife, told her another pack of lies just as I'd told Jody. It didn't make either of us feel good.

I watched him drinking, one leg hooked over the arm of the chair. Was this what I was throwing every-thing away for? An affair with a married man. That's what it was. A man I had no more chance of keeping than the most naive secretary who dates her boss. For all that Benson enjoyed the sex, and whatever crazy excuses he found to come looking for me, this whole fucking mystery might be one big excuse—there was no future in it. He'd go back to Brenda and the kids, and I would... What? Go back to Jody? That seemed increas-ingly unlikely. Whatever had been between us was stretched to the breaking point. One of us was going to finish it sooner or later. Even if I wasn't cheating on him every chance I got, I was pretty sure that Jody was looking for a way out. Love that had seemed so solid and lasting in the heat of danger and its afterglow was disappearing like a mirage.

Eventually he spoke.

"We've got a week."

"Yeah?"

"In DC."

"Okay." What cover story had he given Brenda? Had he left her? Was he planning to return to family life after a week? Were the next seven days the end of something, or the beginning? I didn't ask. From the look on Benson's face, it didn't seem advisable.

He crushed the can in his fist, turned to face me, and said, "Road trip!" He was smiling, at least.

"Yeah!"

"That's what I used to love as a kid. Get some time off, get in the car with a buddy or two, and just take off. Freedom."

"Is that what this is? Freedom?"

He looked into my eyes for a while. I half expected some kind of declaration, but then he said, "We're going to DC to do a job."

"Right."

"But nobody said we can't have some fun while we do it."

Our carefully constructed theories about Armitage, Coburn, Douglas, and Quiller collapsed like a house of cards. Did Benson really give a shit about any of it? Was the threat we'd dreamed up nothing but a chain of coincidences, as unreal as WMD? Perhaps we were doing just what the generals had done—concealing our real objectives behind a smokescreen of excuses. I had no particular reason to care about Dick Coburn. Another dead marine. Big deal. I had one of my own to mourn. And if Harry Armitage made it all the way to the West Wing, so what? Shit floats. I got mugged in Brooklyn, yes, and there was something suspicious about that, but maybe the cops were right. There's war on the streets, and they're using real soldiers to fight it. Al Benson was being blackmailed: he wasn't the first closet case to get it, and he wouldn't be the last. Nothing unusual about it. No ulterior motive. As for Woody Douglas, he was insane, that's all. A victim of the machine. I knew what we were really going to DC for. A seven-day vacation from reality.

We set off early in the morning in my crappy old car with no itinerary, not even a place to stay. We were laughing, excited, singing along to an oldies station, passing a can of coke between us. We stopped at a diner near Yonkers for lunch, filled up on burgers and fries and fooled around in the bathroom, giggling like schoolboys having a pissing contest. It was dark by the time we got close to DC and found a motel. I'm usually happy with the most basic accommodations: if it's got a bed and a shower and a lock on the door, that's enough for me. Benson was a little fussier. "Stop worrying about the fucking money," he said, and booked us into a place with fancy drapes and a bathtub with little jets in it. "We're going to be staying here for a while, we might as well be comfortable. And I'm paying."

Arrogant prick, I thought, but I said nothing. I guess I liked it.

13

Some of us work in gyms when we leave the military, others own them. Kim Evans—Lieutenant Commander Kim Evans, as she was known when she left the navy—opened a gym in the Washington suburbs in the early '00s and had since developed it into a chain serving all the major residential districts around the central DC area. Pilot Fitness Clubs (she wasn't afraid of cashing in on her days as a navy flyer) were upscale establishments for busy professionals, bristling with the latest equipment. The changing rooms were like something out of a five-star hotel, with piles of fluffy towels arranged under gleaming pinlights, bottles of complimentary shampoo and moisturizer, a sauna, and whirlpool. It couldn't have been further from the Strong Box ("Lowell's Premier Fitness and Martial Arts Facility," in case you'd forgotten) if it tried.

Benson made the call and, true to his word, secured an appointment with the owner herself within twenty-four hours. We were summoned to the flagship branch, three floors of steel and glass office in Georgetown, where Evans had her office. Everything about it, from the flowers arranged in tall glass vases to the beautiful desk staff to the leather seats we were asked to occupy, screamed money.

I heard her before I saw her. "Who's this?" Barked, rather than spoken. You can take a girl out of the navy, but you can't take the navy out of a girl. I looked up and saw her, straight out of a TV show: tailored black skirt and jacket, white shirt, black heels, black hair, everything about her as neat and precise as if she'd been on deck.

"Great to see you too, Kim," said Benson, slowly getting up and extending a hand. "You look more beautiful than ever."

She stopped, almost clicking her heels. "If he's a journalist..."

Benson smiled, his eyes twinkling. Evans relaxed a little. "This is my buddy Dan Stagg. A fellow marine. Dan, Kim Evans, ex-navy, but we don't hold that against her, right?"

"Hi, Dan." She unwound enough to shake my hand. "Would you like Max to show you around the gym while I talk to Al?" She gestured toward the young man behind the desk, all thick black hair and flawless skin.

"Sure," said Max, jumping over the desk. His ass was round and hard, his eyes bright blue. "My pleasure. Have a workout if you like."

Ordinarily I'd have been happy to spend the morning working out with a nice little piece like Max, but Benson said, "If you don't mind, Kim, Dan's coming in with me. We have a few questions for you."

"If you're here to talk about my ex-husband, forget it. Every reporter in town has tried and failed."

"Honey, I don't want to talk about your ex-husband. You made the wrong choice, and if I'm big enough to forgive and forget, I'm sure you are."

Evans actually smiled and might have blushed, though it was hard to tell through the flawless veneer of her makeup. Benson was a magician. "You'd better come up then. Max? Bring us coffee in half an hour."

"Yes, Ms. Evans." He jumped back behind the counter. When I looked over my shoulder, he winked at me. And that probably tells you how Kim Evans built Pilot Fitness up to the successful chain it is today. A little charm in the right places goes a long way. I was thinking about how far I could take that charming little piece as we got in the elevator. Benson flirted with Evans all the way. By the time she was showing us into her private office—a glass box with views that a realtor would kill for—she was a very different woman from the suited robot who greeted us. They chatted about everything and nothing—the weather, the news, property prices—and somehow he managed to work a little flattery into every line.

"So, gentlemen, take a seat." She indicated a long, low leather couch. There was a glass coffee table in front of it, at shin-cracking height. "This isn't a formal meeting. Or is it?"

"Of course not, Kim. We're just looking up old friends."

"I see. A reunion."

"Yeah." Benson stretched his arms along the back of the couch, and rested his ankle on his knee. "I'm giving Brenda some time off for good behavior." He didn't mention anything about the men he thought were following him, the blackmail, or the lies he'd told his wife. "Dan and I made contact again through one of those veterans' websites. You know?"

"No," said Evans. "I don't go near them."

"Good idea," said Benson. "No point in living in the past, is there? Leaving the Marines was the best thing I ever did..." And he was off on his favorite monologue about how happy and fulfilling his life was since he left the service. I flicked through a fitness magazine and wondered how soon Max would be back with the coffee.

Conversation drifted around to our shared past.

"Dan was with me in Iraq," said Benson. "We went through a lot together."

"Okay." Evans suddenly looked at me with more interest; I was no longer the hanger-on, the sidekick.

"One of the best men I ever served with."

I knew this was bullshit, but it still made me feel a couple of inches taller. "Come on, Al."

"We were on a mission with your ex-husband, in fact."

"Bad luck."

"No, no, he was a great leader. Inspirational, I'd say."

Evans scrutinized Benson's face for sarcasm. "Inspirational, my ass."

Benson shrugged. "Not everyone liked him. Dan's not his number one fan, for instance."

Whatever Benson's strategy was, he hadn't let me in on the secret.

"Well, at least one of you has a brain, then," said Evans, catching my eye and smiling.

I didn't know what to say, and just smiled back.

"I hope you're not another one with an ax to grind." She ran her fingers through her hair. "Harry's got a lot of enemies in this town."

"And a lot of friends," I said. "I read about his appointment."

"Oh, that. He must be the happiest man in America." She grimaced. "If he can keep the job, anyway."

"Don't you think he's up to it?" asked Benson.

"He's up to any challenge. I just mean that there are a lot of people out there who would love to see him fail."

"Including his ex-wife, no doubt."

"Uh-uh." Evans wagged her forefinger. "I don't have any argument with him. I got what I wanted in the divorce. I did just fine." She gestured around the office; I guess Harry Armitage was footing the bill. "He knows he can rely on me to keep my mouth shut when people come around here asking questions."

"Journalists?"

"Mostly. And guys with a grudge."

"Anyone we know?"

Evans laughed. "You don't expect me to name names, do you? Come on."

"Just curious," said Benson, smiling back at her.

"Is that what this is all about? Coming in here with the old Red Benson charm, putting me at my ease, then when you've got me all nice and relaxed you start asking questions?"

That sounded like a pretty good summary of what had just happened, but Benson pretended to be wounded. "Wow! There's no need to be hostile."

At this point there was a knock at the door. Evans

barked, "Come!" and there was Max, all white teeth and blue eyes and black forelock, with a tray of coffee.

"Here you go, guys." He placed the cups on the table, which involved leaning across me. "Excuse me, sir."

"That's just fine."

He stood up, caught my eye again and smiled. "Anything else, Ms. Evans?"

"Thank you, Max. That's all."

He withdrew, maintaining eye contact until the frosted glass door closed behind him. Something to investigate on the way out, perhaps. If Benson had clocked him, he'd be wanting me to bring Max back to our motel.

Evans walked to the window and looked out over Georgetown. "I'm sorry," she said. "I don't mean to be a bitch. I just don't want to be Mrs. Harry Armitage anymore. I did that job for a long time, and now I quit."

"I'm sorry. It must have been tough."

"Don't try to be sympathetic, Al. That won't work either."

"It's just that when old comrades get together, it's natural to talk. Dan and I have had a great time chewing the fat. That's all it is."

She turned to face us. "Really?"

"What else? Look, it was your misfortune to marry the wrong guy."

"Meaning you were the right guy?"

"Brenda seems to think so. Harry's an asshole."

"Well, that's something we can agree on." Evans sipped her coffee. It was very good coffee.

"What was the name of that guy we were talking about the other day, Dan? You know, the guy in Desert Fox?"

"Who?" I had no idea where this was going, and didn't want to blow it with the wrong response.

"The weapons inspector."

"Oh." I watched Evans's cup stop halfway to her mouth. "Peter Quiller," I said. "Is that who you mean?"

"That's it," said Benson, as if we were just going over some ancient military gossip. "What was that rumor you picked up on?"

I hazarded a guess. "People are saying he was killed by US forces."

Benson snapped his fingers. "That's it. Weird, right? Some nutjob on a blog somewhere says that US Marines were deployed to take out UN weapons inspectors. Crazy, right?"

"Why are you asking me this?"

"Because, believe it or not, fingers are being pointed at Harry. And the people who served with him. And that means me and my buddy Dan here."

"I see."

"And I don't much like people pointing at me," said Benson.

"Me neither," said Evans.

"He ever mention that name? Peter Quiller?"

Evans glanced at her watch. "Means nothing to me. I have another meeting starting in five minutes. So if you—"

"Weird that he would keep it from you. But then I suppose there was a lot you didn't know about your husband."

"What?"

"Perhaps he didn't trust you."

"Of course he fucking trusted me." There was

anger in her voice now. "You know nothing about our marriage."

"Maybe. But I heard plenty."

"Meaning what?"

"Other women. Drinking." Benson balled up his fists, and did a couple of jabs. "Fights."

"Okay!" Evans stood up. "That's enough. At one time he talked about nothing but Peter fucking Quiller, if that's what you want to know. Satisfied? He was obsessed by the man." She was almost shouting, but checked herself. "He said he was a traitor who was in the pay of Saddam. He was proud to have taken him out, and he said he got promoted because of it."

"Hear that, Dan?"

"Yeah. It figures."

Evans's voice was rising again, despite her attempts to keep in control. I guess this had been a long time coming. "He used to read all the same blogs that you do. Still does, I'm sure. And you know what he used to say? He reckoned that the conspiracy theorists, the really wacko ones, were the only ones who were smart enough to figure out the truth. And that suited him just fine, because they were so crazy that nobody would believe them. The ones who say 9/11 was an inside job, that Kennedy was assassinated by the CIA, that Neil Armstrong never walked on the moon. So when those same crazies say that Harry Armitage led a squad of assassins against a UN weapons inspector, nobody listens. He's hiding in plain sight, and he's been rewarded very handsomely for his obedience."

"Right." Benson stood up. "We've taken up way too much of your time. I'm sorry if I touched on old wounds, Kim. All this stuff about Harry…" He waved his hands, as if brushing away an annoying fly. "I really don't listen to it. We all know bad stuff happened out there. It's not news. Come on, Dan. Let's go. We've got a busy day of sightseeing ahead of us."

"Nice to meet you, Ms. Evans." I held out my hand. She took a while to respond, pulling herself together and smoothing down her skirt.

"Of course, of course. Listen, guys, I'm sorry. I just get so damn…" She coughed. "Don't pay any attention to me. I'm a bitter old divorcée."

"No love in your life these days, Kim?"

"Nobody special."

"That's too bad. You're a very beautiful woman. Successful, too." He gestured around the office. "I'm very impressed."

"Don't tell me, Al, if you weren't married you'd ask me out."

Benson laughed. "What? Oh, maybe. But I'm not the cheating kind. I've got everything I need right back home in Pittsburgh."

They kissed each other, and we left.

We were barely out of the building before Benson's phone pinged with an incoming message. He read it, and laughed.

"Yeah, baby! Still got it." He showed me the phone.

Want to have lunch/dinner? Would be good to talk. Kim.

"Maybe she's got something to tell you," I said.

"And maybe she wants a little of this." He grabbed his crotch. "She always used to."

"Don't forget you've got everything you need back home in Pittsburgh."

"Relax, man! I'm not going to fuck her. Unless she asks me very, very nicely."

He must have known how this made me feel. He was enjoying my sullen looks and monosyllabic grunts.

"Oh, come on, Dan! For Christ's sake. What do you want? A wedding ring?"

I didn't answer that one, because I knew that if he said anything else I'd hit him. And once I started, I wouldn't stop. See how bad this was getting?

"Look, I'll take her for lunch. I'll meet you back at the motel at what, four o'clock? I'm not going to do anything. I'll see what I can find out, and we'll have a nice talk about old times, and if she makes a grab at it I'll show her a photograph of the kids. That usually does the trick."

"Is that what you were doing to me, first time we met?"

He stopped smiling. "Yes. If you want me to be honest, that's exactly what I was doing. I got cold feet and I was trying to scare you off."

"Didn't work, did it?"

"Not that time, no. But I wanted you, Dan. I don't want Kim Evans."

If we hadn't been walking down a busy street, I'd have kissed him.

Benson made the call and arranged a date. I went back into the gym and told Max I'd take him up on the offer of a workout. He looked delighted.

"Want to train together?"

Well, that certainly eased the pain. Benson went back

to the motel to change; I went into the nearest store to buy a T-shirt and shorts.

I was kind of hoping for a rerun of the Lee-and-Dan show: working out together, talking about each other's bodies, and moving swiftly to the shower or steam room for a sweaty fuck. Pilot Fitness, however, was not the sort of gym where that happened. There was CCTV everywhere, for one thing; Jesus, if I was on the security detail I'd be taking some of that footage home for private study. The showers had individual cubicles with translucent glass walls, a design I deplore. There wasn't even much to look at in the changing area: everyone, including Max, got dressed and undressed under a towel. When did we become a nation of prudes? I wanted to shout "It's a fucking locker room, guys! Get naked!" For all the fun I had at Pilot Fitness, I might as well have been back in Afghanistan, living under the Taliban.

On the gym floor, however, Max was attentive and chatty. I sensed that he was bored at work and, like all gym employees, underpaid and underoccupied. Under the pretext of showing me how to use the machines "for insurance reasons," he followed me around the floor, occasionally offering a word of advice on technique but more often just gossiping. I made sure that he was left in no doubt about my preferences; I always think it's best to give guys like Max the opportunity to run away as early as possible. He stuck around.

We were on the leg extension machine when the subject came up. I was raising eighty pounds, and every strand of muscle in my thighs was rippling and tensing.

"You've got strong legs," said Max, perching on the next-door machine. "You a runner?"

"Ex-military, like your boss."

"And you kept in shape."

"Yeah. Unlike some of 'em. A year, two years out of the forces, they're buckets of lard. And you should see the top brass. You need to get them down here, whip 'em into shape."

"We do our best. Good to see you've kept up the training. It's really important as you…"

What? *Get older?* He blushed, and I smiled. "Don't worry. You'll be forty one day too."

"Forty? Seriously?"

"Come on, Max. Don't tell me I look younger, because I don't."

"Oh, I—"

"My boyfriend says I look older." I hoisted the weight again, and held it up. "Fucking charming, right?"

His eyes widened a fraction—they were already huge, like some cute little anime cartoon—but that was all. "You're in great shape," was all he said. Professional.

"I have to be, in my line of work."

"And what's that?"

"You could call it security." I wasn't going to tell him that I was several steps down the same ladder as him. "Muscle for hire. Protecting people. Investigating shit."

"Right." He scratched his belly, lifting his shirt up just enough to show a thick mat of dark hair. "Sounds like something out of the movies."

"It's not that exciting."

"Sounds better than working in a gym."

"I can honestly say that the only advantage to my job is that you get a lot of ass."

"For real?"

"On the road. Moving around. No ties." Christ, what bullshit. "I bet you do too, working here. Beautiful women all around you."

"Are you kidding? Ms. Evans would kill anyone who laid a finger on the members."

"Yeah? What about guests?"

He laughed, at least. "You know what I mean, man. Strictly no fraternizing."

"Don't worry." I got off the machine and stretched my quads. "I'm not going to get you fired."

"What do you want to do next?"

I caught his eye and made a *you know perfectly well what I want to do* face. He laughed and blushed, and I said, "Okay, let's do chest. Can you spot for me?"

"Sure."

I loaded up the bar and lay back, enjoying a worm's-eye view up his shirt. "So, is she a good boss?"

"Ms. Evans? She's a good businesswoman."

"I can see that. I mean is she a nice person to work for."

He looked around; there was no one near us. "I wouldn't go that far."

"A ballbreaker?"

Max looked uncomfortable; I guess my Neanderthal vocabulary doesn't go down too well with metropolitan guys like him. "She's very firm, that's all I'm saying."

"Well, it obviously works. She's done well."

"She sure has."

I hefted the weight—one, two, three reps, and back onto the rests.

"Good technique."

"Thanks. So you—what are your ambitions?"

"I don't know. Build up my client base. Manage one of the gyms. This one, maybe."

"You should think bigger than that. A good-looking, smart guy like you should be owning gyms, not running them for other people."

"Not worth the stress."

More reps: four, five, six, back on the rack without a wobble. My chest and arms were burning, and it felt good.

"Ms. Evans get stressed much?"

"She's a ticking time bomb."

"She seemed pretty relaxed to me," I lied.

"It's an act that she puts on for customers and shareholders." He lowered his voice. "Most of the time she's close to the edge. We have to watch what we say. Especially recently."

"What's been happening recently?"

Seven, eight, nine, and I was starting to reach my limits. I grunted as I put the bar back, and Max's hands hovered around it. "Good work. You have a very strong chest."

I thumped my pecs like a gorilla. "Me Tarzan."

"Three more?"

"Give me a second." I mopped my dripping face. "So go on. What's pulling your boss's chain? Money problems?"

"Christ no. It's rolling in, and she keeps the overheads as low as legally possible."

"Then what?"

"She's scared of something."

I let that one sink in for a moment, lay back, and did the last three reps, grunting like a pig and, on the last press, wobbling so much that I needed Max to help me. He came close enough to push my bald head into his crotch.

"Thanks. That was fucking hard." I sat up and rubbed my chest, which felt like rock. "So what spooked her?"

"Not sure. She hired a security company."

"When?"

"A couple of weeks ago. She didn't come into work one day—the official line was that she got sick. But when she came back she was as nervous as hell. In meetings all day long. Didn't talk to anyone. Then these two guys in suits turned up, started escorting her to and from work. It's creepy."

"She still got them?"

"Oh, yeah. They'll be around here somewhere. You probably didn't notice. They're discreet."

"But you noticed."

"I have a lot of time on my hands."

"And you've got a good pair of eyes in your head. Very beautiful eyes too, if I may say so."

"Oh. Thanks."

"Sorry. I forget my manners when I meet good-looking guys like you."

Max busied himself tidying up equipment. How far could I go before he got pissed off?

"Okay," he said, "abs?"

"Sure. Got a medicine ball?"

He gestured to a rack of squeaky-clean balls, ranked in order of weight. At my gym you just pick some stinky old leather thing off the floor.

"Okay, Max. We're going to do this like we used

to in the Marines. Ready?" I clicked my fingers and pointed to the mat. We sat facing each other, feet linked around the ankles, knees bent. "I come up, throw the ball, you catch, go down, up, and throw. Got it?"

"Yes." I threw quickly, catching him off guard. "Oof! That thing's heavy!"

"Come on. You can take it." He could too, and we quickly established a rhythm, up and down, up and down, the ball passing between us wet with each other's sweat, our legs connected. At the top of each sit-up, our faces were a foot apart. I've fucked guys in this position, more or less. It takes some doing, but it's a lot of fun. The image projected over the reality, like a pornographic double exposure. Max's ass clamped around my dick, his eyes rolling back, lips parted as I fucked him.

It's a great way to train your abs.

After about fifty reps we were getting tired, and I, for one, had a hard cock, which is not especially comfortable. I stood up, making sure I had my back to the rest of the room. If Max chose to notice, that was up to him.

He remained seated, leaning back on his hands, looking up at me. His eyes darted between my face and my crotch.

"That was amazing," he said. "I'm really burning."

"Me too." I held eye contact, and let one hand drift down to my cock, rearranging it in my shorts. "Sorry about this. It's always getting me into trouble."

"I bet." He didn't move, didn't smile, didn't frown.

"What about you, Max? You want to get into trouble?"

"I can't."

"Come on. I won't tell if you won't."

"I mean, I have a girlfriend."

"Yeah? I have a boyfriend. I wasn't planning on telling him."

"But I don't… I mean, I'm not…"

"Gay? Right. 'Course not."

Now he did frown. "I'm not."

"Fine. You won't be wanting to suck this dick, then." I made it twitch in my shorts. He watched, didn't move. "Okay. I'll get a shower. Thanks for the—"

"Wait."

I waited, hands on hips.

"I'll…"

"Yeah?"

He got to his feet and pulled up his shirt to wipe his face, giving me a very nice view of the firm, hairy belly. "You can come to the treatment room," he whispered.

"Is there a lock on the door?"

"Yes."

"That's all that matters, then."

"Follow me. And please, just do something about *that*."

I readjusted *that* so that it was barely visible, and followed Max to the reception desk.

"Key for physio, please," he said. "Ms. Evans's guest has a frozen shoulder."

"Okay." The cute girl on the desk clicked around on her computer. "It's free. Twenty minutes?"

"Call it thirty," said Max, sounding breezy but blushing like a schoolboy. It could have been the exercise—let's be charitable. "Thanks, babe." He took the key and spun it around on his finger. "This way, please. Let's get you taken care of."

The treatment room was bigger than some places I've lived in—about fifteen feet by twenty, all gleaming steel and dazzling white, a vase of lilies on the table. Max closed the door behind him, lifted the handle to lock it and pulled down the blind.

"Okay," he said. "We won't be disturbed."

My cock was still hard. I was tempted to push it out the leg of my shorts and shove it in Max's face. But it would be more fun to make him work for it.

"So," I said. "Where do you want me?"

I guess he was expecting me to take charge—the older man, the experienced homosexual, the seducer. Sometimes, though, I think it's good for guys like Max to prove to themselves just how much they want cock. If you let them think it was all your fault and they just went along for the ride, they can pretend it didn't happen. Get them to betray their real desires, and you'll have a lot more fun. Max coughed, cleared his throat, ran his fingers through his thick forelock, and said, "Well, I guess we'd better start off on the table."

He gestured to a massage table upholstered in expensive-looking cream leather. Obedient, I perched on the edge.

"You should probably take your shoes off."

"Okay." I kicked them to the ground. "Anything else?"

"And your—" A cough again, and he licked his lips. "Your shirt."

I peeled it over my head. It was cheap nylon shit, and it crackled with static from my body hair. I bunched it up and threw it on a chair. My muscles were pumped from our workout. I know I'm not a beauty—I have a face like a well-worn boot, I'm bald and beat-up—but if you like 'em rough and ready, I'm your man. It appeared that Max, beautiful big-eyed Max who, as you recall, was "not gay," was the type who does.

"All yours."

"Lie on your front, then. Let's have a look at this shoulder."

"My shoulder? Sure." I did as I was told, pushing my hard cock into the padded tabletop. Max's hands were on me right away, massaging, stroking, pressing. He knew what he was doing. There was nothing wrong with my shoulder, apart from the usual wear and tear, but he made me feel very good. I groaned with pleasure. "Oh, baby."

"You're tense."

"Damn right I'm tense. I've been looking at your sweet ass for the last hour."

"You really like it?"

"Come on, kid. Don't pretend you don't know it."

Max kept on rubbing. "Just don't get many guys saying it like that."

"Plenty of 'em think it, you can be sure of that. I bet ten guys every day walk through those doors and want to fuck you stupid."

I heard him swallow. A drop of sweat fell onto my back.

"Now, listen to me, Max. You're a great masseur. I'd love to lie here all day. But we only have thirty minutes. You want to waste any more of those minutes working on my back?"

"Turn over."

"Yeah?"

"Yes. I want your cock."

He'd said it. That's all I really wanted to hear. No more mind games. I rolled over fast, which was a relief.

"Put your hands down by your sides."

"Like this?"

"Yeah."

He seemed hesitant. "Come on. It's all yours."

He started rubbing my chest, kneading the muscle and pinching the tits. There was no pretense at physio anymore. This was sex. Just to underline that fact, I moved my hand to the edge of the table and pressed it against his thigh. He responded as I hoped he would, shifting his crotch against me. He was as stiff as I was. I squeezed.

That seemed to banish the last of Max's inhibitions. The sleek, smiling professional trainer was ready to risk everything for a taste of cock. His hands ran down over my belly and tugged at the waistband of my shorts. To make things easier for him—I try to be considerate at these times—I lifted my ass off the table. The shorts came down fast, and my cock sprang up.

Either cocksucking is an instinctive thing, hardwired into the human brain, or a lot of these guys who pretend to be straight are lying. Max didn't hesitate to get his lips around the head, and once he tasted me he slid straight down without stopping.

He sucked me from the side, working his head up and down, his forelock starting to flop into his eyes. He looked a lot better like that. I could have come pretty easily—it wouldn't have taken long, and the physio room would be free well within the time limit. But I had other ideas. I wanted him naked, for one thing—all that coyness in the locker room was still rankling—and I wanted to leave absolutely no doubt in anyone's mind that Max was a true-blue cocksucker. The thought crossed my mind that I could fuck him too—but I didn't have condoms, and I guessed that Pilot Fitness, unlike some "gyms," didn't leave them around in handy little dishes.

I pushed him off me. "Strip."

He wiped his mouth on his hairy forearm, pushed his hair out of his eyes, and did as he was told. He was fucking beautiful—slim, defined, a perfect model. His dick was on the small side, curving upward, and very, very hard. He hadn't trimmed his bush, which made it look smaller. I like small dicks. Yeah, I like 'em big too. Medium. Any size. But this... Well, there weren't many I'd seen that turned me on as much.

I got off the table, stood up. "Come here, baby."

He came to me, a smile on his face. I put an arm around his neck, grabbed his dick with my other hand, and kissed him. He wasn't expecting that, but after a second or two he kissed me back. I stroked him, and he relaxed against my arm. He was close too. I pressed my cock against his, squeezed them both together; I was nearly twice his size. Max wasn't bashful, thank god. He reveled in the contrast as much as I did.

"Fuck, man. That's so hot."

I rubbed us together, hard against hard.

"Now on your knees. Suck my cock."

He did as he was told, and it was good. I grabbed his hair, messing it up as much as I could. He'd need another fistful of product to get that back in shape. Looking down, I could see how hard he was; his cock was bouncing around as if one touch would set it squirting. I was close myself. I wanted his ass badly—to taste it, to get my fingers and tongue inside it, to fuck it hard, reaching around to feel his little dick rock hard in my hand...

And that was enough. I said, "Oh, shit," and unloaded in his mouth.

As soon as he tasted my semen, Max's hand flew to his dick. He was about three seconds behind me, cum flying out over my feet. When it was over, he rested his damp forehead against my belly, kissing my softening shaft. I let him do it for a while, wondering if he was going to try for a second round. His cock was still hard, and he was young.

I squatted down and kissed him again, tasting my spunk in his mouth. "How long have we got?"

His eyes were half closed. "Huh?"

"Before they bust down the door."

"Dunno. Five, ten minutes." He spoke like a man in a dream, unwilling to wake.

"Good. I'm going to make you come again."

He didn't say anything, just sighed and leaned against me, sweaty and hairy. I reached down between his legs, under his balls, along his perineum until I found his hole, warm and moist in a nest of soft hair.

"I really want to fuck you, Max," I said, "but that's going to have to wait. This is just a deposit." I spat onto my fingers and rubbed it against his ass. "Ready?"

"Oh, Jesus."

I was in—one finger, right up to his prostate, sliding in like silk. He groaned and squirmed, kicking his legs out like a frog's. His head moved slowly from side to side, looking for something. It didn't take long to figure out what. I was still half hard myself, and I moved around to give Max what he wanted. He took my cock in this mouth, sucking hard, as if he was trying to get a drink out of it.

Another finger joined the first, and I fucked him hard. His thighs clamped around my forearm; good thing I'm strong, because that kind of force could snap a bone. And soon he was coming again, my fingers inside him, emptying another load out of his small, superhard cock, running down his fist and dispersing in his bush.

I kept him plugged at both ends for a long time. He didn't stop sucking, even after his orgasm had subsided.

"You want more from me, you'll have to wait for it," I said. "Now get up and get dressed before we both get busted."

He was shy now, two loads later, but with a flush in his cheeks and his hair hanging limp, he looked even better than before.

"There's one other thing," he said, just before he pulled the blind up. What now, I thought? Please don't tell my girlfriend? Please come back and do it again?

"Yeah?" I was standing close enough to kiss him.

"About Ms. Evans."

"What about her?"

"I shouldn't tell you this. She said that if anyone talked, they'd get the sack. But you and that guy you came in with—you knew her before, right?"

"We served together, yes."

He frowned. He was still naked, and sticky with

three loads of cum. I could see the pulse throbbing in his neck. I couldn't stop touching him.

"You know I said she was frightened?"

"Yeah." I kissed his neck, felt the beating blood.

"Well, there was a reason."

14

"He said what?"

Benson was drunk after a long lunch with Kim Evans, lying on the bed with bare feet and unbuttoned shirt. I kept my distance. There were things to discuss: like what Max had just told me.

"Evans was attacked in the street. Two guys."

He rubbed his stomach. "She didn't mention it to me."

"I'm sure you two were far too busy reminiscing about the good old days."

"Among other things." His hand went under his waistband. Perhaps the company of an attractive woman was reigniting his dormant heterosexuality. "Hey, suck my dick, Danny boy."

Under normal circumstances I'd have been only too happy, but something was wrong with this picture. Okay, Benson looked very attractive lying on the bed; there are very few men who don't look hotter in a motel room. But surely we were in DC for a reason? Benson was supposed to be on the trail of some blackmailers, not to mention investigating the death of someone he said he loved and betrayed. He should have been at least slightly worried about the fact that another of Armitage's associates had been attacked. The suspicion flashed across my mind that the trip to DC was not an investigation but a distraction—or, worse, a trap. I never trusted Benson, not one hundred percent. He could be one of the bad guys, whoever they were. Maybe everything he told me was a lie, and he was working for Armitage, relaying my whereabouts, reeling me in with sex and misinformation. And then what? Dead in DC?

But of course I was getting hard again.

Think clearly, Dan. Summon up those trusty passion-killers, the memories of dead kids, maggot-infested wounds, and bleeding stumps that you've retained from combat zones for just these occasions.

"What do you think, then?"

"I don't know." He massaged the bulge in his pants. "DC is a mugger's paradise. Always has been."

"That's what the Brooklyn cops told me too."

"There you go. Now—"

"Listen to me, Al. Something's going on, and you know it. You can pretend it isn't, we can suck and fuck and make believe that everything's great, but that doesn't change a thing. Everyone who was involved in that mission has been threatened. Dick Coburn is dead. Remember? Dick Coburn."

His hand stopped moving.

"Why are we here, Al?"

"That's a profound question. I don't know. Part of god's big plan. That's what I tell the kids."

"Here in DC."

He sat up, facing away from me.

"Nothing to say?"

Silence.

"Okay, Al. Have it your way. I'm going for a walk."

"Wait. Stay." He still didn't turn. I waited. "There is something going on." He sounded weird, quiet.

"But not what you told me, right?"

He turned around, his face dark with anger. "What the fuck is that supposed to mean?"

Raw nerve, obviously. Doesn't like being caught in a lie. "The blackmail photos. The guys following you and your family. Hey, I don't know. The whole story about you and Dick Coburn."

"You think I made it all up?"

"I don't know, Benson. You tell me."

"Okay." He stood up and adjusted his pants. "If that's what you think, I'll just check out. Don't worry, Dan. I'll pay the bill."

"Sure. Go ahead." I folded my arms. "Have a great life."

We faced each other.

"If you don't trust me..." he began, then looked at the floor.

"Should I?"

"Yes." He looked up. "Yes, Dan, you should. Everything I've told you is true."

"Everything?"

"What is this, a cross-examination?"

I said nothing. Benson may have been my superior officer once, but now I was in command.

"Okay, listen. There are things going on that... I mean, when I told you about the guys who sent me the pictures..."

"Go on. I'm waiting." Was it all lies?

"The thing is, Dan…"

Here it comes.

"I'm scared." Benson looked down at the floor again. His fingers and thumbs were twisting around nervously. "Okay? Satisfied? I'm scared. Me. Red Benson, the big hero."

I thought that was stretching it a little—I had more medals than he did, and I certainly don't consider myself a hero—but I guess when you've had people telling you that you're great for your whole life, you start to believe it. "Fine. We all get scared."

"So scared that I ran. Left my wife and kids and fucking ran."

"I know. You told me."

"Oh, it wasn't just the blackmail. That's bad enough, but all it did was bring about something inevitable. I fucked up, Dan. I fucked everything up."

That was enough; I couldn't keep up the tough-guy act any longer. I took him in my arms, and he pressed his face into my shoulder. Al Benson was crying. I felt his chest heaving, his tears soaking into my shirt.

"It's okay, baby. It's okay. I'm here."

"Jesus." He pulled me closer. "What a fucking mess." His voice was high and broken. "What the fuck am I going to do?"

"I'll tell you what you're going to do, Al. You're going to face up to your problems and together we're going to figure things out, no matter how bad they are."

"We are?"

"Yes. You and me."

"For real?" He sounded like a little boy asking if the tooth fairy would come.

"So help me, god."

He pulled back and looked me straight in the eyes. "Thank you, Dan."

"That's okay."

"I..." He took a deep breath. "I don't know what to say."

"Don't you?"

"Yes. I do." He closed his eyes and took a deep breath. "Shit. Here goes." Eyes open. "I love you."

I could hear blood rushing in my head, traffic on the highway, the sound of the radio in the office. And a huge fucking silence that followed those three words. *I love you.* He loves me. Red Benson, the alpha male, the hero, the poster boy, loves me. Not his wife, not his kids, not his country. Me, Dan Stagg, fuckup, reject, embarrassment.

And that was enough. Whatever happened next with my family, with Jody, with the mission, if there really was a mission, it didn't matter. Benson would get a divorce, I'd give Jody the freedom that he so obviously wanted, and together we'd face the world. If there were asses to be kicked, we'd kick 'em —Al and Dan, Benson and Stagg, brothers in arms.

And so, of course, we fucked.

Afterward we slept, and by the time we woke up it was dark and I was hungry. I'm used to weird sleep patterns; from the age of eighteen onward I've woken and slept when someone else needed me to. It doesn't bother me. I needed food, but that was Okay—there was an all-night diner half a mile down the road, or we could order in. We were naked in bed together, warm, close.

"Do you believe him?" said Benson.

"Who?"

"That trainer who told you Kim had been attacked."

"She's got security goons tailing her day and night. Someone tried to kill her."

"I've got to tell you, Dan—Kim is a very unhappy woman. She's successful, she's loaded, but she is one bitter lady."

"What do you mean?"

"Harry Armitage screwed her up big time. It wasn't a happy marriage. I guess not many marriages are."

I stroked his chest.

"He used to beat her up."

"Seriously? Jesus. He must have been brave."

"He's a psycho."

"And now he's in the West Wing. Great."

"Toward the end of their marriage she lived in constant fear. He was completely paranoid, she said."

"What about?"

"Remember what she told us about Peter Quiller? How proud Armitage had been of that?"

"Yeah. Sick bastard."

"Well, all that changed toward the end. He went crazy if anyone even mentioned Iraq, let alone UN weapons inspectors. Every time there was something on the TV about it, he started yelling and cursing. And one day, right at the end of their marriage, she threw that name in his face—Peter Quiller. She called Armitage a murderer. And he went so crazy she was in fear for her life. That's when she left him for the last time. She thought he was going to kill her."

"Because she mentioned Quiller by name?"

"That's what she thought."

"And now he's got to the White House and suddenly someone's trying to silence her."

"Guess who?"

"You think he's behind all this?" I asked. "You, me, Dick, Douglas and now Evans?"

"He's got a lot to lose. And he has the resources to make all that happen."

"So have the people who gave him his orders."

"You think someone was putting the pressure on him to shut his mouth?"

"I don't know," I said. "But there's one thing I'm sure of."

"What's that?"

"I need to eat something other than your dick."

We had two more leads to follow up in Washington. I'd meet with Naseer Khan, the Newsbuster blogger, and Benson would do the old pals' act with Woody Douglas. I wasn't sure how much reliable information I'd got out of Woody—he was, at best, a fantasist—but if anyone could get to the truth it was Red Benson. Douglas's admiration for his former CO stopped just short of idolatry. Benson made a date for the tour of the 8th Street office.

Khan agreed to meet me at a Starbucks on 14th Street, a big, anonymous place that he referred to as "my office." If this had been at home in Massachusetts I'd have just walked in and looked for the Asian guy. This being Shaw, however, things weren't quite so simple. So I stood in the doorway scanning the crowds until a handsome guy in a striped shirt and tie and rolled-up sleeves materialized in front of me.

"Dan Stagg, right?"

"Yeah. How did you know?"

"Oh, I did my homework." He smiled. "Come on. I'll get you a coffee."

"I bet you already know how I take it."

"Let me guess. Black?"

"How the hell?"

"I know very few servicemen who can be bothered with cream and sugar. Come on. That's my desk." He gestured toward a two-seater table. "I won't be long."

I had time to get a good look at him while he waited for coffee: broad shoulders, big ass and legs, thick black hair on his head and arms and around the opening of his shirt. He looked as if he needed to shave at least twice a day. He was dressed in what I guess you'd call business casual—slacks, a button-front shirt, polished black shoes. There was a sports jacket over the back of his chair, a laptop and phone on the table. Whatever the content of his blog, he looked exactly like every other Washington wage slave. I was expecting a tattooed, pierced hipster with a slogan T-shirt and a statement beard, not this preppy Asian guy with a neat haircut and a Samsonite briefcase. A good disguise, I suppose.

He came back with the coffee and started talking in a low, even tone that merged perfectly with the ambient noise of the cafe. Invisible and inaudible.

"So, Dan, what's on your mind?"

"Peter Quiller."

"So you said." He scratched his chin, which crackled.

"I served under General Armitage during Desert Fox."

"Uh-huh." He looked friendly, open, interested, but not eager.

"We ran a covert mission from an assault ship in the Gulf."

"Right."

"Our target was a surveillance station a few miles near the coast."

Khan nodded, his poker face giving nothing away. He sipped his coffee, I sipped mine, both waiting for the other to open negotiations.

At last he said, "Funnily enough, I read something about that recently."

"About what?"

"Armitage and Quiller. The idea that there might be some kind of..." He looked me in the eye, choosing his words carefully. "Connection."

"And where did you read that?"

He tapped the screen of his laptop. "I monitor some of the more—what should I call them?—fringe blogs out there."

I nodded. Two could play the silent game.

"Of course, most of it's crap. You have to wade through a hell of a lot before you get to the good stuff."

"And you did?"

Khan shook his head. "Maybe. Maybe not."

"Enlighten me."

"The blog is called *Destruction*, which tells you about the underlying agenda."

"He's crazy, I take it."

"He, or she. Destruction's identity is well protected."

"Go on."

"There have always been rumors about Quiller's

death. Usual stuff that you read everywhere—black ops, government-sponsored hits, all the conspiracy stuff. Most of it's simple cut-and-paste with new names added in. But Destruction's stuff seems original."

"In what sense?"

"He—we'll call him he for the time being—is making specific threats against General Armitage."

"Violence?"

"Blackmail."

Another blackmail victim. "I see."

"You're not surprised."

"I'm never surprised."

"Destruction claims to have material relating to Armitage's involvement in Quiller's death that will be made public on the day of his first public appearance as National Security Advisor."

"And when's that?"

"Tomorrow."

I had a sickening sense of urgency; whatever game we were in was entering its final, crucial phase. "And what's he asking for?"

"He doesn't say—not in public, at least. It's very vague. General Armitage had better pay off his debts, remember his old friends, that sort of thing. There's no detail about what form this material might take, and of course nothing specific about the subject matter. But it's enough to get the bloggers going. Armitage has a lot of enemies. You don't get as far as he's got by being liked. He has a reputation as the man they send in to clean up messes that they don't want exposed."

"Who are 'they'?"

"Same as ever. The government, the Pentagon, the

CIA, the aliens who send rays down to control our minds. Take your pick. Destruction has published some crazy shit over the last couple of years—enough to get him locked up, if anyone took him seriously."

"Do you?"

"I'm not sure." For once, his face expressed something in the contraction of his brows. His eyes looked black. "I don't trust him enough to publish anything he says on my own blog."

"But privately?"

"He interests me."

We sat in silence, sipping coffee. I liked Nas Khan. He said little, and thought much. He listened to everything, and only believed what could be proved. He would have made an excellent politician. Perhaps that was his ambition. He was thirty, maybe. Young, smart, handsome. No wedding ring on those hairy brown fingers. Okay, Dan, you've got enough on your plate, but thoughts are free...

"What are you thinking about, Dan?"

Just wondering how hairy your ass is, boy. "The past."

"Ah."

"1998, to be precise."

"Mm-hmm."

"A couple of days before the Desert Fox bombing campaign began, Harry Armitage led a small company of men on a raid on a surveillance station. The stated aim was to disable the facility."

"And the real aim?"

"To kill everyone inside it."

"And how did that go?"

"Mission accomplished."

Khan nodded, drank his coffee, looked out the window, waiting for me to go on. It's an effective form of interrogation.

"Someone told me that one of the people inside that facility was Peter Quiller."

"Ah." He looked back at me. "And do you think that's true?"

I shrugged. "We were never introduced."

"Would you recognize him?"

"No. It was a long time ago, and it happened fast."

"But surely…"

"I killed a lot of men, Mr. Khan."

That didn't seem to surprise him. "Call me Nas."

"After a while, you stop trying to remember."

"I bet."

"So what do you think? Is it possible?"

"What, that you and the rest of Armitage's team took out a UN weapons inspector in a black op? Yeah, it's possible. A lot of things happened off the radar at that time."

"How do you know? You were—what, fourteen years old at the time of Desert Fox?"

"Like I told you, Major Stagg—"

"Dan."

"Dan. Okay. Like I said, I do my homework. I've talked to a lot of military personnel, from serving generals down to ex-grunts with a grudge."

"And what do they think?"

"It's very contradictory. You know how gossipy the armed services are."

"Yes. I found that out the hard way."

"So I understand. I'm sorry about that."

"DADT? That's ancient history, man. I don't dwell on the past." This wasn't true, but I didn't want a confident, handsome young man like Nas Khan thinking that I was a self-pitying victim. I wanted him to admire me.

"There's enough to make me think that Peter Quiller was targeted by our own people. He was a vocal opponent of military action. He was the one they couldn't shut up and pull out. It seems that in the last weeks of his life he shifted his allegiances."

"What do you mean?"

"He effectively stopped working for the UN and started working for himself."

"You mean for Saddam? He was a traitor?"

"Not for Saddam. At least I've never heard that he was in any sense an official Iraqi mouthpiece. But he kept on broadcasting and writing about WMD to anyone who would listen, saying that the case for military information was unsustainable and would lead to reprisals."

"You mean he went rogue."

"That's what it sounds like."

"And the place we found him in...?"

"If it was him. Who knows what that was. There were so many underground groups at that time all over Iraq. Saddam hadn't stamped out all independent voices. There were radio stations even in Baghdad that kept going. Perhaps it was one of them. The underground would have welcomed Quiller with open arms."

"And we found him, and killed him."

"Possibly."

It made sense. Horrible, cold, strategic sense. And if Quiller and his kind hadn't been silenced, and the US hadn't launched military strikes against Iraq in 1998... There was a whole chain of shit that might have been avoided.

I felt like throwing up.

"Want more coffee?"

"No, thanks. I want some air."

"Okay." Khan got up. "I live a couple of blocks away."

I suddenly felt a lot better. A little visit to Khan's quarters—yeah, that would be very refreshing. "Let's go."

We strolled down the busy street.

"Who do you think Destruction is, Dan?"

"Me? Why should I know?"

"Anyone out there who wants to destroy Harry Armitage?"

"I can think of a handful right away. He was never popular."

"Anyone in particular?"

"Try asking his ex-wife."

"I did."

"Ah." We stopped at the entrance to an anonymous apartment building, the door beside a dry cleaner's shop. "You're very thorough."

"I do my best." He opened the door and, smiling, gestured for me to go in. "After you, Dan. Second floor."

The apartment was sparsely furnished, neutral, clean. A bachelor pad, that was for sure. A large, spacious kitchen and living room, a bathroom, and, behind a closed door, what must have been the bedroom. Perhaps I was about to get a tour of that.

"Coffee?"

"I'm all caffeined up, thanks."

"Beer?"

"Only if you're having one."

"I'll pass," said Khan. Good man: keep yourself sober for me. "Okay, water then."

I sat on the oatmeal-colored sofa, arm stretched along the back. *If he sits next to me I can spill the water over my pants...*

He sat on an armchair on the other side of a pine coffee table.

"What did Kim say, then?"

"Ms. Evans was guarded."

"She is," I said. "In many senses of the word. She's frightened of her ex-husband."

"She has reason to be. Armitage would kill anyone who stood in his way."

"Can we count her out then? As Destruction?"

"No. Ex-wives can be vengeful. She could be acting scared as a smokescreen. Who else could it be?"

"You tell me," I said.

"I have two theories. Either it's someone who used to serve under Armitage who has information he thinks could be valuable, and is blackmailing him for money. Or it's someone who used to be Armitage's superior— perhaps someone who ordered the hit on Quiller—who wants to shut him down."

"Any prime suspects?"

"A long, long list. Which I hope you might be able to help me with."

"Okay. Shoot."

Khan opened a laptop, tapped in a few passwords, and sat down next to me—close enough that our legs and shoulders were touching. "Here you go." A list of names filled the screen, but I was finding it hard to concentrate.

"You read them out."

"You need glasses, Dan?" He was smiling, looking up at me from under jet-black eyebrows. He smelled good, fresh and clean.

"Not me. I can see just fine." I leaned over a little, my outstretched arm making contact with Khan's back. Fuck, I felt horny. Two men, a sofa, a little privacy—I've made a lot more out of less.

"See anyone you recog—Hey!"

I'd just moved in to brush my lips against the stubble on the back of his neck; I couldn't resist it. Surely he'd respond. The laptop would slide to the floor, and we'd get down and dirty on the couch...

Instead of desire I saw surprise. Not shock, exactly, not disgust, but certainly not pleasure. Shit.

"Sorry, Nas. I just..."

"What? You think every man is just...I don't know. Available?"

"Of course not." Although, actually, that's just what I think. And I'm usually right. "I'm sorry. I thought you were—"

"We're working together. This isn't some cheap seduction scene." Now he looked angry. "What the fuck. You're not doing yourself any favors, Dan."

"Okay. Jesus, I'm sorry. I made a pass, that's all."

"What made you think I would welcome that?" He was standing up now, bunching his fists as if he was going to hit me. I wasn't afraid, obviously—but I was seriously pissed off with myself. I'd already suspected Al

Benson of using our investigation as a cheap excuse for getting laid. Is that what I was doing? Filling the gaping hole in my life with easy sex dressed up as a quest for justice?

"Nothing. Seriously, forget it. I wasn't thinking."

"You'd better leave."

"Come on, Nas."

He picked the laptop up from the floor and snapped it shut. "Go ahead."

"Okay. I'm going. But give me a second chance, please? I'm not the asshole I seem to be. I'm just... I don't know."

"Someone who sexually harasses people? How's that for starters?"

"All right, Nas. Have it you're way. I'm going. Forget we ever met."

We stood facing each other, arms by our sides. He blinked first.

"Okay." He rubbed his head. "Sit down. I'm sorry I overreacted. Just don't do it again. I don't like it."

"Yeah. You made that clear. And I apologize. I'm a jerk."

"That's right. You're a jerk." He reopened the laptop, pushed it across the coffee table toward me. This time he was keeping his distance. "Now, then. Anyone you recognize?"

Names, names, names. Hundreds of them, scrolling on and on.

"Jesus. Is there anyone you *don't* suspect?"

"Like you say, Armitage pissed a lot of people off."

"I don't know where to begin," I said, then suddenly stopped, mouth half open.

"What?"

"Nothing." But it wasn't nothing. "I don't know. Just a…"

"Yes?"

"A coincidence, I guess." One hell of a big coincidence, Dan. How many Gerald Douglases must there be in the world? Hundreds? Thousands? What were the chances of this being my Gerald/Jerry/Woody Douglas—the one Benson had just gone off to see?

"Right."

"Is every name on here for a reason, Nas?"

"Yeah. They're people who have some connection to Armitage—they served with him, worked in the administration, or otherwise had dealings with him that may have led to some kind of conflict. I only put down the ones who I thought had reasonable grounds to hate him, and who might have access to the kind of information and resources that Destruction seems to have."

"Armitage must be walking around in fear of his life."

"Most people in the White House are. You've seen the security."

"But seriously—this many people with a reason to hate you?"

"You don't get to the West Wing by being nice."

"Right."

Gerald Douglas. Jerry Douglas. Could it be? He hated Armitage all right. Blamed him for his lack of promotion—god knows what other fantasies were whirling around that head. And there was the question of the photograph he'd taken. He said he didn't know where the photo was. He said he was frightened—that

Armitage's people were trying to get to him. What if he was lying? What if Douglas himself, mild-mannered Woody, was the dangerous one? And I'd just sent Benson to see him. I took a deep breath.

"What do we know about Destruction, Nas? Just go over it again."

"Someone with inside information about Peter Quiller."

"Check."

"Someone who hates Harry Armitage."

"Check."

"A Washington insider, with access to classified material."

That was possible, depending on Douglas's levels of clearance. "Maybe. Go on."

"Someone who knows about technology. It's a good blog. Sophisticated stuff. Uses all the feeds. I'd be proud of it."

Douglas was our comms man.

"Come here for a minute, Nas. It's okay. I'm not going to jump on you."

He perched on the arm of the couch and leaned toward me.

I pointed to a name on the screen. "Gerald Douglas. Why's he on the list?"

"Ah." Nas forgot his fears, and sat next to me. "He's an interesting one. Got into a little trouble a couple of years back. Let me think—2011? 2012? There was some suggestion that classified information had been leaked through his office. Personnel files relating to some senior officers."

"But he works in education. How could that happen?"

"Back then he was in payroll."

"Ah." He didn't mention that. "What happened?"

"Things were going missing—records of payments to senior personnel, invoices, insurance details. Just little routine things that caused an almighty headache further up the administration. They were traced back to Douglas's office, but nothing definite was ever proved. He got moved somewhere where he couldn't do any harm, and the trouble stopped."

"And don't tell me—one of his victims was Armitage."

"There were others, but Armitage was the most senior and the most frequent. The others could have been a smokescreen—or Douglas just bears a lot of grudges. I'd kind of forgotten about him, to be honest. What makes you ask?"

"I know him."

"Go on."

"He was one of the team that went ashore in Iraq. He was Armitage's right-hand man. After we'd killed them all, he took a photo."

"I see."

"He was the one who told me we killed Quiller."

"You believe him?"

"I think he believes it. Isn't that enough?"

"It could be. So what do you want to do?"

"I need to make a call. Check up on someone." I dialed Benson's number. No answer. I texted him. No response.

"Shit."

"What's the matter?"

"I've lost someone."

"Well, in that case," said Khan, "it's a good thing you found me."

15

Sometimes, you have to trust people.

If you're going into a combat situation, you'd better trust the guy at your side, even if you think he's an asshole.

When you're fucking, you'd better trust the guy not to hurt you.

And when you're in the middle of a situation that's way out of control, when you've lost your bearings and haven't got a clue how to find them again, you'd better trust the guy with the map.

Naseer Khan was that guy. He had information, he had contacts, and if he didn't know something, he knew how to find out. And so, even though we hadn't exactly got off to a good start when I tried to jump his bones—what the fuck is wrong with me? I'll address that later—I decided to tell Khan everything I knew.

I went through everything: the mission in Iraq pre-Desert Fox, the carnage that followed, and the photograph. I sifted all the information, and a sorry mess it was. I told him what happened to Coburn, to Benson, to Evans, to Douglas, to me. I even told him the other, hidden connections between us: three out of the four guys under Armitage's command were gay. One, Douglas, still lived with his mother. By the end of that debriefing, Nas Khan knew as much as I did, and he seemed to be making a lot more sense of it.

"And you just sent Benson off to meet Douglas?"

"Yes."

"Was he armed?"

"Of course not. He's a software guy, a family man." Khan's eyebrows went up: I'd already told him enough about Benson and me to make him doubt that. "What I'm saying is, he doesn't carry firearms."

"Then we need to find him."

"Why?"

"Because I think you've sent him into danger."

"What do you think Douglas is going to do? Bore him to death?"

"I have a feeling that there's more to your friend Douglas than meets the eye. From what you say, I'm pretty sure that he is Destruction."

"Then he's out for Armitage's blood, not Benson's."

"And you think Armitage is going to sit back and take that? If you and I can figure out that Douglas is a threat, you can be pretty certain that Armitage got there too."

"Okay. It wouldn't break my heart if they got to Douglas."

"You know Armitage's strategy better than anyone. Get in quick, and silence anyone who might talk. That's what you did in Iraq: there were no witnesses. And if

Armitage finds out that Douglas has been talking to Benson, he'll kill two for the price of one. And then he'll come for you. And probably me. He warned you once. He won't give you a second chance."

"That's kind of far-fetched."

"And anyone else he thinks you might have talked to. Your family and friends and partners. And mine. He's not going to take any more risks until he destroys the evidence of his war crimes and all the people who might know about it."

"But I don't have the fucking photograph. Benson doesn't. Neither does Douglas."

"He lied. How else would he be so confident that he could bring Armitage down?"

"Then why didn't he use it to stop Armitage's appointment altogether?"

"I think he's waiting until tomorrow—when Armitage makes his first public appearance alongside the president. The timing couldn't be better. Wait until they're about to address the press, and then, just a minute or two before they go on, release the photo to the major news services. It'll be the equivalent of setting off a bomb in a crowded marketplace. Maximum impact."

"Shock and awe."

"You said it. Once a marine, always a marine."

"Even a jerk like Woody Douglas."

"They train you guys well. So—let's get going."

Suddenly Khan was the man of action—Khan in his slacks and pressed shirt, with his desk at Starbucks. I was the sidekick. The game had changed. "What are we going to do?"

"Find Douglas and Benson."

"I don't know where to start."

Khan tapped his briefcase. "But I do."

I've mentioned before that Jody dragged me kicking and screaming into the twenty-first century by telling me how to switch on a computer. And I thought I was doing pretty well, Googling stuff and looking up blogs. Once Khan got going, however, I realized that I was still at the cave-painting stage of technology.

"Where was Benson meeting Douglas?"

"At his office. He likes to show off his little empire."

"Okay. Got the number?"

I started fiddling around with my phone, wondering how the hell I found a number that I'd dialed maybe twice and only written down on a scrap of paper, long gone.

"It's all right," said Khan before I'd barely opened up my logs, "I've got it." He tapped the screen of his laptop. "Douglas, Gerald, bursar's office. Direct line. Let's try it."

"How the fuck…?"

"Let's just say I have access to things I shouldn't have." He made the call. "Ah, good afternoon. This is Anthony Williams from premises management. Could I speak to Gerry Douglas, please?"

Anthony Williams? Khan just smiled, and made a "hold on" gesture.

"Oh, right. I'm sorry to hear that. Any idea when he'll be back? Sure, I can hold." He moved the phone away from his mouth. "He's out sick, apparently."

"Since when?"

"Since yesterday."

"But he told Benson to meet him there."

"I know, but—Ah, hi. Right. Okay, do you have a number for him? No, of course not. I understand. Okay, thanks for your help. No, it's fine, it can wait. Goodbye." He ended the call. "They won't give me his home number, which of course is right. I don't suppose you have his address?"

I shook my head. "I met him at a bar in Friendship Heights. He said that was near his home."

"Douglas is very careful, isn't he? Protecting personal information. Do you have any reason to believe he was telling you the truth about the location?"

I thought of the crappy bar he'd taken me to—anonymous, gray, empty. I thought of the sandwiches his Mom made for us—or was that all part of the cover? The mama's boy who never left home. *He wouldn't hurt a fly...*

"No reason at all."

"This might take a little longer. But if I can get his social security number, maybe—"

"Don't tell me you have access to that too?"

Khan tapped the side of his nose. "You won't tell, will you?"

"I can keep a secret."

Khan laughed and tapped away. If he was still annoyed at me, he was hiding it well. I guess he was like me—never happier than when he had a mission. He set about his detective work with the kind of enthusiasm most men bring to online porn.

"I'll try this one. Might give us an address. Hmmm..." He scrolled down a screen dense with text— names, addresses, numbers. "Could be." He clicked on an entry. "Gerald Douglas, date of birth 1975. Does that sound about right?"

"I guess so."

"Lives alone."

"Not with his mother?"

"Not anymore. Mrs. Anna Douglas deceased 2004."

"Jesus. You think he keeps her body in the cellar?"

"Let's go and find out. It's the best match we have."

"And you think Benson might be there?"

"It's not a bad place to start."

The address was nowhere near Friendship Heights, which dismayed me but seemed to make Khan optimistic. He'd already decided that Douglas was a high-class operator, adept at covering his tracks. I thought he was an asshole whose mom still made his lunch.

We drove west out of town, into the Virginia suburbs, an address in Falls Church. The traffic was bad, and if Benson really was in danger from Armitage's hit squads then we weren't making great progress in rescuing him. If Khan could get us to the right address, I'd do everything in my power to secure Benson's safety—but if we remained stuck behind a line of trucks and buses, my combat training would count for nothing.

It was already six o'clock by the time we got there.

"You sure this is the right place?" It looked like something out of a Spielberg movie—green lawns, brightly painted fences, the letterboxes in orderly rows down the street. Not the kind of place you could picture trouble.

"I'm not sure about anything," said Khan. He'd been quiet and nervous for the last half hour; if he was mistaken about the location, I may have lost Benson for good. I was calm, but that was my training. If I allowed myself to worry about a man I might just conceivably want to spend the rest of my life with, we were all screwed.

"Here we go. Number 425." I pulled up. "Looks quiet."

Khan frowned and avoided my eyes. He'd fucked up.

I went to the front door and rang the bell. Nothing: no footsteps, no voices. "Hey, Douglas, you in there?"

No response. Khan sat in the car drumming his fingers nervously on the window frame.

I went around the back. Trash cans neatly stacked against the wall. Flowers in beds and pots, well watered. Everything perfect, everything tidy. And one broken flowerpot, fresh shards of terracotta, the earth recently spilled, still moist. I turned the corner. The screen door was smashed to matchwood, the screen ripped where a boot had gone through. The back door was open. I looked into the kitchen. Shattered plates, overturned chairs. I stopped, listened. Not a sound. The house appeared empty. I searched each room as quickly and quietly as I could—praying as I went through every new door that I would not find Al Benson's corpse on the floor.

There was nothing. Nobody. No body. No blood. Just cupboards emptied, drawers turned out, carpets ripped up, chaos.

I went back to the car and reported to Khan. He seemed relieved. "I knew this was the place."

"It could just be a burglary."

"Yes, Dan. It could. But I don't think it is."

"Armitage's men?"

"If it was, we know what they were looking for."

"The photo."

"And Douglas himself. But he isn't here."

"Where to now?"

"Somewhere safe."

"And Benson?"

"I'm counting on the fact that he's got Benson with him."

"But why would he do that? Al's no threat to Douglas."

"Sure of that?"

"Fuck. I'm not sure of anything anymore."

"Just remember one thing, Dan. We're dealing with a lunatic. Gerry Douglas—Woody—Destruction—whatever we're calling him—is a desperate man."

"What are we saying—he's taken Al hostage?"

"Maybe, if he thinks he's a threat. Or he's just giving himself a little collateral. A hostage can be useful in these situations, if it comes to a showdown."

"Armitage doesn't care if Al dies. He'd probably welcome it."

"What about the police? The FBI?"

"You think it's gone that far?"

"It could have been the Feds who came looking for Douglas. Blackmail's a serious business, whatever the rights and wrongs of the situation. And when the victim is someone in the White House, they don't fool around."

"You think they're in Armitage's pocket?"

"Dan, everyone's in the White House's pocket." We drove away from Douglas's house, through the quiet suburban streets.

"Where to now?"

"My place. And don't get any ideas this time." He laughed, and gripped my shoulder hard. "I'm not inviting you back for that."

"Shouldn't we be out looking for Al Benson?"

"Sure." Khan rested his elbow on the back of the driver's seat. "Washington's a big place. Where would you like to start?"

"I don't fucking know. You're the man with the ideas."

"All I need is high-speed fiber-optic broadband, Dan, and a few little toys that I keep in my cupboard. You can go driving around on a wild goose chase if you want to. I have work to do."

It was dark when we got back to Khan's place. I drove around the block a couple of times before stopping, eyes open for anything like surveillance. It looked clear. Nobody in a parked car, nobody around the doorway.

The apartment was as quiet as we'd left it. Nothing had been touched.

"So what now, Sherlock?"

Khan sat at his desk, turning on various computers. It was neat and sleek, and yet he seemed to command all the information in the city. "I need to do a little hacking."

"Mind if I watch?"

"Sure. Pull up a chair."

"I won't touch you."

"Look," said Khan, "about that. I'm sorry for over-reacting."

"I'm the one who needs to apologize."

"You already did. You're one of the millions of jerks in this city who is led by his dick, right?"

"Bull's-eye."

"And you probably think I'm one of the other kind—the uptight straight idiots who freak out at any mention of sex."

"The thought had crossed my mind."

"Well, I'm not."

"Uptight, or straight?"

Khan smiled. "An idiot, I meant."

"Oh, okay." This left interesting room for maneuvering—after we'd rescued Benson, perhaps. See: planning ahead as usual.

"The fact is—oh, wait a minute." He tapped around on his keyboard. "Let's get these passwords in." Various pop-ups flashed and disappeared. "Okay, we'll give that a moment and we're in. Now, where was I?"

"About to tell me why you're not an idiot."

"Oh, yeah. Well, you might not think it to look at me, but I was in the army for a while."

"Okay. Figures."

"But I left."

"Uh-huh." *Same reason as me?*

"Something bad happened."

"I know the feeling."

"I was raped."

Clang!

"Shit. I'm sorry."

"There was an inquiry of sorts, but nothing was done. Senior officers closed ranks. In the end they told me it would be better if I pursued a civilian career."

"So they gave you an honorable discharge and a good reference."

"Yeah. And that's why I get nervous if guys hit on me."

This probably wasn't the time to ask the question that was going around my head—*but are you gay?*

"I'm so sorry."

"Please stop apologizing. You didn't rape me."

"Who did?"

"Dan, I let go of that a long time ago. It was just a bastard with senior rank." He scratched his forehead, the only sign of stress. "And before you go out there with guns blazing, he's dead."

"Right."

"And that, in a roundabout kind of way, is how I started Newsbuster. There were a lot of people who wanted him dead—I wasn't the only one. When I got out, I started digging around. It's surprising how much you can find out if you really want to. And the better the technology gets, the easier it is to do. Like here." He pointed at his screen. "Our friend Destruction's Twitter account."

"What's he saying?"

"Come and look."

I can't stand Twitter. Jody uses it to talk about TV shows, fashion, the weather, all the trivial shit he enjoys. It drives me nuts. But suddenly I was interested.

Armitage your time is up #warcrimes #desertfox

Harry Armitage special security advisor and butcher #warcrimes #desertfox

Armitage look over your shoulder Destruction is coming #warcrimes #desertfox

Armitage forget Al Qaeda your enemy is close at hand #destruction

And so on.

"It's got to be him," said Khan. "Look. He's posting every five, ten minutes or so. He's getting ready."

"When does Armitage make his first official appearance?"

"Ten a.m., at a press briefing with the president."

I looked at my watch. "So we have a little over twelve hours."

"Hope you weren't planning on sleeping much."

"I can get by. But I need food." I'd barely eaten all day, just a sandwich that I grabbed after my workout with Max.

"There's stuff in the fridge," said Khan. "Go and fix us something." He was intent on his screens. I'm not used to being the one who gets the food, but like I said, sometimes you have to trust people. Sometimes the other guy is in charge. I didn't mind. Perhaps letting Benson fuck me so much was turning me into a mellower person. There was fruit, vegetables, whole-meal bread and cooked chicken in Khan's fridge—not the kind of greasy junk I tend to eat.

In the five minutes it took me to put food on plates, Khan made some kind of breakthrough. He was smiling when I went back to the living room.

"He's using a smartphone."

"Yeah?"

"Don't you see? He's Tweeting from a phone."

"Great." The significance of this passed me by.

"We can track him."

"Seriously? I thought that kind of thing only happened in movies."

"Honestly, it's not that hard. Just a question of having the right software."

"You just walk into Radio Shack and ask for tracking software?"

"Of course not. You have to steal it." He clicked around some more. "It's a felony to download this stuff, but my security is a hell of a lot better than the police's. And Destruction's, for that matter. What kind of idiot uses a GPS phone to make his blackmail threats? He must want to get caught."

"How do you know it's a—oh."

A map had appeared on screen with a pulsing red dot. "There you go. Hello, Woody." Friendship Heights—a few blocks from the bar where we met. What did he have? A hideout? Another apartment?

I grabbed my jacket and prepared to scramble. Khan sat quietly, munching a piece of fruit. "Come on, man! Let's get him!"

"Whoa. Hold on a second. You want to send yourself into danger as well as your friend?"

"But if he's got Benson..."

"If he's got Benson, he's not going to hurt him. He's not making any demands, is he? Just warnings. Look." He pointed to another screen, where the *Destruction* blog was displayed. "He's updating here as well. There's no mention of a hostage situation. But look at this." A clock counter ticked away the seconds. "Twelve hours, fourteen minutes, and eleven...ten...nine...eight..."

"Until Armitage's press call."

"You've got it."

"So what do we do? Sit on our asses?"

"We watch, and we wait. And we eat. I'm monitoring the police and the White House. And Armitage himself."

"How the fuck..."

"And as soon as anyone makes a decisive move, I'll

know. In the meantime, we're as safe here as anywhere."

"Safe from what?"

Khan gestured toward his screens. "We're watching them. They're watching us. As soon as Armitage begins to suspect that we know anything about the situation, he'll act."

"You mean if he realizes I'm with you? Someone else from Iraq who knows about the photo?"

"Exactly."

"Jesus."

"But until we get the knock on the door, we sit tight."

So we sat and ate and drank coffee, we said very little, and I tried not to think about how attractive Khan was. I'm sure he wasn't having the same problem. The hours wore on. He was coping better than me; perhaps he spent a lot of nights like this.

At 3:30 in the morning, as I was dozing on the sofa, I heard a repetitive beep like an alarm clock. I opened a dry eye. Khan was on his feet.

"Get up. We're leaving."

"Why? What happened?"

"They're on to us. And unless I'm very much mistaken, someone's coming to visit." He threw my jacket at me. "I'm not really in the mood for company. Come on."

The streets were quiet and wet with fine drizzle that haloed around the lamps. There was very little traffic. Within two minutes of Khan's alarm going off, we were half a mile from his apartment. He'd brought two laptops and a three smartphones with him. I was wishing I had a weapon—but my gun was back at the motel, and Khan vetoed any idea of going to pick it up. Benson had used his credit card at the hotel—and that, said Khan, was enough to bring Armitage's men down in a hurry.

This was new to me—the idea that every transaction, every phone call, revealed your whereabouts to the world. Khan took it as a matter of course.

"And how do you know they're not tracking us? You've got phones."

"Because I'm smarter than your average felon. I disable shit. I take out accounts in fake names. I don't like people knowing my business."

"And what is your business, if you don't mind my asking? Apart from writing your blog."

"I'm a dealer."

"What?"

"Relax. Not a drug dealer, or an arms dealer for that matter. I sell software."

"Illegal software?"

"If you want to get personal."

"Doesn't that worry you?"

"Not in the slightest. And I don't notice you having much respect for the law. Shoot first, ask questions later—that's your style, isn't it? I read about your work on the Marshall case."

"That was a combat situation."

"And this isn't?"

"Okay. And what else?" We were getting close to Friendship Heights now, and if I was going to get killed I at least wanted to know something about the guy I was spending my last moments with. "You married, single, or none of the above?"

"I'm single." Khan laughed. "I wondered how long it would be before we got around to this."

"All right. I'll mind my own business."

"It's fine. I've been single for just over a year. Before that I was with a guy for three years, and before that I was with a woman. Now I'm quite happy to take a break, thank you."

"I see."

"And before you ask, I'm the kind of guy who only has sex in a relationship."

"That's me too."

"Not that I mean you were…you know."

"I'm not. Don't worry. I've got my hands full."

"Right."

We drove on in silence, the air thick with *what ifs*.

"Park here. That's the place." I pulled up in an alley. Khan pointed across the intersection to what looked like an office building. "Somewhere in there."

"What now?"

Khan handed me a phone. "Here. Brand-new burner. No GPS, no tracking. You don't call me, I call you. Find somewhere you can remain unseen."

"Where are you going?"

"There's a twenty-four-hour Starbucks three blocks from here. That'll do as an operational HQ."

"You're brand loyal, I'll say that much for you."

"Free Wi-Fi, and very difficult to track."

"Okay." I felt a tightness in my chest, a tingling in my hands—I was going into battle. Familiar sensations from long ago.

"And listen, Dan, if anything happens… I mean, if I don't see you again…"

"Shut up, Nas. It'll be…"

I never completed the sentence, because he leaned across from the passenger seat and kissed me on the mouth—a long, hard, real kiss. "Just to say there are no hard feelings."

Fuck that: I had hard feelings, but now was not the time to indulge them. "Later."

I locked the car, and we walked in opposite directions.

There was a tiny park across the road from the office building—ten feet square of scrubby-looking grass surrounded by railings, the sort of place where homeless people sleep. I jumped the fence and scouted around: it was empty. I guess the homeless don't bother coming this far out of town. I made for the cover of a bush, sat down, and waited for my orders.

It was cold, and the ground was damp.

I felt very far from home—wherever home is. That dump in Lowell? My family? Jody? Al Benson? Lee? Where, who, what was home? Homeless people sleep here, I said—and that was me. Homeless, and starting to feel sorry for myself.

The phone vibrated; Khan had turned the ring off. Considerate.

"Anything to report?"

"Nothing. All quiet."

"I hacked Destruction's Twitter account."

"Okay. Was it easy?"

"His password is his mother's name."

"Even I could have guessed that."

"I've got him on the run."

"What did you do?"

"A little misinformation. I tweeted something about a photograph."

"Jesus, Nas. Was that a good idea?"

"We've got to start calling the shots here."

"What's your plan?"

"I want to bring things to a head tonight, as soon as possible. If I can make Douglas panic, we can neutralize the threat to Armitage."

"Is that a good idea?"

"Look, it doesn't matter to me if he gets the job. He's a bastard and a crook, but no more so than anyone else in the West Wing. What matters is that we rescue your friend. If Armitage feels safe, then everyone is safe."

"Why does that matter to you?"

"I don't know. I guess I like you."

I felt like a first-class shit. "Thanks."

"And I don't want blood on my hands. So I'm going to keep screwing with Douglas's head for a while and hopefully flush him out. What's happening at your end?"

"Nothing… Wait." A car that passed by the building a minute ago had just come back. An unremarkable black VW, one driver, one passenger. "I think we may have company."

The car slowed in front of the building, then moved on. If he came back a third time, we had trouble.

"I'll call you back, Dan. Something's happening here."

"Nas…" But he was gone.

Silence. A snatch of birdsong; in the east, the sky was getting light. A good time to go into combat, or to raid a suspect's premises. I held myself ready, eyes and ears alert, muscles straining.

Was Benson up there? Was he safe, or injured, or lying dead somewhere? Among all the confusion of the last twenty-four hours, that was all I really cared about. Danger sharpens your focus. It was Benson I wanted.

I waited for the car. Nothing. A few pedestrians: office cleaners starting their day. A bus, a sanitation truck, a patrol car, just what you'd expect. An ambulance sped past, sirens screaming until they faded in the distance.

The black VW again. Slowing to a stop.

You don't call me. I call you.

That was the basic operational briefing, and however much I wanted to alert Nas to this latest development, I knew he had his reasons.

Nobody got out. They waited. I waited.

My phone buzzed.

"Destruction is moving."

"What?"

"He's left the building."

"Not from the front. The VW is back."

"Can you get around to the back without being seen?"

"Of course."

"Then go. Hurry."

"What happened?"

"Douglas panicked. He's going to release the photo now."

"Where's he going? Why can't he do it from here?"

"I'm pretty sure he doesn't have it there. Follow him if you can."

"What—good old-fashioned on-foot following? Not cyber shit?"

"Hurry, Dan. They'll be looking for him too. And be sure of one thing: they will not let him post that photo."

"Why the fuck didn't we just go in and get them?"

"Because Douglas is armed, and Benson is in danger. He said so. I have no reason to disbelieve him."

That was all I needed. I jumped the railings and ran quietly down the street, avoiding lights, giving the VW a wide berth. I made it to the corner without being seen, and sprinted the two blocks to the back of Douglas's building. There was nobody—silence—no trace. My heart beat like a hammer.

And then, a shout, short and quickly muffled. I stopped still, held my breath, trying to figure out the source.

I crossed the street, silent as a cat.

A scuffle, the sound of footsteps, the bleep of a car being unlocked with a remote key.

Over there, maybe fifty, sixty feet away. The flash of indicators. Two men, one of them hooded.

Douglas and Benson.

The engine started as I ran toward the car, arms pumping, wishing to fuck I had a gun to shoot the tires out. And I got there just in time to touch the rear fender as the car sped away. I yelled "Stop!" at the top of my voice, but it was too late.

And from behind me, the sound of running.

16

Two men in black were running across the street toward me. Black pants, black sweaters, black hats. Ring a bell? We'd been here before. Combat-trained muscle, maybe not the same guys who jumped me in Brooklyn but surely from the same source. I kicked their asses last time, but this time they had guns.

Two guns approaching fast. They only had to shoot, and I was finished. But they didn't. The thought flashed across my mind that they didn't know who I was. Unless they were the Brooklyn boys, they'd never seen me before. Perhaps my mug shot was on some kind of "Enemies of Harry Armitage" list, but they weren't expecting me to be here, in Washington, on Douglas's tail. Were they?

"Jesus," I shouted, taking a chance. "Did you see that? That fucking guy nearly ran me over!" They glanced at each other and lowered their weapons as they stepped onto the sidewalk. "Are you cops? Did you get his license plate? Christ, it ain't safe to walk the streets anymore. Fucking lunatic."

I thought I was doing a pretty good impersonation of a nighttime crazy, but my two new friends still looked suspicious.

"You know what those people are?"

They grunted.

"They're fucking Democrats, that's what they are. All of them should be sent to a fucking camp. They want to force us into gay marriages and stop our god-given right to carry firearms. Good for you, boys! Keep 'em in plain sight! Show these commies that they can't trample all over the Second Amendment the way they did everything else."

They were relaxing, starting to smile, convinced that I was a harmless wacko.

"Let me see that gun," I said, making a grab. "Just let me hold it. It's so long since I held a gun, a real gun, a beautiful weapon, not since those bastards put me in prison."

"Fuck off," said the nearer of the two. "Don't touch me."

"Crazy freak," said the other, pushing me away. That was all I needed. I got hold of his hand, interlaced my fingers, and whipped it down hard, tearing the tendons in his wrist and snapping a couple of intermediate phalanges. He screamed and dropped his gun, which I kicked into the street. The other guy aimed a kick at my groin, but I dodged just in time, blocking him with his buddy, who took the force of the blow in his upper arm; another break, with some luck. In the stumbling that followed I jumped on his back and grabbed his windpipe, squeezing until he was down on his knees. With both of them on the floor it was easy to finish: kicks and stamps to the stomach and hands left one unconscious and the other howling in agony.

And now I had two guns to play with. Nice little compact Smith and Wesson .45s. Very handy. Someone had excellent taste in weapons.

I had firepower, but I'd lost my target. Douglas and Benson could be anywhere by now. And then, as the white noise of battle cleared, I heard the distant buzz of a vibrating phone. I'd dropped it during the fight—it lay on the pavement, the screen cracked but, thank god, still working.

"Hi."

"I thought I'd lost you. Where are you? What's happening?"

"I made a couple of new friends. They were kind enough to give me their guns."

"Douglas is on the move."

"I know. I saw him leave. He has Benson."

"They're heading toward Capitol Hill."

"Thought they might be."

"I don't know what he's planning anymore."

"I have a hunch he's going to his office."

"Why?"

"What better place to hide stuff? Nobody takes any interest in Douglas's job. They don't go snooping around. If he's got the photograph anywhere, it's there."

"He'll be sending it out online."

"You mean he could do it from anywhere?"

"Yeah. But if he's as smart as I think he is," said Khan, "he's not carrying it with him. It'll be hidden on a drive somewhere."

"Is he near 8th Street?"

"He could be going that way."

"Okay. I'm going there." I ran back to the car, safe and sound in its alley. Thank god the streets were quiet, because I was about to do some very illegal driving. As soon as I hit Connecticut Avenue all I had to do was break the speed limit all the way downtown.

Khan stayed with me.

"What's Armitage doing?" I asked.

"Sitting tight. Twitter's going crazy with the Destruction stuff. I've been fanning the flames."

"How?"

"Slipping in a few details that Douglas probably doesn't want to reveal just yet. Making it a police matter. I've mentioned Peter Quiller in connection with Armitage's name, and I may just have typed the word *murder*."

"So how many people are after Douglas now?"

"You, Armitage's men who may or may not be FBI, and now the DC police as well. I kind of tipped them off that Douglas is planning a revenge killing."

"Jesus, Khan, are you the crazy one?"

I turned left onto K Street. Nearly there. Watching out for blue lights.

"You better pray that the cops get to him before Armitage's men, if you want to save Benson."

"And if I get there first?"

"I don't know, Dan. You might be walking into a trap."

"If Armitage thinks he's going to get three for the price of one, he can think again. I've already dealt with four of his goons."

"You were lucky."

You don't say *lucky* to a Marine. We win because we're right, because we're better, stronger, faster. Not because we're lucky. The ones who get killed were just not good enough. Luck doesn't come into it.

"I'm turning onto 8th Street now. Stay with me."

I concealed the phone and the weapons in my jacket and parked the car.

"Hey," I said to the security guard at the marine barracks. "Did anyone come in here just now?"

"I'm sorry, sir. I'll have to ask you to step away from the building. This is a government facility."

"As a government employee, I'm well aware of that."

"May I see your ID, sir?"

"CIA," I said, which at least bought me time. "I repeat, did anyone come in here?"

"I'm not permitted to discuss that." He was reaching for his walkie-talkie. The time for talk was over.

"Sorry, pal," I said, twisting his arm behind his back. Okay, I was going to be in a shitload of trouble in the morning, but at present all I cared about was rescuing Benson. If Douglas didn't hurt him, then Armitage's men surely would. And I judged I was just minutes ahead of them.

When I'd administered the old field anesthetic—a blow to the guard's head with the pistol—I spoke on the phone.

"Khan? I'm in."

"I heard."

"Do you think the judge will listen to me if I say it was justified?"

"I doubt it. Now hurry. I've got movement on Armitage."

"What does that mean?"

"He's being taken to the White House now."

"How do you know these things?"

"Friends in the right places. I'm just calling in a few favors. One of the secure transport team."

"He must owe you big time."

"He does. He was my boyfriend."

"Useful friend to have." I was arriving at Douglas's floor now, breathless from the stairs—but it was safer than taking the elevator. I stopped and listened. All quiet.

Maybe I was wrong. Maybe Douglas was somewhere else.

"Khan." I whispered, just in case.

"Yes."

"Why would Armitage be at the White House?"

"Personal safety, perhaps. Or he's preparing to issue a statement. Maybe the president summoned him."

"Because of Destruction?"

"They monitor everything. Almost as well as I do."

"You should get a job there."

"That's my plan."

"Yeah, you—"

I heard something. The creak of a door—not close, but not too far away—and coming, if my memory was correct, from the direction of Douglas's office.

"Stay with me," I said, and crept into the corridor. The lights were dim, the building officially empty. But I was here, and I was not alone.

Douglas. It must be Douglas. And then I saw it—a crack of light around the door, thirty feet down the corridor, the end office.

Douglas's office.

My pigeon had come home to roost.

All I had to do was move slowly, quietly, and take him by surprise.

And then, unmistakable, the muffled sound of a gun with a silencer. A yelp, a shout, and a crash.

The time for stealth was over. I ran to the door and kicked it open.

The smell of gun smoke was strong and fresh. Two men in black stood over Jerry Douglas, who was cowering on his knees, sweat running down his shiny, greasy face.

And on the floor, face down in a pool of blood, was Al Benson.

I shot first, a gun in each hand, kneecapping both of Armitage's men. Douglas screamed and pissed himself, a dark patch spreading quickly over his dirty gray pants. It was a long time since he'd seen action, and he was a coward.

"Thank god, Dan!" he said. "You found us!"

I stood over him. "What have you done to Benson?"

"I... They shot him. I mean..."

He could lie to me later. I kicked him hard in the stomach, winding him. I didn't want to hear his fucking voice, or I might kill him. If Benson was dead... I could feel anger rising like panic, the feelings I had when Will Laurence died, the recklessness and hatred that swamps all your training, all your instincts for survival.

If Benson is dead I will kill them all and then I will kill myself.

The gunman's mantra, repeated before high school shootings, mall shootings, every fucking crazy bastard who's run amok with a firearm.

Stop! Stop!

The voice of conscience? Jiminy Cricket piping up amid the blood and gun smoke?

No. The tinny, buzzing voice of Naseer Khan from the phone in my pocket bringing me to my senses.

"Get an ambulance, Khan."

"On its way."

I rolled Douglas out of the way and felt for a pulse in Benson's neck. Come on. Come on. Where the fuck is it? Don't die, Benson, you bastard, you sick lying bastard, don't die.

And there it was, faint and irregular. A heartbeat. He was alive.

General Armitage made his debut appearance as a Special Security Advisor at the 1000 press conference, standing at the president's side. He made no statement, and took no questions; everything was fielded by the president or his aides. Armitage's next public appearance was "rescheduled," and within a week he was visiting an obscure military installation in Nebraska. Questions about his return to Washington were stonewalled, and the blogs were alight with speculation.

Some of this I learned in a police cell from the lawyer that Benson appointed to represent me. Some came out later, when I was bailed, from Nas Khan. The photograph, if it even existed, never appeared; everything that Jerry Douglas had ever touched was seized by the FBI, his house, his office, his various hideouts located and gutted. Armitage's public reputation was protected, but his career was over. Even without proof of war crimes, his involvement in an attempt to silence members of a 1998 black op was easily established. Benson and I sang like canaries. The charge sheet against me got shorter and shorter until it disappeared altogether.

I spent thirty-six hours in police custody, and became quite friendly with my captors, who seemed like a nice bunch of cops. And in case you're wondering, I did not have sex with any of them. No dicks were shoved through prison bars. No helpless blond twinks were thrown into my cell. In truth, I was glad of the rest. Even Dan Stagg needs time to recharge, and there's nothing like a short spell of incarceration for that. When Khan came to bail me out, I was glad to see him. He even gave his address as my temporary location. "You'll need to stick around for a week or so," he said.

I called the Strong Box and explained that I'd been involved in a major crime, even got my lawyer to call them, but they'd already "let me go" with a half-assed suggestion I could come and do some freelance PT "if I worked things out." Oh, well, no great loss. I called Lee to tell him the news; he was upset, but I promised I'd make it up to him as soon as I got home. I made up a story about an "undercover operation" I'd been involved with, and the poor kid was so impressed he was almost jerking off over the phone. "What, real guns?" he said, with an unmistakable hitch in his voice. Perhaps if he asked nicely I'd show him my weapon.

I visited Benson in the hospital, where he was being treated for a gunshot wound to the shoulder. Muscle torn, tendons damaged, but the bone was intact and everything else would heal. Jerry Douglas—who was not granted bail, nor was he likely to be—had shot in a panic when Benson tried to overpower him. "I'll tell you the whole story later," Benson said, "but right now I need to sleep."

Last of all, I called Jody. I was reluctant, I guess. Everything I cared about seemed to be here in DC or back home in Lowell. Jody—increasingly distant, indifferent, unreliable—already felt like the past.

"Hey, Dan," he said, and started coughing.

"You smoking again?"

"Jesus." He put a hand over the receiver and hacked away. "No, I'm not coughing. I have a chest infection."

That rang alarm bells. I'm as ignorant about sexual health as the next self-deluding jerk, but even I know that chest infections in young men are bad news.

"Oh."

There was a pause, then, "Well, Dan, what do you want? I'm kind of busy."

"What with?"

"I have an appointment, if you must know."

Yeah, I thought: with an eight-inch dick, if I know you. "Oh, fine. Don't let me keep you. Just thought you might like to know that I just got out of police custody, but hey, it'll wait."

"What?" He sounded annoyed.

"It's okay. Nothing for you to worry about. Anyway, nice to talk. I'm sure we'll—"

"Dan." He almost shouted.

"Yes?"

"My appointment."

"Sure, run along, don't let me—"

"It's with a doctor."

My stomach hit the floor. "Oh. Are you okay?"

"No."

I felt sick. "What's the matter?"

There was a long silence. AIDS? Hepatitis? What? *What?*

"I have epilepsy."

"Epilepsy?"

"That's right. You heard."

"What the fuck?"

"It's fairly common after head injuries. That's what the doctor told me."

"How long has this been going on?"

"A few months." He tried to sound careless. "It's okay, it's under control."

"What about the time I came to see you at Pratt? Did you know then?"

"Yes. I'd just got back from the hospital when you turned up. That's why I was kind of out of it. I told Lloyd not to tell anyone."

"And spring break?"

"I had to stay here for tests."

"For god's sake, Jody, I'm supposed to be your..." I hesitated long enough for Jody to jump to the attack.

"I'm your boyfriend, Dan. Your partner."

And I went on the defensive. "Am I? I wonder sometimes."

"Listen, Dan..."

Here it comes. The bombshell.

"The doctor thinks I might be... You know. Ill. Seriously ill."

My anger evaporated, and my throat tightened. "Oh."

"I'm sorry I didn't tell you. I thought you might just leave me."

"What? Jody, for Christ's sake. I want to..." What? Look after you? Love you? Take care of you? I'd nursed him before, I could do it again, couldn't I? But that first time, all that mattered was that Jody didn't die, that we had a future together. Now I had other concerns. Benson. Lee. Khan, even. Fuck, what a mess I'd made while Jody was there in Brooklyn concealing his illness, frightened that I wouldn't stick around if I knew he was sick.

And how right he was. What a fickle, faithless bastard I am.

"I've got to go, Dan. The doctor's waiting for me."

"I'll come and see you," I said, but he'd gone.

Khan, who had discreetly withdrawn to the kitchen during my phone call, stuck his head around the door. "Dan? Want coffee? A soda? Jesus, Dan, are you okay? You look like you just saw a ghost."

And I guess that's when the shock hit me. The shock of it all. Douglas, Benson, the blood, the gunfire, Jody...

I put my hands over my face.

Khan was sat beside me and put an arm around my shoulders. I leaned against him, grateful for human contact. I felt like I was drifting on a stormy sea, and I clung to him like a raft. I cried. Fuck, Dan Stagg who never cries, sobbing on his shoulder like a baby.

"It's okay," he said, stroking my head, my face. "It's okay." He kissed me on the forehead, on the ear. I gasped, and pressed my mouth against his chest, feeling a hard nipple through his shirt. Oh, fuck, I did not need this complication in my life, and yet I did need it, I needed it worse than I've ever needed it before. I lay back in Khan's arms, strong arms that held me, and I opened my mouth to his kiss. His hand went inside my T-shirt, undid my pants, pulling up and down until I was exposed from chest to knees. Khan never stopped kissing, caressing, stroking my dick until I shot a fierce hard load, almost passing out from the intensity of it.

After that we went to bed, mouths locked, hardly speaking, lost in strange worlds of distress and comfort. And then we slept.

"I know you're not free," he said in the morning as we lay together in the bright sunlight. "I'm sorry if I took advantage of you."

"Your turn to apologize, huh? A poor defenseless guy like me. You should be ashamed of yourself." We were both hard again, needing to piss, needing coffee, but needing each other more. Hands ran through hair, over chests, thighs, and asses.

"So what will you do?"

"I don't fucking know. Right now I just want to run away from it all."

Khan held me tight, as if he thought I might disappear.

"Got a private jet or a yacht or anything like that? Something we can just go away on?"

"Sorry, no." He took hold of my cock, gently stroking me. "But there's your car. I have a waterfront place on Chesapeake Bay. We could be there by tonight."

God, it was tempting. To disappear—to cut all my ties. There was nothing holding me back. No property, no possessions that I really needed, nothing but a few emotional messes that would clear themselves up if I wasn't around to make them worse. A place on Chesapeake Bay, and Nas Khan. Happily ever afters have been built on less.

I almost said yes.

But then he started sucking me, and I came, and I started to think again. And we both knew that it would never happen.

Benson was discharged from the hospital a few days later. Brenda was there to take him back to Pittsburgh. I saw them off in the hospital parking lot—it was a gray, humid morning, the air heavy with exhaust fumes. A miserable fucking way to say goodbye to the guy whose life you saved, who told you a lot of bullshit about love and then got into the car with his wife and couldn't even look you in the eye. Couldn't even tell me what happened that day, after his lunch with Kim Evans, when I sent him off to see Woody Douglas. Couldn't explain a fucking thing, blaming it on the pain and the meds, hoping I would keep my mouth shut and ask no questions. And the look in Brenda's eyes as she said, "Hey, Dan, thanks for everything, you really must come and visit with us sometime"—a look I know all too well from my own family, a look that says *Keep away, you're not wanted, you scare us.*

We spoke on the phone when Brenda was out of the house, and he told me what happened. He met Douglas at his home. Douglas seemed "excited" and "irrational" and then whacked him over the head with a blunt instrument. That much was borne out by medical reports. Douglas took him hostage, hooded and cuffed and with a gun in his back as the endgame of his crazy plan played out, driving him to the office and issuing threats that "civilians will die." It was a pointless threat; Armitage didn't care about collateral damage, and if he'd known it was Benson he'd have instructed his men to shoot to kill. Benson's memories were confused: two men burst into the room, there was a struggle and a shot—from Douglas's gun, it seemed—and blackness. He woke up in the hospital.

The police were no more forthcoming. As for Douglas, he disappeared without a trace.

But this was never about Douglas, who was at most an incidental threat. Khan thought it likely that he'd been blackmailing Armitage for years, using his knowledge of past crimes to his own advantage—and whether he had the photo, or knew its whereabouts, we would never find out.

The real threat was always Harry Armitage. When I was interviewed by the police, I told them everything—Dick Coburn's death, the attacks on me and Kim Evans, the blackmail of Al Benson—and I told them everything I could remember about that night in Iraq, the blood and guts up the walls, the pile of corpses, Michael Jackson on the radio, the man with outstretched hands.

That began a long series of interviews with civil and military authorities that continues to this day. Armitage has been suspended pending investigation of a growing list of charges. Perhaps they did find something tucked away on one of Douglas's hard drives. There was evidence somewhere that we weren't being told about. Other allegations from other people, perhaps. Enough to substantiate my claims.

With Khan's help, I pieced together a theory. Harry Armitage did the government's dirty work for years, and got promoted for it. When he made it to the West Wing, it was necessary for other witnesses to be silenced. Perhaps he gave the orders himself, perhaps they came from higher up—but somehow, agents from the FBI, the police, and possibly serving military personnel were assembled as a private SWAT team, targeting individuals who posed a danger to Armitage and, by extension, the entire administration. Quiller's death can't have been the only secret: there could have been hundreds of targets.

Coburn was found somewhere, his recent past as a homeless junkie on the streets of South Jamaica easily discovered, and he was murdered. I never knew where he died, but the body was dumped in a derelict building and burned. Two others died to cover Coburn's death.

I was attacked in Brooklyn, perhaps with intent to kill. Where would they have dumped me? But I fought back and gave them the slip, and by the time they regrouped I was on the road again, with Benson.

Benson, the married closet case, they thought they could silence with threats. They did their homework, let him know that they knew where he lived, where his kids went to school, and then hit him with the blackmail. Khan was pretty sure the blackmailers made it clear to Benson that it was Armitage they were interested in, that Benson's silence on that subject was the price he'd pay for their silence. That's now what Benson told me—but that, I guess, means nothing.

Kim Evans was threatened too: the ex-wife who heard her husband bragging about Quiller and a hundred other crimes. She was scared enough to hire bodyguards.

And that left Woody Douglas. Was he threatened, as he claimed? Or did Armitage fear him enough to leave him alone? Finally, as Douglas's demands became unreasonable, Armitage tried to do what he should have done the first time Douglas contacted him: he attempted to kill him.

But it was too late. The cat was out of the bag, thanks to Nas Khan, and if any one of us died now, all hell would break loose. Douglas disappeared. Custody, perhaps—some unknown dumping ground for detainees who go under the legal radar.

It was hard to believe. The FBI, the police, the military, being used as a private army? An operation so sophisticated it could track me to the Pratt Campus, track Coburn to a crackhouse, and Benson to a bathhouse?

"When you've dismissed every other theory," Nas Khan said, "the one you're left with is probably the truth, however unlikely. The stakes were high, Dan. Armitage had power."

"Not anymore."

"I wouldn't dismiss him just yet. If they can fight this fire, he'll be back."

"Unless someone kills him."

"Don't get any ideas."

Calls for a full investigation of allegations made against Harry Armitage grew in the press for a couple of weeks, but something else pushed the story aside and within a month it was forgotten, the stuff of blogs. Newsbuster, maybe—but Nas kept his powder dry. He's ambitious enough to hold on to secrets until he needs them.

Al Benson distanced himself from me. Too compromising. Perhaps he struck a deal with his wife—you forget Dan Stagg, and I'll forgive what happened. Let's pretend that you didn't leave the family high and dry for weeks while you mapped out a new life and a new identity. Let's retreat behind the facade of our gracious South Fayette home and tell anyone who asks that you did something vaguely heroic in DC that you can't talk about for reasons of national security. If necessary, drop Armitage's name into the conversation.

And that way, everyone would think Benson was a heroic whistle-blower, not a coward who made someone fall in love with him and then pushed him away. Not for the first time. Dick Coburn, Dan Stagg—how many other suckers had fallen into Al Benson's trap?

I survived. I wasn't going to end up on the streets. But I paid a price too: I'd lost Jody. Yeah, perhaps we could get back together. I could nurse him again. I'm good at it. But in my heart, I'd betrayed him. I'd been ready to drop everything and run away with Al Benson—with some dream of my unfulfilled, unhappy youth. Jody, the flesh and blood reality of a relationship, the responsibility—when the chips were down I didn't want it. I was looking for a way out. If not Benson, then Lee, or even Khan. Gambling the possibility of long-term happiness against the certainty of disappointment. Benson, Lee, Khan—none of them offered me a real future. They were guaranteed to fail. And that was what I wanted, because that's what I thought I'd deserved.

That's what I deserve.

* * *

I made a plan to see Jody. A goodbye, I guess. I'd go to Brooklyn, talk to the doctors, do whatever I could to help. And then I'd make some excuses, and we'd go our separate ways.

In the three days before my trip, two things happened.

First, I was contacted by a General Wingfield, USMC, who wrote to invite me to an "informal meeting" to discuss my departure from the Corps and my possible future return. "Due to changes in USMC policy we are in a position to manage a phased return to service for some categories of veterans"—no mention of the word *gay*, but I guess that's what it meant. I nearly threw it in the wastebasket. What do they want—some jaded old jarhead to send out to the latest US fuckup, do their dirty work for them, and live with the nightmares? Fuck that. But then I saw a different path, illuminated with the golden glow of respectability and vindication, Major Stagg once again in dress uniform and polished boots, the apple of his family's eye, accustomed to command, fucking a few twenty-year-olds wherever my duty took me. I saw Lee in a marine uniform, his ridiculous hair trimmed to regulation style—standing to attention, kneeling, lying back. It was an agreeable idea. It was a future. It was a sort of victory.

Second, another email in my inbox from Al Benson. A different address; perhaps Brenda was monitoring the other one. "Hey, Dan, how are you doing? I'm on the mend, should be back at work soon, and if all goes well I'll be in Boston for a big software expo next month. Can we meet for a debrief? Yours, Al."

Sure. Your ass feels empty. You need a big old software expo to get you out of Brenda's clutches.

I didn't answer. Not immediately. What the fuck did I need with Al Benson? He was the past—doubly the past. I could forget him. Except at night, lying awake and thinking about what passed between us, and how real it seemed. *I love you.* We'd both said it. And we meant it.

But I'd said it to Jody a thousand times, and he'd said it to me. Jody had the prior claim.

Jody.

Benson.

Lee.

Nas.

Oh, fuck, what a mess. Run away, Dan. I called General Wingfield's office and made an appointment.

Jody looked terrible. His roommate, Lloyd, had been nursing him to the best of his ability, but if I was looking for a reliable caregiver my first choice wouldn't be a fashion student. Jody was twenty pounds underweight, with dark circles under his eyes. He hadn't been eating properly, or exercising, or sleeping. On his forehead was the fading line of a bruise he'd sustained while falling against a table edge. "I tripped," he said at first, but later admitted that he'd suffered a major seizure while he was on his own in the apartment.

I visited in June. There was no excuse for the delay other than my own reluctance to face the music. I knew as I drove down to the city that this was the end. I'd tell him I'd decided to reenlist. I'd be traveling a lot, and it was only fair to set him free.

It took me that long to figure out that I couldn't face any of them—that I was meant to be a marine, to have no responsibility for myself, only to follow and give orders.

That's what I always wanted, wasn't it? The continuation of the only life I'd known. The last six years were a hiatus, that's all. I waited for the military to catch up with the rest of the world, and now that the only obstacle to my career had been removed I could take up where I left off at Will Laurence's death. I wouldn't have to sneak around anymore; I'd be "openly gay marine Dan Stagg," and if I wanted to fall in love, I could.

The chances of that seemed slim. Sex: yeah, plentiful sex. I'm good at that, and I can even be their friend afterward, but love? Commitment? Not for me. I can't do it, any more than I can tap dance or speak Italian.

Jody didn't see things that way.

"Thank god you're here. I've been losing my mind." He put his arms around me, fell against me, all his weight—not as much as there once was—leaning on me. Total surrender, and total trust. He needed me, and he believed his needs would be met. All the suspicions that I'd used to justify my infidelity were unfounded. He'd been lying to me because he was scared of telling the truth: that he was sick.

I held him and kissed him, and we talked.

The fits started just after Christmas. At first he thought he'd been partying too hard, or overdoing it in the gym. But they didn't go away. They got worse. After the fourth time of falling to the ground, rigid and jerking, he was persuaded to seek medical help. The campus doctor immediately diagnosed posttraumatic seizures resulting from the head injury Jody had sustained a couple of years back. Tests were suggested to discover if he had epilepsy.

He did.

Drugs were prescribed. Side effects included weight loss, insomnia, nausea.

The prognosis? Not good. Shortened life expectancy. Possible remission for a few years, uncertain outcome.

"I can finish my course, and there's no reason why I shouldn't be able to work, as long as I manage the condition and keep taking my meds," he said, but he wasn't even convincing himself. "It might just go away. A lot of people with posttraumatic epilepsy make a full recovery after two, three years. If I look after myself..."

But that was just the trouble. Jody couldn't look after himself. Even in perfect health he needed a lot of management. In his current condition, he needed full-time care. If he was going to finish his course, I'd have to be there with him. There was no one else. His father, perhaps—but he was even less the caring kind than me.

How could I leave him?

"I've been asked to go back to work," I said. No point in lying anymore.

"Wow." He swallowed painfully. "That's amazing."

"Straight back to my old rank, with a very nice financial package to make up for what I lost out on. Pension, everything, just as it was."

"I see." He looked out the tiny window, down to the street where I'd been attacked. "I'm really pleased for you."

"Don't say it like that."

"When do you leave?"

"I didn't say I'm leaving. I said I'd been asked."

"Right." Jody got up and fiddled with his phone. "What do you want? Permission?"

"It's a big decision. Obviously I'm not going to make it without consulting you first."

He turned to face me. "Why? Because I'm part of

that future? Do I come with you to Afghanistan or Syria or wherever they send you?"

"That's not how it works."

"No. It's not."

Silence. What should I do? Back down, tell him I didn't really want it, I was just glad to be asked? Tell him I was there for him one hundred percent, putting his needs first? I didn't know what to say because I didn't know what I really believed.

Or I knew, and was too proud to admit it to myself.

I wanted out of the whole damn thing. Jody getting sicker and sicker, a future of doctors and hospitals, medication and side effects... No fun, no fucking, no point.

That was the truth. I could see it in his sagging sweatpants, loose where they used to be tight. In his flat, greasy hair, his gray skin.

Jody was my responsibility. My duty. But I couldn't face it.

I kissed him, and said, "I'm so sorry," and left.

I went home. Lee came over, so happy to see me, asking no questions, and I lost myself in him. Every sense was satisfied. The weather got hot, but we closed the shutters and turned on the fan and took a lot of showers. We fucked and fucked and fucked until time and sleep started to lose meaning. What was it? Three days? Four? Five? Sometimes we walked to the store together, or drank coffee or a beer, got some fresh air.

We didn't talk much. Lee's not the conversational type. He likes small talk, dirty talk, that's about it. Nothing about the future or the past, about "us."

One morning he said, "I'm going home in September. That's gonna be weird."

"I'm going back into the forces."

"Really? Fucking cool." He thought for a minute. "You still got your uniform?"

"No. Just the boots. I kept the boots."

"Put 'em on."

He licked them, kissed them, rubbed his cock all over the mirror-shiny surface, and eventually came on them. Then I fucked him again, his cock still oozing from the last load.

The next day—or the day after—he came back from the shower fully dressed. "I think I'd better show my face at work," he said. "I can't afford to get the sack."

"Sure. I'll see you later."

"Yeah, 'course." But we didn't. We both found excuses not to meet up—studying, work, appointments, meetings. We'd done it, it was over, move on.

Relief.

This was how it could be. A road map for the future. We'd see each other around perhaps, and if the time was right before we both left maybe we'd have some fun again. Good memories, good times.

Al Benson came back to Boston. He looked old. His shoulder gave him pain, he was still suffering from shock. The light behind his eyes was out.

He was back in the Marriott. Different room, but it might as well have been the same. We went through the motions. I fucked him, and we both came, and then we talked a little. No urgency, no expectation.

If he walked out now, I would not be sorry.

We didn't talk about Armitage or Douglas. Questions hung between us, never to be asked or answered.

"I'm going back," I said.

"I thought you might."

"Really?"

"You were never suited for civilian life, Dan." There was a patronizing note in his voice that would have pissed me off once.

Now I just said, "You're right. I'm looking forward to it. I'm getting rusty and slow."

I looked at Benson—definitely overweight now, his jawline indistinct, torso sagging—and tried to see the man I'd loved. The man for whom I'd been willing to sacrifice anything, even my life, running into certain danger because he was there behind the door in the blood and gun smoke.

"I'm sorry about Dick Coburn," I said. We were back where we began. "He was a good man."

"He was," said Benson, and turned away. There were tears in his eyes.

We were not good men. We would always lie and hide and survive. The good guys—Coburn, Jody, even Lee—get left, and go to the wall.

We had one last meal together, some good ol' Beantown chow, a couple of beers, and a lot of talk about my future and his wonderful career in software, and we said goodbye like two old colleagues who know damn well that they won't bother with the next reunion.

Nas Khan emailed me a few times. I didn't respond. Why bother? I liked him a lot, the sex was great, but it would end. Time to get on with my life. My real life.

* * *

Now I'm ready to go. There's some initial retraining to be done at Pendleton, which made me angry at first, as if I'd forgotten how to be a marine in the years I'd been out. But I probably need it. The Corps has changed, and I'd better learn how. I don't want to be the dinosaur with the medals. I want to be out there leading men. I want to be a general, and I want to do it right, not like that asshole Harry Armitage, who brought the Corps into disrepute.

Maybe if I work hard and keep my nose clean I can make it to Washington myself. I'm not quite forty, though I'm counting the days. I've got ten, fifteen years of useful service in the field ahead of me. A lot of the world to see, a lot of trouble to work out. Do it right, with integrity. Because now integrity is something I can achieve. I can live in the open, hiding nothing, leading by example. And if I get a lot of ass along the way, I'll tell you about it.

I wrote to Jody to let him know where I was going, but he didn't reply. I can call him, of course. Find him online, on Skype, wherever. See how he's doing. I still care.

I'll do it tomorrow. Or the day after that.

About the Author

James Lear is the author of best-selling, award-winning gay erotic novels including *The Back Passage*, *The Palace of Varieties*, and *The Hardest Thing*. After living in America, the Far East, and various European countries, he finally settled in London, where he dedicates himself to helping athletic young men.